"Oh, we slept together, all right,"

Kyle said. "For a few hours, anyway. I wouldn't forget something like that."

"I wish I'd been awake to enjoy it," Jess quipped.

Finally he smiled. "I'm sorry you missed it, too. It wasn't half-bad."

Jess relaxed slightly. "I really wasn't myself last night. And now I feel like I've taken advantage of you. You offer help, and I'm all over you like a rash."

"Taken advantage? Honey, there's something you ought to know about men. When you ask them to sleep with you, it's not taking advantage. When *they* get in bed with you when you're half-unconscious, *that's* taking advantage. You have nothing to apologize for, okay?"

Jess looked him in the eye. "It helped me sleep, to have you there, because I knew I was safe."

Kyle took a long draw of coffee. "You weren't *that* safe."

Dear Reader,

Welcome to another month of powerhouse reading here at Silhouette Intimate Moments. Start yourself off with Lindsay Longford's *Renegade's Redemption*. Who doesn't love to read about a rough, tough loner who's saved by the power of a woman's love?

Move on to Susan Mallery's *Surrender in Silk*. This sensuous read takes a heroine whose steely exterior hides the vulnerable woman beneath and matches her with the only man who's ever reached that feminine core—the one man she's sure she shouldn't love. Alexandra Sellers plays with one of the most powerful of the traditional romantic fantasies in *Bride of the Sheikh*. Watch as heroine Alinor Brooke is kidnapped from her own wedding—by none other than the desert lord who's still her legal husband! In *Framed*, Karen Leabo makes her heroine the prime suspect in an apparent murder, but her hero quickly learns to look beneath the surface of this complicated case— and this fascinating woman. Nancy Morse returns with *A Child of His Own*, a powerfully emotional tale of what it really means to be a parent. And finally, welcome new author Debra Cowan. In *Dare To Remember* she spins a romantic web around the ever-popular concept of amnesia.

Read and enjoy them all—and then come back next month for more of the most exciting romantic reading around, here at Silhouette Intimate Moments.

Yours,

Leslie Wainger
Senior Editor and Editorial Coordinator

Please address questions and book requests to:
Silhouette Reader Service
U.S.: 3010 Walden Ave., P.O. Box 1325, Buffalo, NY 14269
Canadian: P.O. Box 609, Fort Erie, Ont. L2A 5X3

FRAMED

KAREN LEABO

Silhouette®

INTIMATE™MOMENTS®

Published by Silhouette Books

America's Publisher of Contemporary Romance

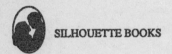

SILHOUETTE BOOKS

ISBN 0-373-07772-6

FRAMED

Copyright © 1997 by Karen Leabo

All rights reserved. Except for use in any review, the reproduction or utilization of this work in whole or in part in any form by any electronic, mechanical or other means, now known or hereafter invented, including xerography, photocopying and recording, or in any information storage or retrieval system, is forbidden without the written permission of the editorial office, Silhouette Books, 300 East 42nd Street, New York, NY 10017 U.S.A.

All characters in this book have no existence outside the imagination of the author and have no relation whatsoever to anyone bearing the same name or names. They are not even distantly inspired by any individual known or unknown to the author, and all incidents are pure invention.

This edition published by arrangement with Harlequin Books S.A.

® and TM are trademarks of Harlequin Books S.A., used under license. Trademarks indicated with ® are registered in the United States Patent and Trademark Office, the Canadian Trade Marks Office and in other countries.

Printed in U.S.A.

Books by Karen Leabo

KAREN LEABO

credits her fourth-grade teacher with initially sparking her interest in creative writing. She was determined at an early age to have her work published. When she was in the eighth grade she wrote a children's book and convinced her school yearbook publisher to put it in print.

Karen was born and raised in Dallas. She has worked as a magazine art director, a free-lance writer and a textbook editor, but now she keeps herself busy full-time writing about romance.

Chapter 1

"What am I going to do with all this junk?" Jess Robinson said on a moan as she sifted through a drawer full of expensive men's socks, some of them never worn. She had already inventoried a drawer full of designer underwear, a closet full of Calvin Klein jeans, shelves full of law books that had hardly been cracked, a cabinet full of men's toiletries.

"I say you pitch all this stuff," said her sister, Lynn, who at the ripe age of twenty, and with half of a university education, knew everything there was to know about the world and human nature. "Better yet, burn it. We could have a cleansing ritual. Maybe even a party."

"No, this stuff is too nice to destroy. Think a women's shelter could use it?"

"What is a women's shelter going to do with men's clothes? C'mon, Jess, just box it up and call the Salvation Army. I'm ready to move in."

"But what if he decides he wants it back?"

"Tough toenails. He told you to do whatever you

wanted with his stuff. If it turns out he made a bad decision, that's his problem, not yours."

Jess sank onto the king-size bed. "I just don't understand why he would leave here with only the clothes on his back. Lord knows his things were a lot more important than his education or his relationships. It doesn't make sense."

"It doesn't have to make sense. You know what your basic character flaw is, Jess?"

"No, but I'm dying to find out," Jess said dryly.

"You take on everyone's problems as your own. I learned about people like you in psychology class. You're called enablers. You enable people to be helpless and dependent because you encourage them to drop all their problems in your lap."

This was just what Jess needed, to be psychoanalyzed by her baby sister. Of course, Lynn wasn't completely wrong. Jess did tend to take on the world's problems, and she'd done so ever since she was a kid. That was why she'd agreed to let Lynn live with her while she finished her degree at University of Missouri at Kansas City.

"Do you have boxes?" Lynn asked.

"In the basement. Does this mean you're going to help?"

Lynn wrinkled her nose. "I'll pack up his jeans and stuff, but I'm not touching his underwear. Honestly, Jess, how could you stand that guy? He's such a dweeb."

Lately, Jess had often wondered that herself. At one time a law student with a bright future, Terry had seemed perfect for her. He'd harbored grand dreams, and she'd been eager for him to fulfill those dreams as quickly as possible. She hadn't even questioned it when he'd asked to move into her midtown duplex with her. He would save rent, he could quit his job and concentrate on school, thus becoming a lawyer that much sooner.

Hell, she'd been crazy in love, maybe for the first time.

But something had gone wrong. He never seemed to graduate. He claimed to spend a lot of time studying in the library, but Jess could sometimes smell beer and cigarettes on him when he came home. When her suspicions had become overwhelming, she'd begun investigating.

Terry was not enrolled at the UMKC law school. He hadn't been for at least two years.

At that point Jess had recognized that Terry was seriously flawed. He was just one of those people, she'd decided, who would never take responsibility for his own life. He blamed everyone but himself for his lack of success.

She'd politely asked him to move out. Caught, chagrined, he'd said he would be gone by the end of the month.

But that month had turned to two and then three. It became obvious that Terry wasn't even trying to find alternative living arrangements. He didn't pretend to look for work or enroll in school. He watched soap operas, drank beer and raided the refrigerator.

She'd put up with it far too long.

The doorbell interrupted her self-castigation, and her stomach tightened. Was he back? Did he want his things? She didn't want to see him again. The past few days she'd prayed he would stay out of her life forever. He needed psychological intervention.

He scared her a little. She didn't believe he was completely nuts, but he wasn't entirely rational, either. She wasn't quite sure where he would draw the line.

"Coming," she called as she trotted down the stairs to the door. But it wasn't Terry standing on her front porch. It was a man she didn't know, with black hair and midnight blue eyes and the squarest, most determined jaw she'd ever seen. Although it was only midafternoon, his face was shadowed with new beard.

"Ms. Robinson?"

"Yes?" Her mouth was suddenly dry. It wasn't that the man was movie-star handsome. His features were too sharp, too startling, for that. But he definitely had presence.

He studied her for a few heartbeats, giving her a casual but unmistakable once-over. "I'm Detective Kyle Branson with the Kansas City Police Department. May I come in?"

"Sure." Just let a complete stranger waltz into your living room, she scolded herself. "Wait a minute. Um, can I see a badge or something?"

He dutifully pulled his wallet from his back pocket and flipped it open, revealing a policeman's shield and a photo ID. Jess studied them briefly. Looked good to her, but then what did she know? With a mental shrug, she opened the door wider to allow the detective inside.

"Is something wrong?" she asked. "Oh, no, someone's died, I know it. If they have, tell me now. I can take it."

"I hope no one's died," the detective said. Rather than reassuring, his words seemed ominous.

Jess perched on the edge of her sofa, leaving available the recliner she'd bought for Terry's bad back. Instead the cop sat next to her, a proper distance away but still close enough to be intimidating. She felt an illogical need to put more distance between them so she couldn't be snared and held by his potent aura of power and masculinity. She resisted the urge to scoot farther away, instead folding her hands in her lap.

"Do you know a Terry Rodin?" he asked.

"Terry? Yes, I do. Has something happened?" Although Jess was positive she had no feelings left for Terry, she felt uneasy at the idea of any harm befalling him. She'd kicked him out, after all, when he had no job and no place to live. What if he'd become suicidal or something?

"That's what I'd like to know. He's missing. This is his last known address."

"He moved out," Jess said immediately. "He said he

was going to stay with his friend Kevin.'' She started to rise. "I've got his address and phone number if you—"

"We've talked with Kevin," the detective said, halting her with his searing blue gaze. "He's the one who alerted us. He said that two nights ago Terry was supposed to move in with him, and he never showed up."

"That's...that's weird."

"You were here when he left?"

"Yes. He took a taxi."

Branson produced a notebook from the inside pocket of his jacket, opened it and propped it on one knee to make notes. "Did he often take taxis?"

"Well, no. He usually took my car, or I drove him, or one of his friends drove him."

"But he took a taxi this time."

"Yes. I offered to drive him over to Kevin's, but he said he didn't...well, he didn't want anything from me. We'd previously been sort of involved, but I'd asked him to move out."

"Sort of involved?" A trace of humor lifted the corners of the detective's mouth. Once again she sensed him appraising her. Did he find her lacking? For some reason, she didn't think so. Branson behaved in a perfectly professional manner, but she couldn't miss the flicker of interest in his eyes.

Jess could feel heat rising in her face. "Very involved, but the relationship disintegrated months ago."

"And he only just now got around to moving out?"

Jess folded her arms. "I couldn't just kick him out into the street. He had nowhere to go, no money of his own. I gave him a few months to pull things together, but he never did. So finally I lowered the boom." And it had been one of the hardest things she'd ever done. Even though she'd come to truly dislike the man, she'd also felt sorry for him. He was majorly dysfunctional.

"Hey, Jess," Lynn called from upstairs, "can I keep Terry's CD player?"

Detective Branson's left eyebrow lifted by a fraction of an inch.

"He left his stuff here," Jess said with a shrug. "I assumed he would come back for it, but he hasn't."

"Obviously."

Jess wasn't sure she liked the look Branson gave her now, as if he was sizing her up for something.

"Jess, did you hear me?" Lynn yelled.

"Not now, Lynn," Jess called back impatiently.

"It's funny that Kevin didn't call here looking for Terry," Jess said, thinking aloud. "Then again, I wasn't Kevin's favorite person. Maybe he didn't want to talk to me."

"He says he tried to call you several times, but you never answered."

"He did? That's odd. Why didn't he leave a message?"

"Apparently your machine wasn't on."

"Well, of course it was on. I never leave without turning it on."

"Never?"

"Well, hardly ever." She didn't push the matter. Perhaps Kevin had tried to call, and she had stepped outside or something without turning on the answering machine. He must not have tried very hard.

"Tell me, Ms. Robinson, where do you think Terry might be?"

"I have absolutely no idea. He has lots of friends and he might have crashed with one of them. Maybe he forgot he was supposed to stay with Kevin. You can never tell with Terry."

"He's unpredictable?"

"Predictably unpredictable. He had a unique way of looking at life, like everyone and everything owed him something, that it was his divine right to be happy, that his needs were more important than anyone else's—" Abruptly Jess cut herself off. Good heavens, where had all that animosity come from?

"Please go on," Branson said with blatant interest.

"I'm sorry. I guess I still have some residual anger to deal with. I started out trying to explain something, which is that only one thing matters to Terry, and that's Terry. If he suddenly decided to bunk with someone else, he would probably arrive at their house unannounced and never bother to tell Kevin he'd changed his plans. That's how Terry operates."

"And you were involved with him?" Branson asked, incredulous. He spoke again before she could answer. "I'm sorry, that was unprofessional and uncalled for."

She answered the impertinent question, anyway. "Terry's also an excellent con artist. I confess he had me fooled for quite a while. Oh, and he loves practical jokes to an unhealthy point. It wouldn't surprise me if he'd disappeared on purpose, just so I would worry."

"And are you worried?"

"No," she said too quickly. "I refuse to be worried." When Branson continued to stare at her, causing a tremor of awareness along her spine, she added, "Well, maybe a little worried. It's strange that he didn't take his prized possessions."

"Such as?"

"His CD player," Jess said, nodding toward the stairs. "His clothes. The only way I can see that he would abandon those things is if someone else is providing them. And I'll bet you dollars to doughnuts that's exactly what happened."

"You mean you think he found him a sugar mama?"

"It wouldn't surprise me."

"Do you mind if I take a look around?" Branson asked.

"Sure, no problem. I might even be able to scare up Terry's address book, if that would help."

"That might help a lot." Branson rose and allowed her to lead him upstairs. Silly as it was, she couldn't shake the feeling that he was looking at her rear end as she walked ahead of him.

She stepped aside and indicated that he should enter Terry's room ahead of her. She followed him in, and there was Lynn, sitting on the floor, sorting through Terry's CDs.

"No, Lynn, you cannot keep anything of Terry's, including his CD player. We're going to box it all up and store it in the basement. Sooner or later, he'll be back. Count on it."

Lynn made a face—until she laid eyes on Detective Branson. Then she scrambled up off the floor and smiled like a beauty queen as she glided across the room. "Oh, hi. Didn't know we had company."

"Lynn, this is Detective Branson. Detective Branson, this is my sister, Lynn."

Lynn held out her hand as if she expected him to kiss it. "Charmed."

Oh, brother, Jess thought. Lynn had only recently overcome her teenager gawkiness, and she was fond of demonstrating her feminine charms to any male within range, just to see how they worked.

Fortunately, Branson seemed to be immune. He smiled politely and murmured, "Nice to meet you." Then he turned to Jess. His polite interest vanished, replaced by a more-than-healthy curiosity. "Did you share the room with him?"

She opened her mouth, but no words came out. How dared he, and right in front of her little sister! What business was it of his whether she and Terry slept—

He cleared his throat. "I don't mean to embarrass you, Ms. Robinson. But questions about a missing person's background and lifestyle are standard procedure."

She reconsidered the harsh words she'd been about to

speak. "No, I didn't share the room with him, at least not during the last few months. I moved into the guest room when we split up."

"Why didn't you make him move into the guest room?" Lynn asked. "It's your house."

Jess could tell by the expression on Branson's face that he, too, was speculating about the answer to that question.

"Because I'm a doormat, okay?" she replied. "Might as well get it out in the open. I was a gullible idiot to get involved with him in the first place, and I was too weak to get rid of him once I was on to him." She was mortified to hear her voice choked with tears.

She expected Lynn and the detective to agree with her, but they were both silent for several moments. Finally Branson said, "Lynn, would you mind leaving your sister and me alone for a few minutes?"

"Sure," Lynn said. She abandoned the pile of CDs and slunk out of the room.

"Sit down," he said to Jess, indicating a straight-back chair.

"Why?" she asked suspiciously. She felt like a kid about to be lectured by the principal.

"Because I want to talk to you."

"You can talk to me while I'm standing up." She knew she was being unreasonably defensive, but she felt so suddenly vulnerable and inferior and downright silly.

"If you're comfortable that way." He sat down on the bed himself, looking perfectly at ease. "Look, there's no reason for you to be embarrassed. I know Terry's type. There are thousands like him out there—men and women who could charm the skin off a snake. Lots of people are taken in."

"But I shouldn't have been," she argued. "I'm smarter than that. I'm Phi Beta Kappa, for God's sake. How could I be so stupid?"

"Hormones are enough to make anyone stupid, myself

included.'' He paused, letting that sink in. ''Everyone makes mistakes. You probably won't do it again.''

''Damn straight I won't.''

''Good. Meanwhile, I need to learn whatever I can about Terry Rodin so I can find the guy.''

''And give him a swift kick when you find him, I hope,'' Jess said, again hearing the surprising bitterness emerging in her voice.

''I'd like to. But kicking private citizens is…you know, against the rules. I could yell at him for you. Would that help?''

She knew he was trying to lighten the mood and put her at ease. To her dismay, it was working. ''I don't think yelling would work. No, brutality is the only answer, I'm afraid.'' She smiled despite herself, then sat at the foot of the bed. It suddenly struck her that perhaps they shouldn't be sharing the bed, even sitting up, fully clothed and several feet apart. To suddenly shift her position now would have drawn attention to the fact, so she stayed put.

The same thought might have occurred to Branson, though she wasn't sure. He did, however, immediately sit up straighter, put both feet on the floor and retrieve his notebook from his pocket.

''What do you need to know?'' she asked. ''I'll tell you all I can. I'll confess that I've occasionally wished violence on him, but deep down I wouldn't want anything to happen to him. He's…disturbed.''

''Distraught because of the breakup between you two?'' Branson asked, his dark blue eyes snapping with renewed interest.

''No, I wouldn't say that. He was angry at me for kicking him out, and he definitely laid a guilt trip on me, trying to get me to feel sorry for him, but he wasn't distraught.''

''So you don't think he was suicidal?''

She hesitated before answering. ''It's occurred to me,''

she finally said. "But I'd say he's more the type to threaten suicide rather than actually carry it out."

Branson scribbled furiously for a few moments, then looked up, skewering her with those startling eyes. "Any other theories?"

She gave the question serious thought, then shrugged. "I really can't imagine where he's gone. He claims to have no family, but I have reason to doubt everything he's told me, so who knows?" She slipped off the bed and went to Terry's seldom-used desk. "He has a Rolodex here. You're welcome to take it. There's not much in it, just a handful of friends and acquaintances, his tailor, his hair stylist—"

"Hair stylist?"

"His appearance is very important to him. I suppose you could classify him as vain."

"And did he have reason to be?"

"He's extremely good-looking," Jess answered without hesitation. That, at least, was one indisputable fact about Terry Rodin. She'd never met a single woman who thought he was less than movie-star material. At one time Jess had taken a certain feminine pride in partnering with such a handsome man. Now it wouldn't matter so much to her. Looks contributed very little to a relationship.

Branson frowned slightly as he scribbled in his notebook. "I'll take the Rolodex," he said, his voice gruff. "Can you tell me about his favorite hangouts? Restaurants or bars he frequented? Did he go to church?"

She stifled a laugh. "No church. And by his account he spent an ungodly amount of time at the UMKC Law Library, although I found out later he probably hasn't been there in years. There is one restaurant he's particularly fond of, called Papagallo's."

"Oh, yes, I'm familiar with it. Mediterranean food?"

She nodded. "He might go there. He claimed he had to eat there at least once a week or go into withdrawal."

"And I suppose you indulged him?"

Now she was not only embarrassed, she was getting downright irritated. She folded her arms and looked Branson straight in those damnably blue eyes of his before she answered. "I gave him my credit card and let him take his friends," she said. "I think we've established the fact that I was stupid, okay? Do we have to keep hammering on it?"

At least Branson had the good grace to appear slightly embarrassed himself this time. "Sorry," he murmured. "I'm not doing it on purpose. But you're an attractive woman, and you certainly don't seem slow. I find it difficult to believe you could be taken in, even a little bit."

He seemed sincere. Jess wasn't sure if she should have been flattered by his assessment or insulted. "Like I said, Terry was good," she murmured.

"What do you do for a living, anyway?"

"Freelance court transcriber."

"It's hard for me to envision anyone getting the better of you." This time his admiration was a little more obvious, a little harder to ignore. Surely he wouldn't be coming on to her, would he?

"Me too," she said, her voice failing. She'd been wrong before. Kicking Terry out hadn't been the hardest thing in the world; facing up to how stupid she'd been was definitely worse. But Branson was forcing her to do just that—out loud. "They say love is blind."

"That it is." He gazed off at a far wall, unseeing, and she wondered if he'd ever loved unwisely. Then she decided that was impossible. He was too controlled, too self-assured, for that. It seemed more likely that he'd never succumbed to that weak emotion at all.

"Are you married?" she asked impulsively, realizing even as the words left her mouth that the question was inappropriate.

He smiled, his eyes twinkling. "No. Never have been. Never even came close."

She offered no follow-up question, in case he thought she was flirting or something. Her momentary curiosity was satisfied.

They talked a few more minutes about Terry. She provided a photo, gave a detailed description of his habits and attitudes, right down to his favorite brand of beer. She actually found herself reluctant to have the detective leave, despite the fact that she'd bared herself to him, almost as if he'd seen her in her underwear.

He made a closer inspection of the room, walking around with an easy grace, looking but not touching anything. Finally he looked down at the carpeted floor. "Did there used to be a rug here? An area rug, I mean, on top of the carpet. There seems to be an outline defining an area that's less worn."

"There—" Jess stopped. "Oh, my God."

"What?" Branson's voice was laced with sudden tension.

"He took my Oriental rug." This was beyond belief. "That bastard took my rug. It was hand-woven silk over a hundred years old."

Scribbling again. "Worth a lot of money?"

"Yes, I'm sure it was, but that's not the point. It belonged to my great-grandmother. Why, out of all the things in this house, would he—"

"Are you sure Terry took it?" Branson asked, once again the consummate cop. "When was the last time you noticed it?"

She thought for a moment. "I don't remember when I noticed it last. It's been in this room ever since I moved in five years ago. And yes, I'm sure it was him. No one else has had access."

"But you didn't notice it was gone until now?"

"Not until you pointed it out." It amazed her that her

powers of observation were so dull, but lately she'd spent very little time in this room.

"And he didn't take it with him when he left two nights ago?"

"Now that I would have noticed. He couldn't have fitted it into the taxi, anyway. It was huge. He must have taken it and sold it at some point earlier," she said, thinking aloud.

"Did he need money?" Branson asked. "Was he on drugs?"

"He always needed money, but not huge amounts. I'm pretty sure he didn't do drugs. But I guess I didn't know him nearly as well as I thought."

Branson nodded noncommittally, made a few more notations in his pad, then stuffed it back in his breast pocket. As he exited the room, he stopped, looking down at the floor in the hallway. "There's a stain on the rug."

"Oh, really?" She was about to comment that it was rather uncalled for of him to point out the shortcomings in her housekeeping skills until she realized he was taking more than a casual interest in her carpeting. He stooped down and ran his fingers over the round, reddish brown spots.

"Is this a fresh stain?" he asked.

"I don't know. I never noticed it before, I guess."

"It looks like blood."

Jess's heart skipped a beat. She bent down to have a closer look, bringing her uncomfortably close to the detective. She caught a whiff of his aftershave. She recognized it as one of the brands Terry wore, and she recoiled.

"It could be blood, I suppose. Terry cut himself shaving last weekend, but I'm not sure the cut was bad enough that he would have been dripping blood."

Branson stared at her in a way that made her decidedly uncomfortable. She knew what he was thinking.

"No way," she said. "Terry was whole and hearty when he left here two days ago."

"And you're sure he hasn't been back?"

"Positive. Well, no, not positive," she said on second thought. "He could have slipped in when I was gone, but what for?"

Branson didn't answer. Instead he asked, "Does he have a key?"

"He did, but he gave it back. I made sure of that. Although I suppose he could have made a copy. But I don't think he's that devious."

"Do you worry that he might return?"

"Frankly, yes, and I want to prevent that at all costs. If he wants his stuff, I'll box it up and deliver it to him, but he's not setting foot through that front door ever again. It probably would take a bulldozer to get him out a second time."

Her attempt at humor fell flat.

Branson rubbed his fingers over the stain one final time before standing. He gave her another one of those appraising looks, as if he wasn't quite buying everything she said. Or as if he was wondering what he might do to make her talk.

His silent assessment made her shiver. She'd done the best she could; why did he make her so nervous?

As she walked him to the door, he said nothing else until he'd stepped onto the front porch. Then he turned and gave her a warning that chilled her to her heart: "Don't wash the rug. Don't touch it. We may want to check it out."

Dear God, did this guy really think some harm had befallen Terry in her house? And did he think…that she'd done it?

Chapter 2

"City Cab," a bored dispatcher answered.

"This is Detective Kyle Branson with the Kansas City Police Department," Kyle said into the phone between bites of a blueberry bagel. "I'm investigating a missing-persons case, and I need to speak with someone who can check the records for—"

"I'll transfer you."

Kyle sighed. This was the sixth taxi service he'd contacted during the past hour. So far, none of them had any record of picking up a fare at 4201 Sycamore, Jess Robinson's address, on the night Terry had disappeared. He hated to admit it, but he'd been hoping to find someone to corroborate Jess's story.

Another woman, this one with a bit more personality, came on the line, and Kyle made his request. While he waited for the woman to search the records, his thoughts returned to Jess. He wasn't sure what to make of her. Normally he had a gut emotional reaction the first time he met a witness or potential suspect, and his instincts seldom proved wrong. However, with Jess, so far the only reaction she'd provoked was of a distinctly physical nature.

He'd noticed her face first—classically beautiful, with large, dark eyes, high cheekbones, pillowy lips, straight, white teeth. Then he'd looked at the rest of her. She had a tall, sleekly muscled build, the kind that made him think she would be athletic in bed.

After that uncensored thought, he'd forced himself to stick with business. But it had been difficult for Kyle to get past her sensual appeal to read the nuances of her expression, body language and tone of voice.

Still, he'd persisted, with some degree of success. She'd seemed guileless enough, politely anxious but not overwrought, eager to be helpful. Yet there was a certain detachment about her, almost as if she was playing a part in a movie. Her reactions were almost too predictable. And the fact that she and her sister had been sifting through Rodin's belongings was…peculiar.

Rodin's leaving his things behind bothered Kyle, bothered him a lot. It wasn't the sort of thing a rational person did, which left him to believe that Terry was either emotionally or mentally unbalanced, or he'd become the victim of foul play.

Unbalanced? Maybe. According to Kevin Gilpatrick, Terry was a happy-go-lucky guy, not exactly steady but not unstable, either, and certainly not depressed about anything, especially his ex-girlfriend. But Kyle hadn't ruled out suicide, especially given Jess's take on the situation, which was very different from Kevin's.

Jess thought her ex-lover needed psychiatric help, which gave Kyle pause. During his twelve years on the police force, he'd seen the handiwork a spurned ex-lover could do, and it wasn't pretty. If Rodin really was unbalanced, Jess would be the natural target of his animosity. He could do anything from writing her nasty letters to filling her car with cement to blowing her head off. On the other hand, if *Jess* was the spurned lover... He closed off that line of thought, for now.

So whose image of Terry Rodin was closer to the truth, Kevin's or Jess's? Maybe neither of them was lying. People saw what they wanted to see.

Something else really bothered Kyle about this case, and that was the stain on Jess's hall carpet. He was ninety-nine percent sure the stain was blood. And she wanted him to believe it had been caused by a shaving cut? Please. He'd already requested that an evidence tech collect the stained carpet. Jess would probably be livid when the guy sliced up her rug, but those were the breaks.

He wished he hadn't had to alert her to the fact that he found the stain significant. If she was to become a suspect—and it looked as if she might—he didn't want her to know about it until absolutely necessary.

The woman on the other end of the phone came back on. "Sir?"

"Yes?"

"We don't have any record of a passenger being picked up at that address on October second."

"And is every fare documented?"

"Yes, sir. Undocumented passengers are grounds for dismissal at City Cab."

"All right, thanks—" A crumpled piece of paper flew at him from an adjacent desk. Kyle caught it deftly in his left hand and threw it back at his grinning partner, along with a murderous glare. "Thanks for your help. Bye now."

"Bye now," Blayney Cook mimicked in a syrupy voice. "Branson, you crack me up."

"Yeah, I'm so funny I'll entertain everyone in the unemployment line after we both get fired for making no progress whatsoever on this case. What have you got on Kevin Gilpatrick?"

Blayney, who at twenty-six was one of the youngest

detectives in the department, immediately sobered. He was a wiseass, up for just about anything that would get a laugh, but he was a damn good investigator when he tried. Kyle had every hope that the guy would someday develop into a first-class detective, probably in homicide, which was where he eventually wanted to be. It was just unfortunate that Kyle was the one assigned to break the kid in.

"Gilpatrick is an orderly at Blue Springs Medical Center. He has about a bazillion unpaid parking tickets on his record and one citation for drunk and disorderly several years ago. Other than that he's clean. He lives in a little rented house in Raytown. The place looked like a normally messy single guy's place, nothing out of the ordinary. He showed me the room he'd intended for Terry Rodin to move into."

"Furnished?"

"No. Gilpatrick said Rodin had planned to bring some furniture from the girlfriend's house, and that he'd rented a truck to carry it. Gilpatrick was waiting around that night, ready to help his buddy move his stuff in once the truck arrived. But Rodin never showed. Apparently the two of them had agreed on rent, and Gilpatrick had even installed a second phone line, so this wasn't a casual arrangement. Rodin was very serious about moving in."

Kyle scribbled a note to himself to check out all the U-Haul–type companies to see if Rodin really had reserved a truck.

"What was your take on Gilpatrick?" Kyle asked.

Blayney scratched his chin, which sported a scraggly beard. "Earnest, worried. Almost a little too cooperative, just inches short of bowing and scraping. Know what I mean?"

Kyle knew well the type of character Blayney was referring to—polite and helpful around authority figures, always saying "yes sir, no sir," in a way that was slightly nauseating. Such behavior always made Kyle wonder what the person was really thinking.

"Did he call you 'sir'?" Kyle asked Blayney, smiling at the thought.

"Yeah, as a matter of fact. Hey, what's so funny?"

"Nothing. Just don't get used to it." Blayney was about as authoritative as Little Orphan Annie.

"So do we have enough to get a search warrant for the babe's house?" Blayney asked, clearly relishing the idea of discovering some type of foul play.

Kyle opened his desk drawer, pulled out a much-abused Yellow Pages, and thrust it at Blayney. "Find out if Rodin rented a truck," he ordered. "I'm going to talk to Ms. Robinson's neighbors. And I wish you wouldn't call her 'the babe.'"

Blayney shrugged, looking a little puzzled. "It's just between us. I wouldn't call her that to her face, or write it in a report or anything."

Kyle nodded. He was being an idiot. All cops were at least a little cynical. Suspects were automatically "scumbags," and that was when the cops were feeling charitable. But it didn't seem right, referring to Jess Robinson as a "babe." She had more dignity than that.

"She good-looking?" Blayney asked.

"Average," Kyle said. He turned and stalked out of the squad room before he could think too hard about why he'd just lied to his partner.

"Hey, Jess, come look at this." Lynn was staring out the bedroom window, a half-folded pair of Terry's jeans hanging across her arm, forgotten.

"What now?" Jess asked, growing more irritated with Lynn every passing minute. The girl had spent far more time gazing out the window than performing any useful task. "Honestly, you're worse than nosy Mrs. Tanglemeyer two houses down. Is that stray dog relieving himself on our lawn again?''

''Much more interesting than that,'' Lynn said smugly, her gaze never wavering. ''The macho cop is back.''

Jess was at the window in an instant, peering down at the empty driveway. ''Where? I don't see anything.''

''Across the street. Talking to Mrs. Stubbs.''

''I wonder what he wants with her?''

''Jeez, Jess, don't you ever watch TV? He's checking out your story! Whatever you told him about Terry, he's seeing if Mrs. Stubbs can corroborate it.''

''Is he talking to all the neighbors, or just her?'' Jess wondered aloud.

''I'll bet he talks to everyone, to see if he can get a consensus of opinion. You know, like, 'Were they a happy couple? Did you ever see them fight? Did she have violent tendencies?' ''

''Lynn! That's not the slightest bit funny.'' Apparently Kyle Branson had finished questioning Mrs. Stubbs. He was putting his notebook in his pocket, although the middle-aged woman was still talking ninety to nothing. He waved goodbye to her and headed down the walkway, but he didn't return to his car. Instead he walked to the next house over.

''What in the world is he finding out?'' Jess asked, guiltily remembering the incident between her and Terry a couple of months ago. Terry had locked her out of the house in her bathrobe when she'd run outside to get the paper, and she'd yelled and knocked loud enough to wake the whole neighborhood, to no avail. Later he'd claimed it was an accident, and that he hadn't heard her knocking and ringing the bell, that he'd been taking a shower.

But she knew better.

She'd had to wake up her landlord next door at 6:00 a.m. to borrow the extra key. At the time, she'd been sure that the whole block knew that Terry had locked her out of the house and that she'd been madder than a she-wolf who'd missed dinner.

"Does this Branson guy doubt my word?" she wondered.

"A good cop doubts everyone's word," Lynn said in her newly acquired "expert" voice. "In my psychology class, we learned how fallible human memory can be. Even if he believes you're telling the truth as you know it, he has to allow for the fact that you might not accurately remember the sequence of events."

"It happened exactly like I told him." Then Jess thought back. During her conversation with Branson, she'd corrected herself several times, she recalled, and had often admitted that she wasn't sure about things.

Wouldn't that indicate innocence to him, to anyone? After all, if she'd been covering up something, wouldn't she have thought about her story and gotten it straight before talking to a cop?

Maybe not. The newspapers were full of stories of criminals too stupid to be believed, like the guy who robbed a bank and wrote the demand note on his own deposit slip.

"Lynn...you don't suppose he really thinks I had something to do with Terry's disappearance, do you?" Jess asked in a small voice.

"You?" Lynn laughed with abandon.

"It's not that ridiculous," Jess said. "After all, I did once...hurt someone."

Lynn sobered. "Relax. That Branson guy is just checking things out, that's all. Playing it safe."

For once, Lynn was making sense, more sense than Jess. "I suppose you're right."

"Do you think Mr. Dickinson will tell him about the time he saw you sunbathing nude in the backyard?"

Jess groaned. "I was *not* nude. I had on a beige swimsuit, and Mr. Dickinson needs glasses." If Detective Branson talked with a bunch of her chatty and highly imaginative neighbors, he might deduce all kinds of unsavory, incorrect things about her life. There was the time one of Terry's parties had gotten out of control and the police had shown up. She'd been out of town.

"There's only one thing to do," Jess concluded. "I'm going to face this guy head-on. If he wants to know everything about my private life, he can ask me. I won't hide anything."

"Not even the—"

"That I'll hide," Jess said quickly. "And don't you mention it, either. No one needs to know about the trial in Massachusetts."

Jess abandoned the box she'd been packing, rolled up her sleeves and headed downstairs. She paused in the hallway to stare at the brown stain on the carpet. She felt a strong impulse to clean the spot despite Kyle Branson's warning.

She would have to wait, though, until the police had run their tests, or whatever it was they did to supposed bloodstains. Anyway, she was on another mission right now. She opened the front door and strode brazenly out into the early-October chill.

Jess caught up with Branson just as he was exiting Mr. Dickinson's house. "Detective?"

He stared at her, first in disbelief, then looking a bit sheepish, like a kid caught looking up a lady's dress. "Ms. Robinson. What a...surprise."

"I could say the same. Just out for a little social stroll, are we?"

"It's called canvassing the neighborhood." He resumed walking toward his next target, the house across the street, which was next door to Jess's duplex. "I'm trying to find out if anyone has seen anything suspicious—you know, strange characters hanging around the neighborhood, any peculiar behavior—"

"Peculiar on whose part?" Jess asked. "Mine? Terry's?"

"Either. Both." He stopped on the neighbor's front porch, where Jess had followed him. When she didn't budge, he took a threatening step toward her. "If you don't mind, I'd like to conduct these interviews in private."

"Oh." Jess shrank back from his intimidating six-plus feet towering over her. She realized that by being confrontational, she was shedding an unflattering light on herself. "Fair enough. I'll just, um, go home and put some coffee on, then. Maybe you could stop by when you're done. I'd like to find out what kind of progress you're making."

"I'll keep you informed," Branson said in a way that made Jess suspicious, as if he was making fun of her. "As a matter of fact, I'd already planned to pay you another visit this afternoon. I might have a few more questions for you."

Jess nodded. He wanted to ask her more about her relationship with Terry. Fine. She had nothing to hide. Well, nothing about Terry, anyway.

Lynn was bouncing down the stairs as Jess came through the front door. "All of Terry's junk is in the basement except for the stuff in his bathroom. I'll start moving my stuff in now, okay?"

"Whoa, whoa, wait. I'm moving into the master bedroom. You can have the smaller room."

Lynn wrinkled her nose. "How come Terry could always get his way with you, but I can't?"

"Terry was a man," Jess said simply, without thinking.

"So?"

"Men can be pretty frightening, even weak men like Terry." Her thoughts strayed to Detective Branson. He scared her, but he also intrigued her. How annoying.

Lynn appeared thoughtful. "Yeah, I guess." Then she

was back to business. "Okay, let's move your stuff over to the master bedroom, then."

"You can start anytime you like," Jess said mildly as she headed for the kitchen, Lynn dogging her heels. "I'm making coffee. Detective Branson is coming over to ask more questions."

"Really? Maybe he'll try and trip you up, get you to contradict yourself."

"What a pleasant thought." As she put a new filter in the basket, Jess dithered over whether to make decaf or regular, then shook her head at her own foolishness. Had she actually been concerned about what Branson would prefer? This wasn't exactly a social call. She grabbed the canister of decaf, figuring it would be kinder on her nerves. She put two scoops into the filter, then filled the reservoir with tap water.

"You could box up the last few things in the bathroom," Jess suggested hopefully to Lynn.

"I told you, I'm not touching anything intimate like toothpaste or that flippin' gold razor you told me he uses. Oh, and, by the way, you'll need a new shower curtain."

"What? What's wrong with the old one?"

"There is no old one. It's not there."

"Not... You mean it's missing? How could that be?"

Lynn shrugged. "Beats me."

Now Jess was really baffled. First her Oriental rug, then her shower curtain. The only logical conclusion she could reach was that Terry had taken them. But why? The rug she could understand. He could sell it for at least a couple of thousand dollars. But why steal a shower curtain?

Maybe he'd torn it and thrown it away, then forgotten to ask her to buy a replacement. Yes, that made sense. Anything could be explained away if you just worked at it, she reasoned.

With a guilty smile, she reached under the sink and plucked out a pair of rubber gloves. "Here," she said, handing them to Lynn. "Now you can box up his toiletries, and his cooties won't get on you."

Lynn rolled her eyes, but she took the gloves. "All right, but you'll owe me."

"You might even find some pine cleaner under the sink. I'll bet the place needs a good disinfecting."

"No doubt. Don't push your luck, sister dearest. I promised I would keep my bedroom and bathroom neat, and I would clean up after myself around the rest of the house, but that does not include scrubbing up after Terrible Terry."

"All right, all right." As soon as the coffee was ready, Jess poured herself a cup, doctored it with cream and sugar, then went into the living room to sit down and await her interrogator.

"Now that's a strange way to think about it," she murmured to herself. She and Branson were on the same side, weren't they? He wanted her cooperation, and she was giving it. He hadn't said a cross word to her, or given any reason to believe he wanted to nail her for something—just that cocked eyebrow that indicated a skeptical nature.

She vowed not to take his skepticism so personally.

Olivia Tanglemeyer was the eighth and final neighbor Kyle intended to question. So far, he'd learned some interesting, if not startling, facts about Jess Robinson and Terry Rodin. Nude sunbathing, huh? Hardly the trait of a murderer, but fascinating nonetheless.

Not one neighbor had seen a taxi pull into Jess's driveway three nights ago, although Maxine Findley claimed she remembered a horn honking.

Maybe Rodin was the vindictive type, Kyle thought as he waited for someone to answer the door. Maybe he'd disappeared on purpose just to scare Jess, as she'd laughingly suggested. Stranger things had been known to happen.

The front door opened a crack, and a white-haired woman peered at him with one rheumy eye above a security chain. "What do you want?"

Kyle immediately displayed his shield and introduced himself, then explained why he wanted to talk to her.

"What do you want with me? How could I possibly help you?"

"You might have seen or heard something that could shed some light on the situation," Kyle said, part of his standard spiel. "It could be something that seems very insignificant to you. May I come in?"

The chain came off. "I'll be of help if I can," the lady said, her manner changing abruptly from suspicion to cooperation. "I'm Olivia Tanglemeyer, by the way, and you can call me Livvy. And your name is Kyle? How nice, I have a grandson with the same name. Come in and sit down. I just took a coffee cake out of the oven. Although I still don't know how I can help. I mind my own business. Most folks around here know me, but mostly I keep to myself...."

Mrs. Tanglemeyer continued with her monologue while Kyle loosened his tie. This was going to be a long interview. Contrary to what the lady had just said, she didn't mind her own business or keep to herself—at least, not according to her neighbors. When she wasn't peering out the windows at everyone else, she was on the phone, trying to glean information and passing along her own juicy morsels.

"And he was a very nice young man, yes indeed," Livvy said as she set a generous slice of coffee cake in front of Kyle. They had settled in the kitchen, which bore that odor of stale grease and natural gas so common to old houses belonging to old people. "He took my garbage out for me a couple of times, although I think that was Jess's idea."

"Mpff," Kyle said. Olivia Tanglemeyer's coffee cake

was dry as a brick, and she offered Kyle nothing to drink, and she talked nonstop, but he stuck around. She was proving to be a wealth of information. "He drove too fast," she said of Terry, "always screeching in and out of the driveway, sometimes at odd hours. Then again, I guess a lot of young men act that way. And the parties. Oh, my."

It sounded as if the old lady spent most of her life peering out windows, looking to find fault. But as for Jess herself, Olivia had only kind words to say.

"She really is a good neighbor. She keeps her grass mowed and is generally quiet, except for those few exceptions I mentioned. Maybe she just has bad luck with men. Her younger sister, the one who's over there now, once told me that a man Jess dated in college stalked her after she gave him the boot. What an awful thing."

Kyle made a note of this, though he wasn't sure what significance, if any, it had.

"Oh, there is one other thing…no, never mind. It's probably nothing." Livvy began nervously wiping down the pink-flecked Formica countertop.

"What? If it's nothing, then it won't hurt to tell me."

Reluctantly, she did. "Well, last weekend—before Terry left, you understand—Jess dropped by to see if I had anything that would get out bloodstains." The way Livvy dithered, it was clear she wished she'd never brought up the subject. "I lent her some spot remover."

"Did she say why she needed it?"

"No, I don't believe so. But it's so easy to cut yourself—by dropping a glass in the kitchen, or cutting up vegetables…" Her rheumy eyes seemed to be asking something of him.

"You're right, it's probably nothing," Kyle said, hoping to put the lady at ease. And maybe it wasn't significant, especially if it happened well before Terry's disappearance.

Maybe it hadn't happened at all, he thought hopefully.

Could be that Mrs. Tanglemeyer imagined things. She seemed sane enough, but she could be dotty as a Dalmatian. She was, after all, eighty-two years old, which she'd reminded Kyle of no less than six times.

Surely, if Jess had killed her lover, she'd done so in the heat of passion. He refused to believe she could ruthlessly plan ahead, to the point of anticipating troublesome bloodstains.

It was almost an hour later when he left Livvy's house with a promise to return soon and sample her poppyseed pound cake. He headed back to Jess's house, looking forward to his interview with her. He already had her on the defensive, and with a few pointed questions he hoped to get her thoroughly flustered. Then perhaps he could ascertain whether she was telling him the whole truth.

When she answered the door, her long dark hair was piled carelessly on top of her head, secured with a single clip. Several loose, wavy tendrils framed her face. She looked expectantly at him, and he was the one who felt suddenly flustered.

"Um, as I said earlier, I have a few more questions, if this is a convenient time."

"No more or less convenient than any other time," she said, her face and voice carefully neutral, he noticed. She allowed him inside. This time, however, she sat in the recliner, relegating him to the sofa alone. Did she do it because his nearness bothered her, or because she wanted to be sitting higher than he was? Perhaps she thought she would gain a psychological advantage by doing so.

Hah. He was a master at interrogation. He declined to sit down. "Is that coffee I smell?"

"It was," she said smoothly. "I drank it all. I was working at the computer, and I drink nonstop when I'm working."

"May I have some water, then? I just ate two pieces of

Mrs. Tanglemeyer's coffee cake. Have you had the pleasure?''

Jess nodded and was on her feet, heading toward the
kitchen. "Enough said."

Kyle followed her. "What are you working on?"

"The transcript for the Roger Drane murder trial. Very
interesting stuff."

"Do you often transcribe murder trials?"

"I've done a few," she said, a note of caution entering
her voice again as she filled a glass with chilled water from
a bottle in the refrigerator. "Most of my work is a little
more mundane."

"But you do quite a few criminal hearings?"

"I'm not sure what 'quite a few' means, but I'd say the
majority of my work involves civil hearings, not criminal."

Still, Kyle mused, she'd probably gleaned quite a lot of
knowledge about police procedure, and how murderers and
other criminals tripped themselves up.

She'd reclaimed her throne in the living room, and Kyle
had downed almost all his water, before the conversation
resumed.

"Did you borrow some stain remover from Mrs. Tanglemeyer earlier this week?"

Jess appeared startled at first, then wary. "Yes, I did.
Terry cut himself shaving and bled on his shirt—I already
told you that, didn't I?"

Kyle nodded.

"The spot wouldn't come out the first time I washed
it."

"Were you in the habit of doing Terry's laundry?" Kyle
asked, trying to mask the incredulity in his voice.

Jess sat up straighter. "Terry didn't even know how to
operate the washing machine," she said. "He usually sent
everything out to be cleaned, but I offered to do the shirt
so the stain wouldn't set. In fact...yes, of course." A tri-

umphant smile lit up her face. "The shirt's probably still in the basement where I keep the washer and dryer. Livvy's stain remover didn't work very well, so I left the shirt down there, thinking I'd have another go at it. Would you like to see it?"

"That might be helpful. It was a small stain, you say?"

She stood and led the way into the kitchen and through the basement door with a confident swing in her hips. "About the size of a quarter, I guess. Small, but very noticeable. He certainly wouldn't have wanted to wear the shirt again unless the stain disappeared."

Jess's basement was clean, tidy and well lit. A clothes rack stood by the old-model laundry machines, where several shirts—women's shirts, from what Kyle could tell—hung. Jess flipped through the hangers, then put her hands on her hips and looked around the basement. Perplexed, she opened the washer and dryer, which were both empty.

"Now, that's odd," she said. "I guess Terry took the shirt with him."

"I thought he didn't take anything with him."

"He didn't, but—"

"If he were only going to take one shirt, why would he take the one with a stain?"

Jess shrugged. "I don't know where the damn shirt is." Now she was really frustrated. That's where Kyle liked his suspects, he thought with little satisfaction. There was no denying now that Jess was a suspect, at least in his mind.

"Is this Livvy's stain remover?" Kyle asked, picking up a plastic bottle from a nearby shelf. It was empty.

"I intended to buy her a new bottle," Jess said, folding her arms across her breasts.

When they returned to the living room, Kyle switched to a different line of questioning. "When Terry left Monday night—did you see the cab?"

"Yes."

"Do you happen to remember which company it was?"

"No. I mean, I didn't actually see the vehicle that clearly, but I saw the lights pull up in the driveway, and the driver honked."

"Was it a long honk?"

Jess shook her head. "No, just a tap on the horn, the way cabbies do."

Kyle felt undeniably relieved that at last something Jess had said was corroborated by another witness. Mrs. Stubbs had described the horn she'd heard Monday night the same way Jess had—as a short, single honk. Unfortunately, that didn't mean he could ease up on his questions.

"Jess, would you describe your relationship with Terry as a calm one?"

Jess closed her eyes, and her porcelain face tightened with tension. For a moment, Kyle regretted his adversarial role with her. An image flashed into his mind. He saw himself rubbing Jess's shoulders, smoothing his hands along her neck, her jaw, her cheeks, easing away the tightness. The mental picture was downright erotic, and Kyle quickly turned away to look out the window until his thoughts were under control.

"At times Terry and I had arguments. Sometimes he just blew up for no reason, and I couldn't help but respond. But that was before we broke up. After I made the decision to break off with him and asked him to leave, things calmed down. We tolerated each other, barely spoke. It was a relief, really." She opened her eyes and stared at him, challenging him to dispute her.

"Hey, Jess!" Lynn called from upstairs.

Jess looked relieved at the interruption. "What is it?" she called back.

"Can I pick out the shower curtain to replace the one that's missing? I don't like this starfish one in my bathroom."

Kyle's senses went on the alert. "You're missing a shower curtain?"

"Mmm, yes, another little mystery."

"From which bathroom?"

"Terry's." Abruptly her eyes narrowed. "For heaven's sake, why are you asking questions about shower curtains and stain remover? What possible impact could things like that make on Terry's disappearance?"

Did he have to spell it out? Couldn't she put two and two together? The crime he envisioned was brutal and cold-blooded, but simple enough. And if it had taken place, Jess was probably the one who'd done it.

"Ms. Robinson, I'd like to take you downtown for questioning," he said as indifferently as he dared. "And I think it would be a good idea if you called a lawyer."

Chapter 3

The "interview room" was gray and featureless, unless one counted the obscene graffiti some previous "witness" had scratched onto the wall. Jess sat primly with her hands folded on the table in front of her, as she had for the past three hours while Kyle Branson had questioned her.

Questioned? That was too mild a description of what that flaming jerk had been putting her through.

"How many times are you going to ask me the same questions?" she asked, her voice cracking from the strain.

"Until I'm satisfied," Kyle replied, studying his nails. He hadn't raised his voice, hadn't physically intimidated her. But the relentless pounding of the same subjects was getting to Jess just the same. And his sheer physical presence was intimidating enough.

"Maybe it's time to break out the hot lights and rubber hoses," Jess said, amazed that she could manage even feeble humor.

The stern uniformed officer stationed at the door almost smiled, and Branson threw her a scathing look.

Jess had waived her right to have an attorney present—foolishly, it seemed now. God, what had she been thinking? She was well acquainted with the legal system. To ask for a lawyer would have made her look as if she had something to hide, and she didn't. Having a lawyer sitting beside her would have put her in the class of "suspect," which was somewhere she'd never intended to be.

She'd made the decision back when Branson had been halfway friendly. He'd somehow managed to convey, without using the actual words, that she didn't *really* need a lawyer despite his earlier warning, that this was routine questioning. Anyway, the only lawyers she knew were friends of Terry's.

She was about to change her mind. The interrogation—and that was the only word for it now—had gotten increasingly aggressive. Branson had confused her so thoroughly that she couldn't help misspeaking, correcting herself, clarifying and then reclarifying in a way that sounded guilty even to her.

There was no denying now that she was a murder suspect.

"I asked you a question, Ms. Robinson," Kyle said, annoyingly polite. "Would you like me to repeat it?"

"No, I heard you fine the first time. But I'm choosing my words very carefully, since you seem to have a habit of twisting everything I say. Terry came downstairs last Saturday with a light blue Polo shirt in his hand and holding a Kleenex to his chin. He said he'd cut himself shaving and stained his shirt, and because it was a favorite shirt and he didn't trust the laundry, would I get the stain out for him? I said okay, no problem, since I was doing laundry that morning, anyway. But I was out of the prewash stuff I usually use, so I ran down to Livvy's to borrow something. She asked what for, and I told her."

"But the stain didn't come out?"

"No. I thought I might try bleaching it later. I put it on a hanger and hung it on the rack."

"Bleaching it?" he repeated. "A blue shirt?"

She sighed. He was doing it again, making her feel foolish. "Light blue. The label didn't say not to bleach. It might have worked."

"Was it that important to you, to get the stain out?"

"It was a challenge, okay? Maybe I like laundry challenges. Maybe it fulfills me to remove stains. Jeez, next you'll be saying I wanted to earn back Terry's love by getting his shirt clean! But even that wouldn't satisfy you. Next you'd ask, 'Were you distracted that day? Too distracted to clean the shirt properly, because the sight of all that blood got you thinking, right? Thinking about killing your ex-boyfriend!'"

Branson said nothing. He appeared a bit surprised by her outburst. She'd been completely docile until now.

"Am I right?" she demanded, coming out of her chair and leaning across the table toward him. "Isn't that what you would say?"

Her words echoed hollowly in the barren room. Only then did she realize how loudly she'd been speaking.

Slowly the detective rose from his chair and leaned toward her. The expression on his face frightened her, and she shrank back.

"Were you distracted?" he asked softly. "Did the blood make you think about killing your ex-boyfriend?"

The questions sounded much more menacing coming from him. She remembered another man who had spoken to her that way, softly, not with violence but with so much power. Seconds later she'd been fighting for her life.

Face-to-face with Branson now, she felt beads of sweat break out on her forehead, even though the room was chilly. Her palms dampened against the smooth wooden tabletop. The hair on the back of her neck stood on end, and she had to resist the urge to gasp for air.

"Would you answer me, please?" he said.

Her knees failed her, and she sank back into her chair. "No," she whispered, wincing as she waited for his reaction.

"What? I can't hear you."

Her voice was no stronger when she repeated herself. She cleared her throat. "I won't answer any more questions without an attorney."

"Now you're asking for an attorney? Was it something I said?"

She wanted to retort. His sarcasm made her want to hit something. But her throat locked up and her eyes misted over, and her whole face flushed hot. Damn, she was going to cry.

"I...know...my...rights," she managed to choke out. Her eyes overflowed, and she hid her face in her hands, utterly mortified.

They were both silent for many long seconds. Then Branson came around the table and sat in the chair next to hers. He leaned down, trying to see her face. "Look, Ms. Robinson...Jess...I know this is hard for you. And I'm sorry I have to be so tough on you." He cast a cautious glance at the policewoman, as if he was worried that she would catch him being nice. But the uniformed officer was staring into space, appearing neutral once more.

"I don't enjoy all these questions," he continued, "believe me. I'm just doing my job."

She wanted to tell him to get another job, then, one that would allow him to be human instead of some lowly subspecies. She wanted to tell him that she wasn't fooled one bit by his phony sympathy. She knew this routine, had seen it in dozens of court transcripts. She wanted to tell him to go straight to hell. She'd asked for an attorney. The game was over, unless he wanted to take some high-powered flak for violating her rights.

But she couldn't get the words out.

"Do you want a glass of water?" he asked, all traces of sarcasm having vanished.

"I told you what I want," she mumbled through her hands.

He sighed. "All right, I'll get you a lawyer. It'll take some time—"

She raised her head and looked at him, knowing her face was wretchedly tearstained, her makeup smeared. Why she should care about that, she didn't understand. "I'll get my own lawyer, thank you." She sniffed loudly.

"All right, then," he said, sounding resigned. "You have until tomorrow morning."

"I can go?"

"You're not under arrest at this point."

She could tell by the tone of his voice that he wished she were. "Do you really think I did something awful to Terry?"

He studied her for a moment. "I don't know."

He seemed about to say something else when someone knocked. Branson nodded to the uniformed officer, and she opened the door.

A man in his midtwenties swaggered in and dumped a pile of small plastic bags onto the table. "Looky what I got," he said, casting an expectant glance at Jess. "A key chain, engraved with the initials TR. A gold chain, fourteen karat. And a man's wallet with some interesting ID."

"Those are Terry's," Jess said, forgetting her own misery for a moment as the implications of these discoveries sank in. "Oh my God, you found him? Is he...is he dead?"

"No, we didn't find him, Ms. Robinson," the newcomer said. His mouth tightened, as if he were suppressing a smile.

"Then where did you get those things?"

The young man smirked. "We had a search warrant for your place and your car, remember?"

Jess nodded. She'd surrendered her house and car keys without a whimper, figuring their search would yield nothing. "Those things were in my house?" she asked.

"Under your mattress."

"Son of a bitch," Kyle said under his breath. He turned once more to Jess. "Ms. Robinson, I'm afraid I spoke too soon. You're under arrest."

In a monotone, Kyle read Jess her rights, even though he'd already Mirandized her before the interrogation. He walked her through the booking process—the fingerprinting, the mug shots. She looked frail and pallid, as if she might pass out any moment. More than once he had to stop himself from touching her, reflexively offering her a supporting hand or a word of comfort.

Good God, what was he thinking? The woman was a cold-blooded murderer, or so the evidence suggested. During the interrogation, he'd almost begun to believe she was telling the truth, that she didn't know what had happened to Terry Rodin. She hadn't acted guilty. Her answers to his questions remained maddeningly consistent, no matter how he flustered her.

Damn his instincts, anyway. In this case, they were just flat wrong.

As a guard led her away to a holding cell, where she would be incarcerated until her arraignment tomorrow, she gave Kyle one final, pleading look. Hell, what did she expect him to do for her? He was a cop, for God's sake. He wasn't in the business of helping murder suspects. He'd done nothing but antagonize her from the moment they met. Did she think he was going to suddenly come to her rescue?

That was exactly what he was contemplating as he walked the case over to homicide. He could at least make sure she had a decent lawyer, that she was able to post bond.

Ah, hell, he had to be out of his mind to let a pretty pair of brown eyes seduce him. Hadn't he learned by now not to make assumptions about a woman because she was beautiful and refined? Hadn't Buck, his former partner, learned that lesson the hard way?

Kyle promised himself that once homicide had control of this case, he would put it out of his mind. He had other cases piling up on his desk.

Lt. Jon Easley, in charge of homicide, assigned the case to Bill Clewis. Clewis would not have been Kyle's first choice. The man was hard, utterly without compassion and a sloppy investigator to boot. He always looked for the easy answer, never went that extra mile.

On the plus side, he was a helluva good interrogator. If anyone could make Jess Robinson crack, Clewis could. The thought made Kyle a little nauseated, and he couldn't help feeling sorry for Jess, guilty or no. She was in for it.

"Problem is," Kyle said to Clewis once he'd gone over the case with him, "I'm not sure if the D.A. can make the murder charge stick when there's no body." He swung one leg back and forth from his perch on the edge of Clewis's messy desk, trying to maintain an air of detachment.

"It's been done before," Clewis pointed out, puffing out his chest and sucking in his gut. "Anyway, if there's a body to be found, I'll find it."

"There's no murder weapon, either," Kyle said. "The evidence team searched her house from top to bottom. They're digging up the yard now."

"Did you do a trace metal test on her hands, to see if she's held a gun recently?"

Kyle shook his head. "Too much time has elapsed."

Clewis nodded in agreement. "'Course you're right. Now, what's this note about blood?"

Kyle winced inwardly. He'd spoken with the evidence team who'd searched Jess's place. They'd used luminol on the stain on her carpet, a chemical that detected the minutest traces of blood, even those that couldn't be seen with the naked eye.

"There's a small spot on her upstairs carpet that turned out to be blood. Not only that, but the luminol showed traces all over Rodin's sink and bathtub. At one time they were both awash with blood, and lots of it."

Clewis smiled unpleasantly. "Maybe a murder charge will stick. She could have taken the guy unawares, maybe when he was taking a bath. She offs him with a butcher knife, then wraps the body in the shower curtain, then the rug. She drags him to her car, drives to the river and dumps him. You checked her car?"

"No blood there," Kyle said. "But there was a little bit in the washing machine." More than that quarter-size stain she'd described could account for.

"Did you check her clothes? Everything in her closets and drawers?"

"No bloody clothes found."

"So maybe she did her dirty deed in the nude," Clewis said with a leer. "Or she might have ditched the bloody clothes."

"If she was so careful, then why would she be dumb enough to hide Rodin's wallet and keys under her mattress?"

"She probably had no idea things would heat up so quickly, and she intended to dispose of them later. She couldn't take a chance leaving them in his room. Anyone who saw them would know he hadn't left without them. And she wouldn't want to dispose of them with the body. She was counting on the body not being quickly identified if it turned up."

"Yeah, that makes sense, I guess," Kyle reluctantly agreed.

Clewis gnawed on his lower lip. "So you think she did it?"

Kyle thought long and hard before he spoke, but he still

couldn't come up with a definite answer. "Sometimes I do, and sometimes I don't. If she did do it, she's one cool cookie and a helluva lot smarter than your average murderer."

"And if she didn't, what are the alternatives?"

Kyle sighed. There weren't many. "Someone else did it, in her house."

"So someone was with Rodin the night he disappeared, because he didn't show up at his buddy's house. Then, after the babe went to sleep that night, this unknown perpetrator dragged Rodin back into the babe's house. Then this unknown perp offed Rodin, wrapped him in the shower curtain and the rug, then left with the body—all without our little suspect knowing a thing."

The theory was patently ridiculous, and Kyle resented Clewis's patronizing tone.

"Without a body, we can't even guess at the time of death," Kyle said. "Maybe the murder took place while Jess was out the next day. She went to help her sister pack and was gone several hours."

Clewis smiled indulgently and shook his head. "No way. That's why I'm a homicide detective and you're in missing persons. Face it, Branson, that sweet-faced little girl offed her boyfriend. And I'm going to prove it."

"Your Honor," the assistant district attorney said, "due to the particularly cold-blooded and heinous nature of this crime, I'm requesting that the amount of bail be set at one million dollars."

Jess's heart went into her throat. Dear God, where would she come up with that kind of money, even the percentage she would need to get a bond? In Massachusetts, her bail had been only twenty-five thousand.

Marva Babcock, Jess's lawyer, was instantly on her feet. "Your Honor, there's been no body and no murder weapon found," she pointed out. "We're not even sure any crime has been committed. The prosecution's evidence is primarily circumstantial. Furthermore, my client is a respected, law-abiding citizen with a career and strong family ties in the area. She isn't likely to flee. I respectfully request that bail be set at twenty-five thousand.''

The judge, a grandfatherly man with eyes of cold steel, frowned, then proclaimed, ''Bail is hereby set at one hundred thousand dollars.'' He looked straight at Jess as he spoke, and she got the feeling he was silently warning her that she'd better not prove him wrong by skipping town.

It was tempting, but of course she wouldn't flee. She'd always played by the book, and even though the rules had worked against her at times, she wouldn't change her ways now. The justice system had once failed to protect her but had eventually cleared her of all wrongdoing. Surely that's how it would work this time.

She nodded solemnly at the judge, indicating she'd heard him loud and clear.

Her gaze drifted toward Kyle Branson, sitting to the right and slightly behind her. She'd noticed him watching her throughout the proceedings. Even when she was looking straight ahead, she could sometimes feel his gaze on her. Oddly, his interest hadn't made her uncomfortable. In fact, despite the way he'd treated her over the past couple of days, she believed that he was one of only a handful of people in the world who didn't automatically believe she was guilty.

He'd been required to testify as to his part in the investigation of Terry's disappearance. After his aggressive interrogation the day before, she'd been prepared for him to annihilate her at the arraignment. But his testimony had been strictly factual, no emotion showing on his chiseled face. She couldn't honestly say he'd tried to shed a more favorable light on her, but neither had he gone out of his way to make her appear guilty.

Unfortunately, the evidence did that well enough, without anyone's help.

Jess had been as surprised and shocked as anyone to hear what the search of her house had turned up. She'd known about the stain on her carpet, of course, and she was pretty sure how it got there. But evidence of blood—and lots of it—in the tub and sink was a shock, and a little harder to find a rational explanation for.

She also hadn't realized that a knife was missing from her good Chicago Cutlery kitchen set.

"A hundred G's," Marva whispered in her ear. "That's good."

Marva wasn't anyone's stereotype of a slick lawyer. She was heavyset, in her midfifties and black. Lynn, of all people, had found her through one of her professors at UMKC. Jess had nearly dropped her teeth when she'd first laid eyes on Marva, but she'd soon had to scold herself for making snap judgments based on appearance. Marva was as sharp and deadly as a poison dart.

The arraignment was over quickly. In fact, the past twenty-four hours had gone by in a blur of phone calls, hasty conferences, food hardly tasted, a hard bed barely slept in. She'd been numb, in shock, she realized now. Thank goodness Lynn had proved to have a head on her shoulders, after all. She'd taken care of everything.

"How soon can you arrange for a bond to be posted?" Jess asked Marva. Two guards stood by, waiting to take her back to her hated jail cell.

"Before lunch—you just wait and see," Marva said, patting her client maternally on the shoulder. "Do you have ten thousand dollars to put up for the bond? If not—"

"I've got it," Jess said, thinking of the little nest egg she'd been saving. This would just about wipe out her savings account. She had no idea how she would pay Marva, but the attorney hadn't seemed concerned. "Lynn, did you bring my Money Market checkbook?"

"Got it right here," Lynn said. "Although, I'm telling you, it was damn near impossible to find anything after those cops got through trashing the place. They just dumped everything on the floor and left it there."

Jess didn't care about the mess. She would gladly spend the next week cleaning up, if only she could be at home. She wrote out a check for ten thousand and handed it to Marva. Then the guards took her away.

Cameras flashed and microphones were shoved in her face as she left the courtroom. She'd been prepared for scrutiny from the press, had already planned out her strategy with Marva. Instead of the standard "no comment" so many crime suspects hid behind, she paused and spoke to the reporters.

"I'd like to talk with you all," she said pleasantly. "I'd like the chance to tell my side of the story. But my lawyer advised me not to. I'm sorry."

"Do you think you'll get off?" one voice from the crowd asked.

"Did you do it?" another, farther back, demanded.

"I can't answer any questions," she said again, then turned to continue on her way. Apparently they believed her, because they didn't follow.

As she turned the corner, she skidded to a stop to avoid hitting a man standing in her path. The man was Kyle Branson.

"Oh," she said, and stared at him idiotically.

"How are you?" he asked.

"How do you think?" she countered. "How would you be in my position?"

"Dumb question, I guess," he said.

She shook her head. "No, I'm the one being dumb, snapping at you like that. I appreciate what you did back there."

He appeared confused. "What did I do?"

"When you testified. You sounded...impartial." He

was standing close enough that she could smell his after-shave. It was a different one this time, not the one Terry had worn. She liked it.

"I haven't exactly done you any favors," he said.

"No, but you could have treated me a lot worse than you did. I'm grateful for any small thing at this point. So have you made up your mind? Do you think I did it?"

"Jess," Marva cautioned, but Jess held up her hand to forestall her lawyer's objections. For some reason, it was important to know what Branson thought. He knew more about the case than anyone. If he believed there was even a chance she was innocent, then a jury might, too.

"It looks bad for you, Jess," he said.

"But…?"

He shrugged. "Beats me why I'm still not sure, but I'm not."

She latched on to his opinion and held it close to her heart. It gave her hope.

"Thank you," she said before the guards urged her away from the detective and on down the hall.

True to her word, Marva managed to spring Jess from jail just as a guard brought her an unappetizing lunch on a tray. She gladly turned her back on the food and waltzed out of her cell with visions of Taco Bell in her mind. The numbness was receding, her senses returning. After fewer than twenty-four hours in jail, she was ready to fight for her freedom.

She spent the afternoon answering questions for Marva, who made Branson's interrogation look like a stroll in the park. With her skillful questioning, she helped Jess to re-member details she hadn't recalled before—nothing that proved terribly significant as yet, but that might eventually.

That evening she spent a couple of hours cleaning up the mess the evidence team had made. Lynn hadn't ex-aggerated. Drawers were overturned, cushions had been pulled off furniture and a hunk of her hall carpeting was missing. Apparently the men had cut away the section with the bloodstain for further analysis.

And they weren't done yet. They were digging up her yard while her landlord, Mr. Glorioso, yelled at them from behind the yellow crime-scene tape. She couldn't blame him. If they applied the same delicate touch they'd used with her house, it would take years to put the landscaping back in order.

It was almost dark, but she could still hear the clanking of shovels.

"I can't take any more," Jess declared at just after eight o'clock. "I'm going to bed."

Lynn looked up from her place on the couch, where she'd been studying one of Terry's law books. Other books were spread out all around her, bristling with scraps of paper where she'd marked interesting passages.

"Okay," she said, "but first listen to this. 'The State of Missouri v. Langley Bostwitch,' 1936. Apparently this guy slit his mother's throat and hid the body—"

"Lynn, please!" Jess exploded. "If I hear one more word about stabbings and hidden bodies, I'm going to scream!"

"But this guy used a great defense and he got off."

"Tell me in the morning. I'm going to bed." At Lynn's crestfallen expression, Jess softened her admonition with a smile. Funny how strong a person could be when circumstances dictated, she mused as she climbed the stairs. She never would have guessed Lynn would prove such a veritable pillar of strength and common sense.

As tired as she was, Jess had trouble falling asleep. She kept going over and over the days preceding Terry's disappearance, trying to remember anything—anything at all—that might have been overlooked. She didn't come up with a single useful scrap, however, and shortly before midnight she managed to fall into an uneasy sleep.

At about two, the phone jarred her instantly awake. Her

first thought was that maybe Terry had been found alive and well and they were going to let her off the hook. Even as she grabbed for the receiver, she realized she was being hopelessly optimistic.

"Hello?" she answered cautiously.

"Why did you kill me?" The voice was a hoarse, muffled whisper, like someone speaking through layers of gauze.

Terry? Speaking to her from the beyond? She shook her head to clear it of the last vestiges of sleep. A spirit wouldn't need to use the telephone.

"Who is this?" she demanded sharply. A phone prank. It had to be.

"Why did you kill me?" the voice repeated.

"Terry?" It really did sound like Terry. Her heart pounded furiously.

"I loved you. We could have worked things out—"

"Shut up!" She knew she should just hang up. But she couldn't help responding in anger. "This isn't funny."

"No, murder isn't funny. At least tell them where you hid the body, so I can rest in peace."

Jess hurled the vilest insult she could think of at the caller, then slammed down the phone. Who would play such a vicious prank?

An immediate answer came to mind. Who had delivered twenty pizzas to his former employer's office and charged it to the employer's credit card? Who had used weed killer to write obscenities on the neighbor's lawn when he'd had an argument with said neighbor over his yowling tomcat? Who had made chocolate pudding with Ex-Lax and served it to an old girlfriend he'd been mad at?

Terry. Of course, Terry, the ultimate practical joker. The son of a bitch had set this whole thing up to frame her for his murder.

Chapter 4

Kyle's stomach was tied in knots as he watched, through a two-way mirror, while Bill Clewis verbally abused his murder suspect in the interview room. Not that Kyle hadn't been just as tough on her when he'd been the one in charge of interrogation. The difference was that Clewis seemed to enjoy his suspect's discomfort.

"I have no idea what happened to my knife," Jess said, her voice a monotone, her hands folded demurely on the scarred table in front of her. She'd displayed little emotion during the ordeal. In fact her attorney, Marva Babcock, had shown more outrage than Jess, frequently objecting to Clewis's relentless hammering when it became repetitive.

"And when was the first time you noticed it missing?" Clewis asked.

"I didn't notice. I was told that the evidence team was taking my set of knives, and why."

"You're a very neat and precise person—is that a fair statement?"

She thought a moment. "Yes."

"And you enter your kitchen...how many times a day?"

"Maybe between five and ten."

"Yet you didn't notice that knife missing?"

"No. I haven't done much cooking in the past few days."

"When was the last time you remember seeing that knife, Ms. Robinson?"

She sighed. "I don't know. I'm not even sure precisely which knife is missing. I cooked some chicken a couple of weeks ago, and I used the deboning knife from the same set. If any of the knives had been missing then, I probably would have noticed."

"Besides deboning chicken, what do you use those knives for?"

There was a pregnant pause. "Carving up ex-boyfriends."

"Jess!" the attorney scolded. "This is no time for sarcasm."

"Vegetables," Jess said hastily. "I make a lot of salads. And I'm sorry, but what do you want me to say? Does it really matter what I use a knife for, unless I really did use it the way you think I did?"

"I think we should call a halt to this session," Marva said. "My client is close to exhaustion."

"Amen to that," Kyle mumbled.

"Just a few more questions," Clewis said. "Fifteen more minutes, all right?"

"Fine, just get on with it," Jess said, slumping back into her chair.

Of course Clewis would want to continue, Kyle thought. When the suspect was exhausted, that was the best time to catch her in a lie.

As Clewis went over old territory, Kyle jotted in his notebook: "Interesting that she didn't invent a story about the knife, like, 'I lost it years ago,' or 'I accidentally bent the blade and had to throw it away.'"

"What are you doing in here, Branson?"

The voice behind him made him jump. He swiveled and found Lt. Jon Easley, head of homicide, standing beside him, chewing on the mangled end of a Bic pen. He'd quit smoking a couple of months ago and had immediately put on twenty pounds, adding to his already impressive girth. Horn-rimmed glasses, a white crew cut and polyester suits added to Easley's less-than-cool image, but there was no sharper cop in the whole department.

"Clewis wanted me to observe the interrogation," Kyle replied, returning his gaze to the shell-shocked woman and her tormentor. "He thought I might be able to spot inconsistencies from when I questioned her."

"And?"

"Nothing. She's remarkably composed today, cooler than when I talked to her."

"Composed? What about that 'carving up ex-boyfriends' crack?"

"That was the first time in four hours she's said anything out of the ordinary. Either she's telling the truth or she's one cool cookie."

"Which do you vote for?"

Kyle pursed his lips. "Not sure."

"Wait," Jess said as Clewis started to close his notebook. "There's something else." She exchanged a hooded glance with Marva, who simply closed her eyes as if praying for patience.

Kyle leaned forward.

"This could be interesting," Easley said, echoing Kyle's thoughts.

"Yes, Ms. Robinson?" Clewis said with his pseudo-polite smile. "Did you just happen to remember something?"

"No. It's something that happened last night. My attor-

ney doesn't want me to bring it up, but I think you should
know. I got a phone call last night. A crank call.''

"Go on.''

"The man said he was Terry. He talked in this funny
voice, and he asked me why did I kill him, where did I
hide the body.''

Clewis wasn't even taking notes, but Kyle did. "And
what,'' Clewis asked, "did you reply?''

"I figured it was an ugly prank, and I called the guy a
bad name and hung up. But then I started thinking—could
it really be Terry?'' Warming now to the topic, Jess was
leaning forward, her face more animated than it had been
since she'd walked into the room. Her cheeks pinkened,
and her eyes sparkled.

And Kyle shifted uncomfortably in his chair.

"You see,'' she continued, "Terry has a fondness for
practical jokes, as I've told you. And I was thinking,
wouldn't this be the greatest practical joke of all? Faking
his own death, then framing me for it? Calling me up to
taunt me?''

"Why would he do something like that?'' Clewis asked,
totally skeptical.

"To pay me back for breaking up with him, for kicking
him out of my house. Don't you see?''

Clewis leaned back in his chair and steepled his hands
below his chin. "You expect me to believe that this man,
this scorned man, would abandon all of his material possessions, steal your knife, your shower curtain, your rug,
plant blood in the bathtub and washing machine—all to
frame you for his nonexistent murder?''

"I don't expect you to believe anything,'' Jess said
coolly. "I'm presenting a possibility to you. And while it
sounds far-fetched, you don't know Terry the way I do. A
practical joke of this magnitude is perfectly consistent with
his personality.''

"I'll, um, keep it in mind,'' Clewis said with barely

concealed amusement. He stood and stretched. "You can go now. I'll be in touch." He sauntered out of the room.

"You were right," Jess said dejectedly to Marva. "He didn't believe me. That's exactly what Terry's counting on—that no one would believe such a crazy story."

Beyond the two-way mirror, the breath caught in Kyle's throat. "It sounds like Jess is telling the truth about that crank phone call," he murmured.

"Don't be so naive," Easley said, still lurking behind him. "She knows there's a two-way mirror. She knows others are probably observing her."

Kyle didn't want to believe that. Her emotions seemed too real to be some kind of elaborate put-on. Then again, he had little experience with criminal minds, other than the drunks and druggies and petty thieves he'd encountered when he was a patrol officer. His entire investigative career had been in missing persons.

Kyle had had numerous opportunities to transfer to a different division—auto theft, burglary, homicide—but he'd preferred to stay right where he was. Finding people was challenging to him, and rewarding. It was the only area of police work that, more often than not, yielded a happy ending—returning a runaway teen to her family, locating the old person who'd wandered away from a nursing home. He liked tying up loose ends.

This homicide stuff was something else again. He didn't think he was cut out for catching murderers. It wasn't that he had a problem believing a *stranger* could kill. Hadn't he been suspicious enough of Jess before he'd started to know her? But when it came down to suspecting someone you knew, someone you were starting to like just a little…

Like Melissa, his former partner's wife. Widow. He'd known the woman had a drug problem, but he'd refused to see the violence lurking below her surface. Because he'd known her. Liked her. Wanted to believe the best in her. And then it had been too late.

Thankfully he wouldn't have to worry about any such inner conflict with Jess Robinson. Once he reported his observations from the interrogation to Clewis, he was officially off this case, and back to his comfortable role in missing persons.

Jess's back hurt, and her throat ached from so much talking. She didn't even want to calculate how many hours that ogre Clewis had kept her in that uncomfortable chair, browbeating her until it was a given that she would lose her temper.

Oddly, though, this interrogation hadn't seemed as painful as the one she'd had with Detective Branson. She'd known from the start that Clewis was out to get her, that truth and justice were less important than winning, getting the better of her.

But when she'd first met Kyle, she'd sensed a man who was digging for the truth—tough when he had to be, but not vindictive. So his brutal questions had felt more like a betrayal.

"What now?" she asked Marva, once they were safely alone in the elevator.

"We try like hell to find that turkey ex-boyfriend of yours. You really think he's alive?"

"With every bone in my body. This whole setup has Terry's fingerprints all over it."

"Do you have the means to hire a private investigator?"

"Marva, I don't even have the money to pay you," Jess said, exasperated.

"Don't you worry about that. We'll work it out. This is a high-profile case, and if I get you off, the publicity will have my phone ringing off the wall. That'll be payment enough. But a P.I. wants cash up front. What about relatives? Parents?"

"I'm afraid I exhausted their resources with my previous legal defense in Massachusetts."

Marva shook her head. "Man, for a little white-bread girl from the suburbs, you sure know how to get into trouble."

"I know how to pick my men, you mean," Jess said. The elevator opened onto the first floor, and Jess started to step out, but Marva stopped her.

"Uh-uh. Reporters, waiting like vultures." The doors closed again. "I'll take you the secret back route." Sure enough, Marva led Jess up to the second floor, along several obscure corridors and down a dimly lit staircase. They went through a door marked Official Personnel Only, and ended up at a back door near a Dumpster. Not a reporter in sight.

Jess looked up at the skyline and got her bearings, then tried to remember where she'd parked. "Thanks, Marva. I'll see what I can do about scraping up some money for a P.I. and give you a call. Hey, I could have a garage sale and sell all of Terry's things!"

Marva's eyes widened and she clutched her chest as if she was having a coronary. "Think, girl. From now on, every move you make, you think about how it will look to a jury. Got that?"

Jess's heart sank. "Right," she said, properly chastised. "I'll find the money somewhere else."

They parted company, and Jess made her way through the parking lot, dotted with anonymous-looking government-issue cars and Kansas City Police Department squad cars. It was three o'clock—shift change. Doors were opening and slamming, engines were starting up.

She wasn't sure what made her pause and focus in one particular direction, at one particular tall man with raven hair and a certain way of carrying himself that demanded attention as he walked toward an unknown destination in the parking lot.

She followed him, not knowing why. "Detective Branson?"

He swiveled, and his eyebrows flew up at the sight of her. "Ms. Robinson."

"Jess. I think you can call me Jess now that you're no longer investigating me. That's right, isn't it? I mean, you dumped me over in homicide."

"That's correct. Is there something I can do for you?" he relaxed slightly, though his navy blue eyes remained wary.

"I guess I...no, not really." What did she want? she wondered. Why was she standing here like some major geek, just staring at his handsome face?

"Do you have questions? I can't tell you anything about the investigation, but if you have any general questions about the process—"

"Do you know any private eyes who work on credit?"

The out-of-the-blue question seemed to surprise him. He put a hand to his chin in a gesture of deep thought that struck her as exaggerated. All right, so maybe it was a stupid thing to ask. Who could blame her for trying?

"Not offhand. What do you need investigating?"

"Oh, it would take too long to explain."

"I've got time. I'm off duty. Have you had lunch?"

Lunch! She hadn't even had breakfast. She'd been positively nauseated this morning at the thought of submitting herself to more questioning. Suddenly her stomach felt as if it might cave in on itself if she didn't get something in it.

She was on the verge of accepting when she thought about the sorry state of her pocketbook. She patted it. "I'd probably better go home and have a peanut-butter sandwich."

"My treat," he said hastily.

"Why?"

He shrugged, then resumed walking, expecting her to follow along. "Why not? Couldn't hurt my reputation any to be seen with a pretty woman."

.She did follow. She was drawn to him even as she feared him. "What about being seen with a murder suspect?"

He shrugged again. "If anyone looks at us twice, maybe they'll think I'm trying to extract information from you."

"And is that what you're doing?"

He opened the passenger door of a red Mustang. "I'm off duty. If you crumble and confess, I'll be obliged to pass along the information to the proper authorities. Barring that, I'm not planning to run and tell Clewis about every word out of your mouth, if that's what you're worried about." He smiled at her.

And her heart, at least, crumbled, just a little around the edges. If she'd seen that smile just once when he was interrogating her, she would have tried harder to please him. It was a very appealing expression, especially on such a formidable man.

"You should smile more when you question a suspect," she said, climbing into his car without further hesitation. In for a penny, in for a pound, she figured. "Especially women suspects. You'd charm the truth right out of them."

He appeared slightly embarrassed by her comment, maybe even puzzled. He looked now as if he were making an extra effort not to smile as he closed her door.

Really, *she* was the one who should have been embarrassed. She hadn't meant to sound flirtatious, but that was probably how he took it. She vowed to keep the rest of this meeting strictly business. And what business, exactly, did she have with him?

She wanted to tell him about the phone call—that was it. Clewis either hadn't thought it was important, or he flat-out hadn't believed her. She wanted to get an honest, professional opinion from someone who didn't have a stake in her guilt or innocence—someone who could listen impartially.

"You like greasy hamburgers?" Kyle asked, adjusting the vents on the car so that some of the warm air from the heater poured in her direction. His personal police scanner squawked and crackled, and he turned it down.

"Sure." Beggars couldn't be choosers, she reasoned.

"Town Topic is not too far."

"Sounds fine."

On the short drive, she restricted her conversation to comments about Kansas City's ever-changing skyline and the growing popularity of the downtown theater district. It wasn't until they were ensconced in a red leatherette booth in the deserted Town Topic diner that she found the courage to bring up her new theory about Terry's premeditated disappearance.

"I got a phone call the other night," she began, between bites of a chili-cheese dog that tasted like heaven. "At 2:00 a.m. I think it was from Terry."

"Oh?"

She proceeded to describe the phone call, word for word, as best she could. "The voice was muffled, like someone put a cloth over the receiver. But it *could* have been Terry. It *sounded* like Terry—not so much the voice, maybe, as the cadence. The accent. The word choice. You know what I'm talking about?"

"Sure," he said. He took a bite of his hamburger and stared out the window, as if fascinated by the passing traffic.

Then it hit her. Throughout her entire explanation, he hadn't once looked at her, eye to eye. And that wasn't his style. He was a direct-gaze kinda guy.

She went out on a limb. "You already knew about this, didn't you?"

"What makes you say that?" But his face turned slightly ruddy, answering her accusation.

"You were watching through the two-way mirror." She wiped her mouth with a paper napkin and threw it down on the table. "Why did you let me go through that whole long explanation? Why didn't you stop me? Oh, never mind. What was I thinking, believing you might have an inkling of understanding? You cops stick together."

She started to scoot out of the booth—destination unknown—but he grabbed her wrist.

"Wait. Please." His grip was loose, not at all painful. Nonetheless, it sent a shock wave of panic through her.

She jerked free. "Don't do that. Don't *ever* do that. I know you're stronger than me. You don't have to prove it."

Rather than reacting with anger, which was what she expected, he appeared merely bewildered. "I didn't mean to hurt you, just to stop you from leaving. Yeah, I observed your interview with Clewis. I was looking for inconsistencies in your story, but I didn't see any and I told Clewis so. I'm on your side, lady, and I'm about the only one who is."

"You believe me, then?" She knew she sounded as eager for a word of support as a puppy is for a pat on the head.

"Let's just say I'm keeping an open mind."

"And everyone else already has me convicted," she said glumly. She sat back down on the edge of the booth, poised for flight if need be.

"It's a sensational case. Detectives and D.A.'s make their careers with cases like this—provided they get solved. Ultimately everyone wants to get to the truth. It's just that some of us pursue it a little more zealously than others." The expression of distaste on Kyle's face indicated exactly what he thought of Bill Clewis's methods.

Oddly, that little bit of nonverbal communication made Jess feel the first tentative bond between herself and Kyle Branson. "So if you were observing, you know he didn't believe me about the phone call. He probably forgot about it the moment he walked out of the room."

"Probably."

"Do you believe me?"

"I don't disbelieve you. But you'll have to forgive me if I don't swallow your theory about his framing you for a nonmurder. That's pretty outlandish."

"As I told Detective Clewis, if you knew Terry, you'd realize it's exactly the sort of outrageous stunt he would pull. But, no, I don't expect you to swallow the theory whole. If you'd just acknowledge that it's even an outside possibility, I'd feel better."

He nodded. "I can go that far."

Hope welled up in her heart. "So what should I do to prove it? I mean, I can't afford a P.I., so it's up to me to figure out where the bastard's holed up. What would you suggest?"

He appeared to give her request some thought. "Make a list of every friend and acquaintance of his you can think of, no matter how tenuous the link. Get their addresses. Don't call them, though. You'll want to show up unannounced."

"You mean, just drive from house to house hoping to blunder upon him?"

"If he's alive, he's got to be somewhere. Don't be afraid to ask questions. Be rude, if you have to. Intimidate. Try to catch someone who's being evasive or won't meet your gaze—like you just did with me. With a little guidance and some long hours, you can be your own P.I."

"You really think I can?" His suggestions excited her. He was such a quick thinker. Why hadn't she thought of canvassing his friends' houses? It made so much sense.

"If you think you've figured out where he is, don't move in yourself. He might be dangerous."

"Who, Terry?" Jess snorted. "I'll call the cops, then sit on him till they get there."

"He might be dangerous," Kyle repeated, emphasizing

every word. "You yourself said he needed psychological intervention."

"Yes, but—"

"If your theory proves true, he's gone to a great deal of trouble to hurt you," Kyle reminded her, "and in my opinion he's a very sick man. He might be dangerous. Don't underestimate him. Don't approach him on your own. Call the cops. Promise me you'll do that."

The intensity of his gaze skewered her like a shish kebab. "I would feel real bad if something happened to you as a result of your following all this advice I'm giving you. You're going up against someone who's potentially dangerous without any protection, without any backup. Don't take chances."

"All right," she agreed, although no matter how hard she tried, she couldn't picture Terry as a violent person. Vindictive, petty, conceited, but never violent. She shivered, more as a result of the way Kyle was looking at her than from any real fear of Terry.

"Bill," Kyle said the next day as he approached Clewis's desk.

Clewis looked up. "Yeah?"

"I have some interesting information about the Terry Rodin case." Yeah, he'd promised Jess he wouldn't go running back to Clewis with whatever she'd had to say to him yesterday at lunch. But he wasn't tattling about some incriminating slip of the tongue, he reasoned. He was telling the lead detective on her case something that might help clear her. And that was different.

Clewis smiled faintly, the way he would with a troublesome but amusing dog. "Yeah?"

"I think there's a good possibility Jess is innocent."

Clewis rolled his eyes. "This is news? You thought she was innocent yesterday."

"Yeah, well, I'm even more convinced now. She

wanted me to recommend a private eye, to help her find Terry—alive. I don't know that Terry *is* alive—'' Kyle kept thinking about all that blood in the tub and sink at Jess's house, and the wallet and keys under her mattress "—but I think she believes it. And I think that phone call she told you about is for real.''

For a moment, Clewis looked confused. "What phone call?"

"The crank call? The guy who said he was Terry, looking for his body?"

"Oh, that," Clewis said dismissively. "Why didn't she bring it up first thing? Why did she wait until the end of the interview, when her position looked hopeless? It was a last-ditch effort to introduce some doubt into the case. A failed effort, I might add.''

"She said her attorney didn't want her to bring it up, simply because it *did* sound nutty.''

Clewis shook his head. "Don't be so damn naive, Branson.''

That was the second time in twenty-four hours that someone had accused him of being naive. He wasn't, dammit. Melissa Palladia had cured him forever of the rose-colored-glasses syndrome. He was simply considering the evidence, considering all theories, all possibilities, looking at the case from every direction. It was what a good investigator did.

"So did you recommend a P.I.?" Clewis asked, only mildly interested now. He hunched over in his chair, his gut hanging over his belt, going over some report. Lord, didn't any of these homicide guys get exercise?

"Turns out she doesn't have the money to pay a P.I.," Kyle said. "So I told her how to do the investigation herself.''

"Yeah, I'd like to be a fly on the wall watching *her* do an investigation. Don't make me laugh.''

"But that's just it, Bill. Someone should be watching

her. If she goes through with it—if she really makes an honest effort to find Rodin, wouldn't that indicate she's sincere about it?''

Clewis looked up sharply, then flipped a shock of greasy brown hair off his forehead. "You trying to tell me how to do my job?''

God save him from homicide detectives' egos. "Just a friendly suggestion. If you find the guy alive, your case is solved.''

"And I'm a laughingstock," Clewis added. "I don't want to find him alive. I want to find him dead, and I want to nail his murderer. That's what my job is about.''

Kyle winced. That was some attitude for a law-enforcement officer to have—wishing someone dead for the purpose of bolstering his own reputation. He considered commenting on the hypocrisy of it all but bit his tongue. Bill Clewis wasn't someone who could be swayed. After all the years he'd been in this department, he wouldn't change the way he thought about his job.

Suddenly Clewis looked up sharply. "Do *you* want to shadow her?''

"No. That is—''

"Wait a minute, you've given me a great idea," Clewis said, sitting up straighter and pushing aside the report he'd been reading. An expression of pure inspiration pervaded his face. "You're already in good with the babe, seems to me. Yeah! You could hang out with her after hours, cozy up to her, sympathize with her, maybe get her to confide in you...find out where she hid that damn body.''

"No," Kyle said more emphatically. "That's not what I had in mind.''

Jon Easley chose that moment to walk past Clewis's desk.

"Hey, Jon, c'mere a minute," Clewis said. "Branson here just offered to assist with the Rodin investigation.

Think you can spring him from missing persons for a few days, maybe a couple of weeks?''

Oh, hell, Kyle thought miserably. His fate was sealed now. He was either going to help clear Jess's name...or jettison her toward a murder conviction.

Chapter 5

"Ah, here's a fascinating item," said Lynn. They were sitting on the living-room floor, poring over the boxes of Terry's stuff they'd packed only a few days earlier. "A birthday card from someone named Brianna. With lip prints."

"Lemme see that," Jess said, holding out her hand. Lynn gave her the card, then watched expectantly as Jess examined it. "The postmark is from last year," Jess said, bristling with outrage. "That was six months before we broke up!"

"Now, you're not really surprised, are you?"

Jess expelled an angry breath. "Just continually amazed that I could be so stupid."

"Lighten up, Jessie. You're being too hard on yourself. Everyone makes mistakes."

"No, not like this," Jess said pensively. "I'm in a league of my own."

She should have held on to Terry's Rolodex when she'd had a chance, Jess thought, scrutinizing the return address on a yellowed envelope. Instead she'd turned it over to the police, and now, to identify his cohorts, she had to rely on her memory and the odd notations made in Terry's old calendars.

The doorbell pealed. Jess, her nerves bowstring tight, first jumped, then pointedly ignored the interruption, returning to her box of junk.

"Aren't you going to get that?" Lynn asked.

"Why? It's probably just another reporter."

Lynn hopped up and dusted off her jeans. "But maybe it's not."

"Bet you a buck." Jess really didn't want to know who was ringing her doorbell a second time. Even if it was just the paperboy, she wasn't in any shape to be civil. Truth was, she wanted to crawl under a rock and hibernate until this whole thing was over.

What a temptation. She could get into her car and drive, just drive as fast and as far as she could, and hide out until Terry tired of his game and surfaced. Where would she go? Somewhere warm, maybe Florida. She pictured herself on a beach, coated with suntan oil, sipping a piña colada—

"You owe me a buck," Lynn said, rudely interrupting the pleasant fantasy.

"I...what?" Jess looked up, orienting herself to reality. And what reality. Kyle Branson was standing in her living room, giving her that faintly amused expression that was becoming habitual, at least around her. From her vantage point on the floor he looked at least seven feet tall and pure muscle beneath his raincoat. "Is it raining?" she asked.

Lynn snorted. "Get with the program, Jess. It's been raining all morning." She stood slightly behind Kyle, watching with blatant interest. Jess had told her of their impromptu lunch the day before, and since then Lynn had been speculating wildly about Kyle's interest in the case—and in Jess herself.

Jess stood and dusted off her hands, struggling to come up with a more conventional greeting for her unexpected guest. "Good morning. Do you have any news?" she asked hopefully.

"No, I'm afraid not," Kyle said. "I brought you a present." He reached into his raincoat pocket and pulled out a gray box, an electronic device of some sort. When he handed it to her, their fingers brushed. She felt his innocent touch right down to her toes.

"What's this?"

"A caller-ID box. I've already set it up with the phone company. This will automatically trace your incoming calls. Have you heard any more from your mysterious caller?"

"Actually, yes," Jess said, examining the device. "At least, I think it might have been him. The phone rang several times last night, but I refused to answer."

Kyle frowned. "I hope he doesn't give up, now that we have the means to catch him."

"So I have to answer the phone if he calls back?"

"The caller-ID box will trace most incoming calls, even if you don't answer. But you need to talk to the guy if you want to verify that he is your crank caller."

Jess gave an involuntary shiver. She didn't want to hear that voice again, begging her to tell where she'd hidden the body. It gave her the willies.

"Hey, it'll be okay," Kyle said softly. "A voice on the phone can't hurt you. He can only trip himself up."

Jess shook off the uneasy feeling. "You're right, of course. So how does this thing hook up?"

"It's easy. Just plug the box into the phone jack, then plug the phone into the box. Let the phone ring at least twice before you answer or the box won't have time to trace the call. Want me to hook it up for you?"

"Sure," she said, even though she was certain she was capable of doing it herself. If she could hook up her complicated array of computer equipment and tape recorders without assistance, this little box wouldn't be a challenge. But, she admitted silently, she wanted to give the handsome detective a reason to hang around a little longer. "The phone's over there, beside the sofa."

"Don't you have a phone in your bedroom?"

"Well, yes, but—"

"I'm assuming that's where you are when the caller strikes. You don't want to have to come running down the stairs in the middle of the night to check the box."

"You're right." She nodded and headed for the stairs. She didn't know why she was so uneasy at the thought of Kyle going into her bedroom. After all, he'd been in there before. But it wasn't *my* bedroom then, she thought. It had still been Terry's.

"Whoa," Kyle said as he entered the room behind her. "I see you've made a few changes." He looked around the room, taking in each detail, trying to record them with a cop's trained eye. Unfortunately, he was absorbing the feel of Jess's bedroom with a man's instincts.

The space looked completely different than it had during his first visit to the duplex. No trace of Terry Rodin remained in the room, now decorated with mauve and green throw rugs and curtains. The pictures on the wall, sensuous pastel watercolors, were different, reminding Kyle purely of Jess. Even the furniture had been rearranged. Jess's jewelry box and a tray of perfume bottles sat atop the dresser. A wicker rocker with frilly lace pillows occupied a corner where an exercise bike had stood. The huge bed was festooned with more pillows. Even the scent that hung in the air was Jess's, distinctive and one hundred percent feminine.

"Lynn did this while I was in jail," Jess said. "She cleaned up the mess made by the evidence people, then moved all my stuff in here. The rest of the house was still a wreck, but she wanted me to have this one nice place to come home to. She's been incredible through all this..." Jess's voice caught.

When Kyle looked at her, she turned away and began pointlessly rearranging things on the dresser.

He couldn't imagine what she'd been going through. He'd never been on this side of the fence before, observing what the legal system did to an individual. He'd never even thought much about it before. If a person was guilty of a crime, he supposed they deserved to be put through the wringer. But if he or she was innocent...

Yeah, he thought derisively, how many innocent people were arrested? A lot of them got off, through plea bargaining or on technicalities, or because the D.A.'s office simply couldn't *prove* they were guilty. But ninety-nine percent of those charged with crimes were guilty as sin.

Still, at this moment, he wanted with all his heart to believe he was looking at the one percent that was innocent.

He touched her shoulder, wanting to offer comfort.

She jumped and shied away from his touch. "Don't." The single word wasn't an order but a plea.

He dropped his hand. "I only wanted to offer sympathy. I didn't mean to make you uncomfortable."

She looked up sharply. "You're the enemy," she said suddenly. "You're with the police, and the police want to prove I'm a murderer. Why should I accept your sympathy?"

"I'm off the investigation, remember?" The lie was bitter in his mouth, but regardless of his personal beliefs about Jess, he still had a job to do. He had to stick close to her, "cozy up to her," as Clewis had termed it. If he hadn't believed that his continued involvement would eventually lead to the truth, he never would have agreed to do this. He hoped like hell "the truth" equaled Jess's innocence, and that what he was doing would somehow prove it. That was the only way he could stomach telling lies.

He'd worked undercover before. The narcotics division had recruited him a couple of times to do some small stuff. He could play a part, lie when necessary, be the nice guy or the brute as the situation demanded. But this—pretending to be something he wasn't for Jess—was harder, for some reason.

"So you're bringing me presents," she said, pointing to the gray box, "out of the goodness of your heart?"

"Yeah, as a matter of fact." That, at least, was the truth. Clewis wouldn't approve purchasing the caller-ID box, so Kyle had paid for it himself.

"Why?"

"Because I'm not sure you're getting a fair break. Bill Clewis isn't one of my favorite people. He's into winning, earning feathers in his cap. He won't even consider the possibility that you're innocent. Essentially I'm doing the job *he* should be doing, which is to cover all the bases."

"Oh, I get it." Jess put her hands on her hips. Her whole body posture challenged Kyle. "If the box doesn't catch my caller, it means I made the whole thing up."

"And if it does, we might find Terry and you're off the hook. Look, dammit, I'm trying to help you. And you're looking a gift horse in the mouth."

She slumped, defeated. "You're right. I don't have many people in my corner, so when someone happens to wander in, I shouldn't chase them off." She paused, took a deep breath. "I'm sorry. I'm not thinking very straight."

"Apology accepted," he said. This time when he touched her arm, she didn't object. She even gave him a tremulous smile. The simple gesture nearly brought him to his knees with a wanting so sharp that it cut him to the quick. Her scent, her warmth, the trace of trust in her eyes all conspired against him. He felt a protective instinct as well as a much more primitive desire to conquer and claim.

Kyle quickly removed his hand. Now, where was the damn phone? The sooner he completed this task and got the hell out of her bedroom, the better.

Jess sat up in bed, heart pounding, adrenaline flowing, her fight-or-flight instinct in full bloom. Then she realized it was the phone. She reached for it, then stopped herself. Kyle had said to let it ring twice. When it rang again, it seemed loud enough to bring the house down. She let it ring a third time before answering with a cautious "Hello?"

"Jess. Oh, Jessica, how I've missed your voice. Why didn't you answer the phone last night? Were you sleeping with someone else?"

Terry. No doubt about it. All traces of sleep fog fled from her mind. "Who's calling, please?" she demanded as she fumbled for the bedside lamp. Where was the dratted switch? Kyle had instructed her to act scared and angry when her crank called back. He was aiming for a certain reaction, Kyle theorized—terror. If she gave it to him, if she fooled him into thinking he was in control, not she, he would keep calling back. And that's what they wanted. That was how they would catch him.

Under no circumstances was Jess to hint that she was on to his game.

"You know who it is," the voice said. "It's cold here, so cold."

"Please don't do this," Jess pleaded. "Who is this? What have you done to Terry?"

A choked sob, then nothing. He'd hung up.

Jess finally located the lamp switch and twisted it. She peered at the LCD readout on the caller-ID box. Triumph surged through her, followed by disappointment. The phone number blinked at her, tantalizing. The box worked! But beneath the number were the words "Pay Phone."

Dammit! Terry wasn't stupid. He was a step ahead of her. Anticipating that she would try to trace the calls, he'd outwitted her. Still, the phone could probably be located via the number, and Terry's whereabouts narrowed down.

Using a pad and pen she kept by her bed, she quickly jotted down the number, then wavered as to what to do next. Kyle had given her his home number. He'd said that if the caller struck and she got results to call him. He would jump in his car, drive to the source of the call and arrest the responsible party for harassment. Even if it wasn't Terry, it would put an end to the crank calls.

But there was nothing Kyle could do with this information, at least not until morning. Her crank wouldn't keep hanging around the pay phone all night.

Impulsively, she picked up the phone and dialed Kyle's number, anyway. She wanted to hear his reassuring voice. She wanted to express her impotent fears. Which was downright stupid, she realized. A homicidal maniac could break into her bedroom this moment, and Kyle's voice wouldn't protect her.

Still, she didn't hang up.

He answered on the first ring, sounding instantly alert. "Branson."

Immediately Jess felt foolish for calling. This could have waited. She was on the verge of hanging up when he spoke again.

"Jess?"

"Yes." Her voice sounded absurdly breathy. She cleared her throat. "How did you know it was me?"

"I don't give too many people permission to call me in the middle of the night. Did he call?"

"Yes. And the box says it's from a pay phone."

"Mmm. What's the exchange?"

"Three-five-three."

"Raytown. Know anyone who lives in Raytown?"

The answer was easy. "Kevin. Of course. He's mixed up in this thing with Terry. Terry probably put him up to filing the missing-persons report." She switched off the lamp and burrowed back under the covers. "Is there any way to prove it?"

"Mmm," was all Kyle said.

"Couldn't you just go knock on Kevin's door and demand that he produce Terry? Kevin would have no qualms about conspiring with Terry for his stupid practical joke, but he sure wouldn't protect Terry if it meant getting in trouble with the law."

"I can't just go knocking on doors in the middle of the night without a warrant or probable cause."

"But I can," Jess said, suddenly filled with anger again. "I'll go over there and rouse his buns out of bed. He thinks he's so smart, using a pay phone. He'll *think* pay phone when I get done with him." As she made her plans she was already turning the lamp back on, climbing out of bed, reaching for the dresser drawer for clothes.

One word from Kyle stopped her. "Wait."

She froze like a guilty child trying to sneak out of church. In that single word he'd packed enough authority to stop an elephant from charging.

"You can't go barging over there in the middle of the night," he said. "It's not safe."

"But Terry and Kevin wouldn't—"

"We've already discussed this. Terry isn't rational. You have no way of predicting what he might or might not do. Just because he's never harmed you physically before doesn't mean he's not capable."

Jess experienced a sudden flashback, and the force of the memory nearly knocked her off her feet. She sank back onto the bed as the cop's long-ago voice floated through her memory:

"Has your ex-boyfriend ever hurt you before?"

"No."

"Then why do you believe he'll do so now?"

But the police investigator had been from Barnstable County, Massachusetts, not Kansas City, and the ex-boyfriend hadn't been Terry, but Phil Cattrone.

The investigator had been wrong to discount her worries.

If she'd been so worried about Phil based on nothing but vague threats—worried enough to ask the police for protection—why wasn't she more concerned about Terry being a physical threat?

"Jess?"

"All right, I won't go over to Kevin's house. What else can be done?"

"I have an idea...but you might not like it."

"I'm desperate. I'll do anything."

Kyle didn't respond right away, causing Jess to wonder exactly what possibilities he might be considering.

"A stakeout," he finally said. "Find the phone booth, hide your car and watch with binoculars to see who shows up at two in the morning."

"Oh, yes, that's a great idea," Jess said, her enthusiasm immediate. "But what should I do if he shows up? You seem to think it might be dangerous to confront Terry—"

"I'll confront him."

"So...I'll bring a cellular phone with me on this stakeout? And if Terry shows up, I call you? What if you can't get there in time?"

"No, Jess, that's not the plan at all. I'll do the stakeout with you."

"Okay, so you think she's really getting phone calls in the middle of the night," Clewis said between bites of a corned-beef sandwich. He paused to wipe a smear of mustard off his chin. "What does that prove? It's just a crank."

They were in the tiny enclosure of Lieutenant Easley's office. The smell of corned beef permeated every molecule of air—and there hadn't been that many to start with.

"If nothing else, it's harassment," Kyle pointed out. "She's got enough problems without losing sleep because of some fanatic."

"And that's supposed to be a good enough reason to do a stakeout?" Clewis said. "Since when does the department okay stakeouts to catch a crank phone caller?"

"When the crank caller is connected to a possible murder," Kyle said, his voice rising on every word. Clewis's continuing closed-mindedness was getting on his nerves. The guy had big-time tunnel vision.

"Possible murder?" Clewis retorted, then shook his head at Kyle's obvious naivete. "You are either soft in the head or hard in the—"

"All right," Easley broke in. "That's enough, Clewis. Branson, you know as well as anyone this stakeout business is a long shot. Who's to say the caller will strike again?"

"He's called three nights in a row."

"Who's to say he'll use the same phone?"

"Criminals develop habits. Besides, the pay phone is within walking distance of Kevin Gilpatrick's house, and Jess thinks he might be involved. She says she and Kevin were never on good terms." Kyle didn't go so far as to suggest that Gilpatrick was hiding Terry Rodin. He didn't figure Easley or Clewis would go for a conspiracy theory.

Easley gnawed thoughtfully on his pen. The thing was mangled so badly that Kyle doubted it was still functional.

"Okay, here's the deal," Easley said. "I'll okay this stakeout for one night, and one night only."

"But—" Clewis started to object, but Easley held up a hand to forestall him.

"Hold on, Bill. Let me finish. The only reason I'm agreeing to your idea, Branson, is so you can legitimately spend some time with our suspect without arousing her suspicions. If she sits in a cramped car with you for hours on end, maybe she'll let her guard drop. Maybe she'll slip and reveal something."

"Or maybe she'll break from the torture," Clewis interjected. "I sure as hell wouldn't want to spend the night in a car with you, Branson."

Kyle bit his tongue to keep from replying.

"If this thing drags on for more than one night," Easley said, "you're on your own time."

Kyle nodded. "Fair enough." It was a compromise he could live with. Maybe one night would be enough. *Or maybe one night spent with Jess Robinson would never be enough.* Surprised by the errant thought, he stared out the window until he could banish all thoughts of his hands tangled in thick brown hair, and pale thighs wrapped around his hips.

Clewis shot a sour look at Kyle before tossing the remains of his sandwich into Easley's trash can and exiting the room.

Kyle started to follow when Easley stopped him. "Branson. Just one more thing."

Kyle turned back. "Yes?"

"You're a smart guy, a good investigator. I wouldn't mind having you in my department on a permanent basis. But you've got a lot to learn when it comes to suspects. Some of them can charm the socks right off you. A few tears, a catch in the voice, a little prolonged eye contact, and it's easy to fall."

Kyle nodded stiffly. There was no point in arguing with Easley. But Kyle's belief in Jess's innocence went far beyond a good acting job. He was looking at the facts, too, facts that didn't add up to a simple conviction.

"One other thing," Easley said, and for once he threw down his chew stick. "I'm not advocating that you sleep with the woman. That would be unethical." He stopped there, leaving Kyle with the impression that should an opportunity present itself, Easley would look the other way.

Anything for the cause, Kyle caught himself thinking with a half smile as he left the room. Immediately he was flooded with guilt.

Chapter 6

"He's late," Lynn said, pointedly checking her watch. She sat on the living-room floor, the law books that had become her constant companions spread out on the coffee table. "Are you sure this is such a good idea?"

"Why wouldn't it be?" Jess shot back defensively. "I want to catch the crank caller, and this appears to be the only way."

"But why do you have to go? Why can't Kyle do it by himself?"

"He might need me to identify the caller," she explained. "Anyway, it's not like he's getting paid to do this. He's losing sleep on his own time. Since he's doing it for my benefit, it's only fair that I come along and keep him company."

"Hmm," Lynn said.

"Also, he said if our caller 'makes' him, having a woman along would look less suspicious."

"*Makes* him?" Lynn rolled her eyes.

"You know, if he notices Kyle hanging around."

"I know what you mean. I just wondered when you'd started using police jargon. And when Detective Branson turned into Kyle."

Jess felt her face warming. All right, so what if she was a little bit fascinated with the detective? He gave her something interesting to focus on besides her own miserable situation. He gave her hope.

"Anyway," Lynn continued, apparently not expecting an explanation from Jess, "if he's any good at what he does, no one will spot him."

"And how did you get to be such an expert on police work?" Jess asked, hoping to turn attention away from herself.

"By reading all these books! All right, maybe I don't know that much about police procedure. But from reading these briefs, I can tell you one thing. The police aren't on your side. And I'm not sure it's such a good idea for you to get chummy with a cop."

"But he really *is* on my side," Jess said softly. Or was she being incredibly naive? Recalling how Kyle had interrogated her that day she was arrested, she winced. He sure as hell hadn't been on her side then. "He at least wants to find out the truth. That other detective just wants to nail me, and to hell with truth."

"That's not unusual, from what I can tell," Lynn said. "The casebooks are full of instances where an innocent person was prosecuted because the police jumped to conclusions and went after the wrong guy. I'm making a list for Marva."

"You're kind of enjoying this," Jess concluded.

Lynn looked up sharply. "Enjoying the fact that my sister has been charged with murder? Hardly."

"But you like the research. Ever thought of going to law school?"

Lynn shrugged. "Marva said if I did, I could clerk for her anytime."

Jess couldn't help smiling. At least some good might come of this whole mess. Maybe her baby sister had found a calling—finally.

The pealing doorbell chased the smile away. Oh, Lord, he was here. It was almost midnight, and she was going out the door with a man who made her insides go hot and liquid. And she was taking along a blanket.

With some effort, she reestablished the smile and opened the door. "Hello, Kyle."

"Evening, ladies," he said as he stepped inside.

Jess had never seen him in casual clothes, and the effect was devastating—worn, snug jeans that delineated every muscle in his thighs, a gray wool sweater that made her think of warming her hands beneath it, an open shearling jacket that added to the daunting size of his upper body. She mumbled a pleasantry and took a step backward, nearly clipping herself on the coffee table.

"It's getting cold out," he said as his gaze took in the women, the room, the law books, as if he was looking for something. Clues, maybe. The man was first and foremost a cop, and Jess couldn't lose sight of that fact. He could take anything she said and twist it to his advantage. He'd already proved that he could.

Then why did she find it so easy to believe in his honorable intentions now? Maybe she was as naive as her sister accused her of being. She already knew she was a lousy judge of character. Why should this be any different?

"I'm wearing thermal underwear," she said in response to his weather report.

He quirked one eyebrow, perhaps thinking her discussion of underthings was inappropriate.

She quickly continued. "And I have a thermos of coffee. And gloves, and even a blanket." Realizing how that sounded, she added, "Maybe two blankets would be better."

Lynn smirked. Kyle looked up at the ceiling as if he

found her acoustical tiles fascinating. Jess realized she was digging herself deeper.

"I'll get another blanket," she said firmly, heading for the stairs.

"Don't bother," Kyle said, his voice rife with amusement. Her heart thumped wildly until he said, "I have an extra in the trunk. I think we'll be plenty warm."

Why was she so darn easy to flummox? Men knew it. Everyone knew it, and it seemed as if they all delighted in embarrassing her.

Damn, now she *was* getting paranoid.

"We should be going," Kyle said. "Lynn, you know what to do?"

She nodded. "I let the phone ring twice, I pick it up, and I pretend to be Jess and get all flustered."

"That's it. And lock the door behind us. Never know who might be lurking around."

Not wanting to alarm Lynn, Jess waited until she and Kyle were outside before voicing yet another of her doubts. "You don't think Lynn could be in any danger, do you?"

"Not any more than the average citizen."

"I thought I noticed someone following us today when we went to the grocery store."

"Wouldn't surprise me, but it probably wasn't a bad guy."

She had to think a moment. "Oh. The police are following me?"

He was slow in answering. "I'm not involved with the investigation, so I don't know exactly what they're doing, but having you followed would make sense."

Jess shivered. "No wonder Marva warned me to watch my p's and q's." It wasn't the first time Jess had lived in a fishbowl. Back in Massachusetts, she'd been a hot media topic and a favorite feminist cause for several weeks. Phil Cattrone's family had hired private investigators to shadow her every move, trying to dig up dirt—any kind of dirt—that would strengthen the state's case against her.

Thank goodness her life was so staid. The P.I. hadn't been able to find any skeletons in her closet. Not back then.

Kyle opened the passenger door of a white LeBaron, and she climbed in. "Wait a minute, where's your Mustang?" Moments later she spotted the elaborate radio equipment on the dash and console. "This is a cop car."

"Yeah," Kyle drawled as he slid behind the steering wheel. "The fire-engine red Mustang is a little too obvious for a stakeout."

"But how did you get this one? Do they let you take cars home overnight?"

"No. I went and picked it up just now."

"You mean the police know about the stakeout? Detective Clewis, I mean," she clarified, since Kyle was the police, too.

"Of course. I wouldn't undertake this on my own without telling someone. If we actually find Terry, we'll need backup."

"I see." Somehow, this revelation disappointed her. She'd taken comfort in the thought that Kyle was on *her* side, not Clewis's. "Are you getting paid?"

Another long pause. "Yeah. Does that bother you? I've convinced Clewis and Lieutenant Easley, his superior, to give this plan a shot."

"Then I guess it shouldn't bother me." But it did.

"Even if they hadn't approved the overtime, I'd be here," he added.

She wanted to take comfort in his loyalty. But in the back of her mind she could hear what Lynn would say to that: Loyalty? What makes you think he owes you any loyalty? Get a grip, sis. He's got an angle.

She didn't want to believe that. Couldn't he just be a

nice guy who wanted her to have a fair chance? Couldn't he?

They drove in almost total silence toward staunchly middle-class Raytown, about twenty minutes. As the LeBaron's energetic heater warmed the car's interior, Jess thawed a bit, too.

She had to take Kyle at face value. It wasn't in her nature to be suspicious of kindness, of good deeds, no matter about her past. She saw the worst of people every day in her work as she transcribed tapes from trials of every description—people suing anybody and everybody for the almighty dollar, criminals lying through their teeth, con artists ripping off old ladies. Yet she'd never lost her belief that people were basically good until proven otherwise.

She needed that faith. Without it, what would be the point?

"This is the place," Kyle said as he drove slowly past a darkened discount store. A duo of phones sat against the brick wall near the front entrance, with only a small Plexiglas shield between them for privacy.

"Looks quiet enough," Jess said.

"Too quiet. No place for us to hide." He drove around the block twice before settling on a parking spot on a side street. They had a full view of the parking lot and the phones—from several hundred feet away.

"How will we recognize Terry from this distance?" Jess asked.

"I'll admit it's not an ideal situation. But the way I figure, anyone who stops to make a phone call here this late at night is suspicious." He pulled out a pair of binoculars from under the seat. "We can get a license plate, if he's driving, and you might be able to ID him with these."

"Let me try." She held the binoculars up to her face and twiddled with the focus for a few moments. "Good-

ness, I think I could ID a gnat with these things. Okay,
I'm convinced. This'll work. Now what?''

"We wait. And we freeze. That pretty much describes
a stakeout. Waiting and freezing. Or frying, in the summer." He turned off the ignition. Without the constant
blast of the heater, the air inside the car quickly cooled.

Jess resisted reaching for the blanket in the back seat.
She didn't want to wimp out this early in the game. She
needed something to get her mind off the cold, off the
tension, off the feel of her own nerves grating against each
other. "So what made you decide to become a cop?"

"My dad was a cop," he answered. "It was pretty much
preordained that I would follow in his footsteps." His
voice was casual, but his gaze remained riveted on the
phones across the street. He seemed to be taking his job
very seriously.

"Do you ever wish you'd done something else?"

He paused before answering. "Nah. I like the work."

"Don't you worry about the danger?"

"Not anymore. Missing-persons work isn't all that haz-
ardous. Not like when I used to patrol on the east side.
Now *that* was dicey."

"Were you ever hurt?"

"Not bad."

His answer made her wonder exactly what "not bad"
entailed, but she decided it was really none of her business.
Or maybe she didn't want to know. She didn't like thinking of Kyle's handsome face being bruised or his strong
bones broken. Now that he was on her side, she didn't
want to think of him as anything but invincible.

She found herself wanting to touch him, to reassure herself he was real, solid muscle. "Want some coffee?" she
asked overbrightly.

"Sure."

It was something to do, something to keep her hands

busy. She poured them each a paper cupful. "I forgot to bring sugar or creamer."

"I take it black. Thanks." He took a long sip, despite the fact that the coffee had to be still scalding. "Good."

Jess blew on hers. She struggled for another avenue of conversation—not that she didn't have a million questions she wanted to ask him, but she didn't want to be tediously curious. So she remained quiet, cautiously sipping her coffee, watching the parking lot, stealing glances at Kyle's strong profile and experimenting with fantasies about whether his lips were firm or soft, whether he closed his eyes when he kissed, what that thick, black hair might feel like between her fingers.

When she became aware what she was doing, she almost choked. Granted, she'd been fascinated with Kyle Branson from the moment he'd arrived on her front porch—fascinated, intimidated, a little frightened. When had those feelings intensified to blatant desire?

There had to be a logical explanation. Lynn—the self-proclaimed psychology expert—would know. It was probably some transference thing, gratitude transformed into lust, something like that. The assurance that a logical explanation could be found didn't help one bit. Her imagination continued to wander with abandon into dangerous territory.

She stared determinedly out the windshield. That's when she spotted the man strolling at a leisurely pace across the empty parking lot.

"Hey, look—"

"I see," Kyle said, the words clipped. He handed her the binoculars. "Look familiar?"

She struggled to bring the man's image into sharpness. Keeping her eye on a moving subject wasn't like focusing on an immobile telephone.

"Well?"

She saw a slender man wearing a cap, a jacket with the

collar turned up, jeans. "Hard to tell. It could be Terry. But maybe not." She couldn't see his hair color, couldn't be sure of his height. The unidentified man headed straight for the phones. "What do we do?"

"We wait until he's done with the phone. Won't do any good to confront him if he hasn't completed the call. He could claim he was about to call for time and temperature. Let me see the glasses."

"Wait, he's...no, never mind." The man had never turned to face her. He was leaning against the brick wall with his back to her, ready to use the phone. Jess surrendered the binoculars, then squinted anxiously out the windshield. The parking lot wasn't well lighted, and she couldn't make out much.

"What time is it?" Kyle asked in an unemotional, all-business tone.

Jess consulted the dashboard clock. "Twelve thirty-five. A little early."

"No law says he's compulsive. He's chatting away to someone. Doesn't look nervous, by his stance. And...he's hanging up." Kyle all but shoved the binoculars at Jess. "Time to see what he's all about. If I say 'down,' you get down. I don't want to see your head above the dashboard. Got it?"

"Yes. But I don't think he's—"

"We don't even know who he is, much less if he's dangerous."

Good point, Jess thought.

Kyle pulled the car across the street into the parking lot, not too fast. Their pedestrian didn't appear to be paying attention to them until they drew close. Then he swung his head around to stare, his face hard with suspicion.

"It's not Terry," Jess said the moment she got a good look at the guy. Disappointment coursed through her. Of course, it wouldn't be this easy.

Kyle rolled down his window. "Excuse me, sir? I'm with the Kansas City Police. May I have a word with—"

At the word "police" the guy turned and bolted. Kyle stepped on the gas and chased him, yelling "Stop! Police!" out the window in between colorful curses. Not that the car couldn't outrun a person on foot, but there wasn't any way to stop the guy's headlong flight except run him down.

Abruptly Kyle slammed on the brakes, threw the car into Park and opened the door. "Stay put," he ordered Jess before leaping out after their suspect, who had a hundred-foot lead on him. Kyle ran like a sprinter.

Jess stared, fascinated. It was like watching *Wild Kingdom*, a jaguar after a gazelle—except that prey and predator were men.

The suspect reached the edge of the parking lot, crossed an alley and scrambled over a low brick wall enclosing a housing development. Kyle, having gained ground, vaulted over the wall in one easy movement only moments later.

Seconds ticked by, stacking one on top of the other to form several agonizing minutes during which Jess saw and hard nothing.

The police radio, the volume turned down to a whisper, looked inviting. She could call for help. If she could even figure out how to use the darn thing. Or she could use the cell phone and call 911. Or…she could disobey Kyle's order, get out of the car, and look for him.

Was it really necessary for her to worry? she wondered. Surely Kyle knew what he was doing. But if anything happened to him while he was trying to help her cause, she would feel terribly responsible. Terrible, period.

After picturing herself trying to explain the situation to some skeptical cop or clueless dispatch operator, she decided on her third option. She would run to the wall and just peek over it to the other side, to see if Kyle was in trouble.

She wrapped her scarf around her neck and opened her door, leaving the engine running. No movement anywhere around her. She got out, swiveling her head this way and that as she made her way across the dark parking lot, her heart in her throat.

The lot seemed as broad as a football field. The distance covered by the two men in mere seconds seemed to take a million footsteps for her to get across. And when she reached the wall, she realized it was well over five feet tall. She couldn't even see over it, much less climb over it as the men had.

Instead she crept down the alley, her senses alert for any noise, any movement. It seemed she walked forever, pulling her scarf more tightly around her neck to ward off the cold. She'd forgotten gloves, and her knuckles ached.

The wall ended abruptly when it reached the street that backed up behind the discount store. Jess paused, trying to decide exactly how to proceed from here. Feeling like a third-class spy, she started to lean around the wall with exaggerated caution. But a man's hard body barreling around the corner blocked her view and very nearly knocked her down.

Jess gave an involuntary shriek. "Oh, God, you scared me to—you're bleeding!"

"It's not that bad," Kyle muttered, holding his hand up to a cut on his cheekbone, frighteningly close to his eye. He continued his pace without slowing. He was breathing hard, his breath steaming the air. And he was clearly irritated. "I thought I told you to stay in the car."

"I was worried about you." She trotted to keep up with him. "You were gone so long, and… What do you mean, it's not bad? You're dripping blood all over the place. What happened? Where's the guy? Did you catch him? Did *he* do that to you?"

When Kyle didn't respond, Jess realized she'd thrown too many questions at him at once. And from the looks of things, he didn't want to answer any of them. He walked in sullen silence back to the car, got in the open driver door and slammed it.

She followed suit on the passenger side.

Kyle flipped on the dome light and peered at his wound in the rearview mirror. "Damn."

"'Damn' is right. You're not in any shape to drive." Jess rummaged around in her purse for a package of tissues. She found one, opened it and pulled out the whole wad. "Here, let me at least clean it up for you so you can tell what you're looking at." She reached up to dab at the blood on his cheek.

He enclosed his hand with hers. "Give it to me. I'll do it."

"Don't be a baby." While they argued, the cut oozed more blood. Jess felt suddenly woozy. She surrendered the wad of Kleenex. "Okay, you do it."

"Jess?" His surliness was gone, replaced with concern.

"Sorry. Blood makes me a little queasy sometimes." It had ever since her little set-to in Massachusetts.

That got a chuckle out of him. "Wouldn't Clewis get a kick out of that? The woman he thinks stabbed her boyfriend to death gets sick at the sight of blood?" He swabbed at his face.

When Jess got brave enough to peek at him again, Kyle still looked like an escapee from a slasher movie. "You have to go to the hospital."

"No way. It looks worse than it is."

"You'll have a scar if you don't get it stitched up by a doctor."

"Would a scar be so bad?" He pressed the tissue to his face to stanch the bleeding. "Might give me some character."

"You already have character. And yes, a scar would be bad if you got it on my account. Humor me. The emergency room, please?"

"What about the stakeout? It's early yet."

"I'm not sitting in a car with you all night while you bleed to death."

He sighed. "All right. See if you can crank up that heater a bit."

Relieved, she began fiddling with the heater controls as Kyle shifted into Drive and steered one-handed. Only then did her curiosity about the events leading up to his injury return. "So what happened?"

"He was a scared kid with a joint in his pocket. That's why he bolted. He was calling his mother to let her know he was on his way home. Apparently he'd missed curfew."

"Did he hit you?"

"No. I took a big, heroic flying leap and tackled him to the ground. Only between me and the ground, I lost. I hit a rock or something. Big drama, huh?"

"Do you know for sure he was calling his mother? And why didn't you arrest him if he was carrying drugs?"

The irritation was back. "I delivered him personally to his front door and met the lady face-to-face. From the looks of things, he was going to get worse from her than he would have from the judicial system. Hell, I'm not up to arresting some juvey with a joint tonight, anyway."

"Sorry. I didn't mean to tell you how to do your job."

"I'm just sorry the stakeout is a bust. The department okayed this for one night only."

"Oh. You didn't tell me that." She considered her options. "I can do it on my own tomorrow, now that I've learned how."

Kyle actually laughed. "I'll be there with you."

"I'll pay you," she said hopefully, relieved that he'd offered without her having to grovel. She had a strong feeling about this caller. He was the key to solving this case, and so long as there was a chance of apprehending him, she wasn't giving up.

"Pay me with what? You already told me you couldn't afford a P.I."

"I'll owe it to you, then."

"No, thanks. Consider it a favor between friends."

She thought about this for several minutes.

"Since when did we become friends?" she finally asked when he'd pulled the car into a parking space. "That's quite a switch from where we started."

He laughed again. She wasn't sure if she liked making him laugh, especially when that wasn't what she intended. Although, come to think of it, she did like the sexy dimple that appeared along with his smile.

"I think we became friends when you started worrying about me."

Jess felt suffused with a sudden warmth that seared her from the inside out, driving out the numbing cold that had settled in her bones during her parking-lot trek. "I'd worry about anyone risking his life on my account," she said, looking at her toes.

"Oh, Jess, you wound me. I thought I was special."

She laughed too, then, because he was trying to be funny. But he'd hit on a startling truth. He *was* special. At some point during this ordeal, he'd started to mean something to her—something more than a symbol of her salvation from a murder conviction—more than just a sexy bod.

Not smart, Jess. Kyle Branson was exactly the type of man she'd spent the past few years avoiding—powerful, charismatic, determined. If she fell under his spell, she would be completely at his disposal. He could do whatever he wanted and she would be helpless to prevent it. He could stalk her, abuse her, and who would believe her word against a cop's?

With Kyle, she would be in an even more vulnerable position than when she'd gotten involved with Phil Cattrone. She shivered.

"C'mon, let's go inside where it's warm and get this over with," Kyle said, apparently misinterpreting her shiver. "I'm only doing this to save you from having to look at a scar, you know. You may not care for blood, but I really, really hate needles."

Chapter 7

Kyle hadn't been kidding about needles. He really hated them. Seeing a person in white approaching with a hypodermic made him want to act like a six-year-old—dive for cover, throw a tantrum. And *this* needle was coming at his face.

"Close your eyes," Jess whispered. She'd come with him into the treatment room because he'd asked the triage nurse to let her. He'd wanted company, he'd said. What he'd really wanted was someone to hold his hand.

And that was exactly what she was doing. He followed her advice, closing his eyes and concentrating on the smooth feel of her skin against his palm, the delicate fingers wrapped around his. He tried to discern her light, floral fragrance above the Betadine. He even tried to sense the warmth of her body sitting near him.

His focusing on Jess's feminine aspects produced predictable results—a tightening in the groin that threatened to become embarrassing. He quickly thought about needles again, solving the problem.

"I'd never have figured you for a wiggling patient, Detective," the sober young doctor said. "I make the prettiest sutures in the whole city, but you're going to ruin my handiwork if you don't hold still."

"Sorry. Why is it that stitches always hurt more than the original injury?" At his good-natured complaint, Jess gave his hand a squeeze.

"Because you've run out of adrenaline by the time you get to the hospital," the doctor replied in all seriousness as he tied another stitch. "Adrenaline is a great anesthetic." He snipped the thread. "There, only four stitches. It was a clean cut, despite how you did it. There won't be much scarring, if any."

"Thanks, Doc." With reluctance he released Jess's hand. His little ordeal was over; no reason now for her to touch him, unless she just wanted to.

He wondered if she did, if she'd gotten nearly the pleasure from the feel of his hand as he'd received from hers...or if the whole thing had been perfectly innocent on her part.

Probably the latter. In her current situation, she wasn't likely to be dwelling much on him—or any man—as a sexual object. Who could blame her? After the way Terry Rodin had treated her, she had a right to hate the whole gender for the rest of her life.

He gave his insurance card to the cashier and they got the hell out of there, away from the smell of antiseptic and too many people.

It was 3:00 a.m.—long past time to take Cinderella home, go home himself and shower and get back to work just in time for his regular shift.

They hardly exchanged a word on the drive back to midtown. He pulled up in front of her duplex, scanning for anomalies, anything out of place. The porch light blazed. All was quiet.

"Same time tomorrow?" he asked her.

"Think you'll be up to it?"

"Sure, no problem." He could grab some sleep after his shift later today. If he didn't have to work overtime. If his pounding head allowed him any sleep.

"All right," she said. "I've got a list made of Terry's friends, and I'm going to start paying them visits, like you suggested."

For some reason, this bit of news gave Kyle an uneasy feeling in the pit of his stomach. Yeah, he'd suggested this line of attack for Jess. Now he wondered whether it was safe for her to go poking around.

Those telephone calls bothered him. They indicated a real cruel streak, a vein of mental illness.

"Why don't you wait—"

"I can't wait. The state is busy building a case against me. I've got to do something."

"Can you take someone with you?"

"Lynn will go, if she doesn't have classes. Otherwise, I'm on my own. Amazing how friends sort of disappear into the woodwork when one becomes a murder suspect."

Kyle didn't suppose he could dissuade her. "Be careful, okay?"

"I usually am." She smiled faintly. "Now look who's worrying."

"I guess that means maybe we are friends." The urge to lean over and kiss her was strong. Too strong. She drew him like a black hole sucks in light. He moved slowly, giving her the chance to escape if she chose. Instead she stared at him like a deer frozen by headlights.

He aimed for her cheek. At the last possible moment, she turned her head and offered him her mouth.

It was a brief but explosive kiss, the merest brushing of lips that had the same effect as a fistful of firecrackers. Kyle suddenly couldn't get enough oxygen into his lungs. His already woozy head felt as if it might spin right off his body and fly into space.

Jess placed a hand on his shoulder, then gently but firmly pushed him back. "No more, okay?" She was practically gasping for air.

When he didn't agree right away, instead staring at her pink, moist lips and contemplating how best to exploit them again, she all at once grabbed her thermos and bolted from the car.

Kyle stared in disbelief for a second as she ran up the walk to her porch. In moments she was safely locked behind her front door. "Well, hell, that was smooth, Branson." He must be losing his touch.

He put his car in gear with some reluctance and headed for home, his brick ranch house in South K.C., near Swope Park. The area was checkered, had some crime problems, but his immediate neighborhood was nice, with lots of old-timer residents and mature trees in every yard. He always looked forward to coming home, to puttering around with his never-ceasing home-improvement projects.

No time for puttering now, he thought with a sigh.

Kyle cracked open a window to let in some fresh, if cold, air during the drive. It was only after he put some distance between himself and Jess that he fully realized what had happened, what might have happened, and he cursed violently at himself.

What had he been thinking? He hadn't been out to a movie with the woman. He'd been on a stakeout, trying to find evidence to save her from a murder conviction. He could muddy the situation irretrievably if there was even a hint that he was involved with her. Easley and Clewis might welcome a deepening of his relationship with Jess, but only because they hoped she would confide something incriminating to him.

That made it doubly important that he not get involved with her. He couldn't risk compromising whatever information he did turn up, good or bad.

* * *

The inevitable questions hit Kyle the moment he entered the downtown station. And he had to explain, at least ten times before eight o'clock, that he'd fallen on a rock while chasing a suspect that turned out not to be a suspect, while working on a case that wasn't really his.

If that wasn't bad enough, he received a royal summons from Easley just as he'd started to follow a hot lead on a missing teenage girl.

"So how'd it go?" the lieutenant asked, staring pointedly at the stitched-up cut on Kyle's cheek. He was chewing on a fresh pen this morning. The thing bore only minimal teeth marks.

"A total wash." Kyle related the bare facts of the disastrous stakeout.

"What'd I tell you?" Clewis crowed, standing in the doorway stuffing his face with a jelly doughnut. "But never mind that. You make any progress with the babe?"

Kyle clenched his fist, then stuck his hand into his pocket. If he heard Jess referred to as a "babe" one more time... "None. She's not exactly warming up to me." Even as the blatant lie left his lips, Kyle wondered why he was lying. It wouldn't hurt his position any to tell them that Jess was opening up, that he'd actually kissed her. Easley might even okay a second night of stakeout if he thought another purpose was being served.

Clewis snickered. "Now why doesn't that surprise me?"

"Stuff it, Clewis," Easley said, echoing Kyle's thoughts. Kyle's disgust toward the homicide detective was growing by exponential proportions. "We have another detail for you, if you're interested," Easley continued.

Kyle shrugged. "Sure." Just so it got him out of this room before he decked someone.

"We've had a guy watching Jess."

"Yeah, and she spotted him, too. She mentioned it last night."

"I hope you played dumb," Clewis said.

"Since I didn't know anything about the tail, what else could I do?"

"Anyway," Easley said, "we need that man back on another case."

"And you want me to tail Jess?" Kyle wasn't sure he liked the idea.

"It's mostly surveillance, not tailing," Clewis said. "She doesn't go anywhere, except for one trip to her lawyer's office. There are lots of cars parked on her street, so it's not difficult to blend in."

Hah! Kyle thought. He would bet that nosy Mrs. Tanglemeyer spotted the strange vehicle within ten minutes of its parking on her street. Not that that would be a problem today. He happened to know Jess's agenda, and she didn't plan to stay home. He'd be tailing her all over town. "Okay, I'll do it."

"On one condition," Easley said. "It's pretty obvious you want this girl to be innocent. Do I have your word you'll report every single move she makes, even if it tends to be incriminating?"

"Jeez, Lieutenant, I might be naive, but I'm not crooked."

"All right, all right," Easley soothed.

But Kyle wasn't finished. "I don't think she killed her boyfriend, but if she proves me wrong I'm not going to withhold information. I don't like her that much." Another lie.

Kyle's collar was starting to feel tight.

"Go check out a car, then. We'll send someone to relieve you for the next shift."

Kyle made a swift escape before Easley changed his mind. Sitting in a car for six or seven hours, watching Jess and unable to make contact with her, wasn't his idea of fun. But if anyone was going to keep an eye on Jess Robinson, he'd just as soon be the one to do it.

"I'm really sorry I can't help you, Jess. I haven't seen him in over a year." Dean Shane, a former law-school buddy of Terry's, had been third on Jess's list of Terry's friends and associates to check out that day. The first one hadn't been home. The second one had moved away.

She remembered meeting Dean at a party a couple of years ago and liking the thin, balding man. He'd been surprised to see her on his front porch this morning—and who could blame him? It was disconcerting to be suddenly confronted with a murder suspect. But once he'd gotten over his surprise, he'd been cordial and concerned. He'd offered Jess coffee and a quiet place to sit for a few minutes.

"If there's anything I can do to help..." Dean said.

"Oh, you've helped already," she replied. He'd given her a handful of mutual acquaintances of his and Terry's, their addresses and phone numbers. More people to visit. She would be at this for days.

"If it means anything, I don't believe all that crap they've printed in the paper," Dean said. "Terry's a loose cannon. In fact, when I first met you, I remember being surprised that he'd hooked up with someone so nice."

Jess looked down at the toes of her boots.

"If Terry's missing, I'm a lot more inclined to believe that he disappeared on purpose than that someone killed him, especially you."

"Thanks, Dean. That means a lot." She drained her coffee cup. "I have to go. Lots more visits to make today. You have my number if you hear anything, or something occurs to you?"

"Right."

Jess made her way down the front stairs of Dean's apartment building. Cold wind whipped up under her broomstick skirt, making her wish she'd worn slacks. When she'd looked out the window this morning, the bright sun and blue sky had lulled her into a false sense of security about the temperature.

Sitting behind the wheel of her car, she crossed Dean's name off the list, then sighed as she realized who the next candidate was. Brianna, of the lip print. Jess had found her address scribbled on the back of an envelope. Well, nothing to do but give her a try.

Brianna Trehorn lived in an old frame house near the university. Judging from the three mailboxes lined up by the front door, the grand-old-lady house had been divided up into apartments suitable for student housing.

Jess rang the bell. Seconds later the front door swung open on squeaky hinges. A young—very young—blond woman stared at Jess from behind the screen door, her smile frozen on her face.

"You."

"Excuse me?"

"Terry's girlfriend. God, I told him he was crazy to stay with you, and now you've proved me right. You've got your nerve, coming here. What, did you come here to gloat? Did he threaten to leave you and you killed him? If you couldn't have him, no one could, is that it?"

The young woman's hostility stole Jess's breath right out of her lungs. She supposed she ought to be getting used to it by now. But it still surprised her when someone spewed hate toward her. What had she ever done to inspire hate?

"Excuse me, are you Brianna—" she began, but the other woman cut her off.

"You know damn well who I am." Tears welled up in her big blue eyes. "Now get away. Get off my porch, or I'll call the cops, you…you murderer. Evil, you're evil!"

"But I just want to ask—"

"Bruno!" Brianna yelled over her shoulder. Jess heard a noise that sounded like a stampeding rhinoceros. Before she could even register what was happening, Brianna opened the screen door and a mass of black hair and muscle exploded outside, all snarls and fangs.

Jess screamed and found herself balanced on the porch railing. "I'll leave, already," she cried out, feeling the rottweiler's breath on her legs as it growled and snapped just inches short of making contact. "Call him off."

Brianna didn't do a thing. When Jess could tear her gaze away from that of the huge black dog, she saw Brianna standing behind the screen, looking faintly amused.

"Call him off!"

Both women, and even the dog, swiveled their heads toward the commanding male voice coming from behind Jess. Oh, God. She knew that voice.

"Kyle?"

"Police," Kyle said. "Call him off or I'll shoot him. I mean it."

"No!" Brianna cried. "Bruno, come! Bruno, sit!" Since the dog did neither of those things, Brianna was forced to come out on the front porch and haul the beast away by its collar.

Kyle reholstered his gun inside his jacket as he climbed the stairs to the porch. "Lady, if you're going to own a dog that mean, you need to have him better trained. He could kill someone."

"I know," Brianna said from behind the screen. "Why do you think I have him?"

"If he hurt someone, you could get in a lot of trouble." Without sparing Jess a glance, he offered a hand to help her down from the porch railing. "Lawsuits, criminal charges—"

"I was protecting my home," Brianna objected. "From a murderer."

"Oh, yeah, she looks real menacing to me. But I don't see a gun or a knife. You'd have a hard time pleading self-defense. Just a word to the wise."

Jess, recovering her voice, thought to ask, "Aren't you overreacting just a bit, Brianna? You're not hiding something inside that house, are you? Or someone?"

Brianna merely looked confused. "What?"

Kyle shook his head. "Never mind. Jess, I think we've worn out our welcome here." He took her hand possessively and led her down the porch steps toward her car. "One of Terry's friends?" he asked when they were out of Brianna's earshot.

"A lover, I think."

"Whew. Jailbait, almost."

"She's awfully paranoid. She could be hiding him."

"Mmm, doubtful. When you suggested as much, her confusion seemed pretty genuine."

She stopped at her car. "I want to know for sure. Can't you get a search warrant or something?"

Kyle shook his head. "Judges don't grant search warrants based on a whim. Hey, you look cold. I'll buy you a cup of coffee."

Jess was on the verge of accepting when she realized that Kyle's appearance was just a little too convenient. "You were following me."

"Well, yeah."

"You're a lousy tail. I spotted you almost immediately." She scanned the street. "You were in that silver Grand Am."

"That was me."

She couldn't even put her outrage into words. Last night he'd been on her side—or so he'd pretended. She'd held his hand while he got his stitches. He'd *kissed* her. Now he was back to being a stupid cop.

"Someone has to do it," he said. "Today my number came up."

"You're trying to catch me doing something incriminating!"

"I just rescued you from a woman-eating dog. Doesn't that count for anything?"

Jess sighed. She supposed she should thank him for that. Another thirty seconds and she might have become a giant Milkbone. But he'd been spying on her. Finally she settled on a compromise. "Thank you for rescuing me. But I'll buy my own coffee. And you can forget about the stakeout tonight. I know whose side you're on, and I can't help but think that the more time I spend with you, the deeper the risk." All kinds of risk.

"Even if you're innocent?"

"Yes. I've seen how easily innocent words and acts can be twisted. The less I give you guys to work with, the better." With that, she climbed into her car and slammed the door. She didn't want to look at him, at his face, his eyes entreating her to change her mind about him. She wanted to believe he was on her side, but the evidence to the contrary was overwhelming.

So much for her Pollyanna attitude. She had to get tough, shrewd. Like Marva. Even Lynn. She roared off without a backward glance, but three blocks away she had to pull over to wipe her eyes.

How was he going to explain this one to Clewis and Easley? Kyle wondered as he followed Jess, not even bothering to keep distance between the two cars. She knew he was there.

He'd blown his cover because Jess had been about to be devoured by a dog? How believable did that sound? Not that his cover needed that much blowing. She'd already identified his car as following her.

So why did he bother to continue to tail her? He supposed he wanted to protect her. Lord only knew how many other "Briannas" there were, waiting to vent their anger over Terry's disappearance on the easiest scapegoat.

Next time it might be worse than a dog.

Still, he checked in at headquarters with his cellular, thanking his lucky stars that Clewis was out to lunch and he would only have to deal with Easley.

"Come on in," Easley said. "If she knows you're there, she sure won't do anything to incriminate herself. We'll let your relief catch up with her on the next shift. Maybe he'll do a better job of staying hidden."

"He'd have to." Kyle tried not to resent the dig. Tried and failed. He'd done a good job tailing Jess. She was just too sharp not to notice when she was being followed. She'd spotted yesterday's tail, too. Still, no point trying to defend himself. The only way he could redeem his reputation at this point was to prove Jess was innocent and Terry was alive.

When that happened he would turn "I told you so" into an art form.

Sitting in the dark in Lynn's old brown Toyota—which Terry most likely wouldn't recognize—Jess kept her eyes trained on the deserted parking lot. She'd been here two hours already, and she'd discovered one very significant thing: stakeouts were really boring. She was already short on sleep, and it was all she could do to keep her eyelids from drooping as she watched the pay phones, using a pair of cheap binoculars she'd borrowed from Mrs. Tanglemeyer.

"About as exciting as watching corn grow." She could remember doing just that, growing up on her parents' Kansas farm. She guessed that meant she was well suited to this kind of work.

At 1:00 a.m., she drained the last of her coffee and wrapped herself up in the blanket she'd brought. The weather wasn't as bitter as it had been last night, but it was still plenty uncomfortable.

By one-thirty, she was wondering how long she could

stand the boredom. Only three cars had passed in the past half hour.

By one forty-five, she was swearing to herself that if he didn't show up by two she was out of here.

At one-fifty, a car pulled into the parking lot, and Jess completely forgot about warm fuzzy house slippers and electric blankets. The car was an '80 Firebird, the body so dented and bearing so many different paint colors that it couldn't be classified. Once seen, the car wasn't soon forgotten, and she'd seen it before.

It was Kevin Gilpatrick's car. With her hand trembling, she picked up her briefcase phone and dialed 911. She'd already decided what she would say to get the police to send out a patrolman.

"Yes," she said when an operator responded, "I'd like to report an attempted burglary at the K mart on Eastern Springs Boulevard. I can see the guy across the street from my bedroom window. Looks like he's trying to pry open a door."

"All right, ma'am, could you hold a moment please?"

Jess disconnected immediately. If she provided no other information, they would have to send someone over to investigate.

A man exited the car and sauntered to the phones. Through the cheap binoculars, Jess couldn't tell much about him. Like the teenager from last night, this man was slender, in jeans, jacket and cap. It could have been Terry. Or half a million other guys.

She couldn't stand it. She had to find out. She started up the car. No reaction from her mark. Easing the Toyota into gear, she crept away from the curb, lights off. Unfortunately the Toyota's engine was anything but quiet. As she drew closer, her suspect couldn't help hearing it.

Suddenly he swiveled around, and she recognized the face.

Kevin.

He dropped the phone and made for his car. Before he could take even two steps, the roar of another car's engine stopped him in his tracks. A bright red Mustang surged across the parking lot toward them both.

Jess hit the gas, fishtailing toward Kevin's car to prevent his escape. The Mustang attacked from the other direction, boxing in the Firebird. Kevin could do nothing but slump in defeat.

Kyle jumped out of the Mustang, gun drawn. "Police. Up against the car. Jess, stay put," he added when she opened her door.

Kevin seemed to know the routine. Resigned, he placed his hands on the roof of the Firebird and spread his legs. Kyle quickly patted him down, then holstered the gun beneath his jacket. "Okay, you can turn around, Mr. Gilpatrick."

"I wasn't doin' nothin', man," he began, but Kyle silenced him with a look that could have frozen molten lava.

"Just out for a stroll at two in the morning?"

Seeing no danger, Jess stepped out of her car. Kevin stared at her, surprised.

"Who were you calling?" Kyle tried again.

"None of your business."

"Kevin, Kevin, Kevin. Phone-company records will verify the number you dialed. Jess's sister will testify as to what you said. Do you know what the penalty is for harassment?"

Kevin's face crumpled. "I was just—" He sobbed. "I just wanted her to tell where she put the body so he can have a decent burial."

Kyle looked over at Jess. "You want to press charges, right?"

"Yes. No, wait." She approached Kevin, drawing closer until she was almost nose to chin with him. "I won't press charges if you'll come clean, Kevin."

"Come clean about what?" he asked defiantly.

"Where are you hiding Terry?"

"That's my line."

"Look," Jess said, "this practical joke has gone on long enough. It's not worth getting arrested over. I know you're hiding him. And when we find him, your butt will be in a sling, too. Conspiracy. Fraud. Lying to the police."

For an instant Kevin's gaze faltered. In that split second, Jess knew beyond any doubt she was right.

Then his face hardened. "You call murder a practical joke?" He spat at her, and she jumped just in time to avoid being hit.

Kyle grabbed Kevin's arm. "All right, that's enough, Gilpatrick. Any more of that crap and I'll arrest you whether Jess wants it or not." He turned to Jess. "How about it?"

She thought for a moment. "Let him go, if he's that determined to drag himself down with Terry. Y'know, Kevin, if you expect loyalty from him in return for helping him get his revenge against me, you'll be disappointed. He'll never be your best friend. He'll use you like he does everyone else."

Again she saw the slightest glimmer of hesitation in Kevin's eyes before he looked away from her.

You're mine, she thought smugly. Sooner or later Kevin would realize she was right, and he'd turn Terry in. Of course, that didn't help her now.

"Jess," Kyle said, "could you move your car so Mr. Gilpatrick here can leave?"

She was more than happy to. Now that the rush of excitement was dissipating, she felt like wilted lettuce. All she wanted was to get home and get into bed.

"Park right over there, on the other side of my car," Kyle said in a tone that brooked no argument. "I'm not done with you."

Chapter 8

Jess watched as Kevin Gilpatrick's taillights disappeared into the distance with a shriek of rubber against pavement. Damn. Something wasn't right. She knew Kevin's voice, had heard it on a number of occasions on the phone when he'd called for Terry. He hadn't been the one to place those first two crank calls.

It was Terry's voice she'd heard. Had this confrontation with Kevin been carefully orchestrated to put another nail in her coffin? To wear her down, give her hope and then dash it to the ground?

Interrupting her thoughts, Kyle climbed into the Toyota's passenger seat without invitation. He dominated the car's tiny interior. Jess felt as if she could almost swoon from his sheer presence, his heat, even the scent of excitement and anger that came off his skin.

And, she made no mistake, he was angry.

"Thanks for taking care of that for me," she murmured. "Where were you and that car hiding? I never saw you, and I looked around pretty carefully."

"Never mind me. What did you think you were doing just now? How many times do I have to remind you that we're dealing with dangerous people here?"

"I needed to see who it was," Jess said, her arms folded defensively across her chest. They didn't ward off either the cold or Kyle's penetrating stare. "I knew the car was Kevin's. I thought for sure Terry was the one driving. I had to know, even if it meant scaring him away before anyone else saw him. I had to know if he was alive."

"You still have doubts?" Kyle's anger escalated another notch. Could she blame him? He'd stuck his neck out for her on the basis of this theory she had about Terry's framing her for murder.

She didn't answer his question for a long time. Finally, in a voice that was barely there, she said, "Sometimes. When I'm lying in bed late at night, I worry that I'm wrong. I *know* it was Terry's voice I heard on the phone. But then I start wondering about the blood. The police said that at one time there was a lot of it in the sink, in the washing machine. Where did it come from?"

"That's what we'd all like to know. The sixty-four-thousand-dollar question."

Something about Kyle's tone of voice hit her the wrong way. Over the past few days she'd been viciously interrogated, harassed, maligned in the newspaper and attacked by a dog. The slender hope she'd been clinging to—that she would catch Terry making the calls—had been blown to smithereens.

And now Kyle, who seemingly on a whim alternated between her champion and her accuser, was doubting her again.

She'd had enough. She longed to simply tell him to get out of her car. But she couldn't quite bring herself to do it. Standing up to someone like Kyle required more brass than she could muster at the moment.

"I want to go home now," she said instead, her voice

thick with unshed tears. She despised the weakness in her that made her cry when she was angry.

"What? I don't even get a thank-you for saving your—"

"No. I didn't invite you to this party."

"You could have been hurt," he said with quiet authority.

"I'm already hurt. My friends have deserted me, my business is practically dead, my bank account is empty, my father's blood pressure is through the roof from worrying about me. Frankly, it couldn't get a whole lot worse. Physical injury would be…a step up, I think." She couldn't hold back anymore. The tears spilled out of her eyes and the sobs erupted from her throat.

"Aw, Jess, don't." Somehow he managed to pull her against him in the awkward confines of the car. She didn't resist. She didn't have the strength or the will. It was preposterous that she should accept comfort from the very person who'd made her cry in the first place, but it seemed easier than fighting him.

"I was worried about you," he said in a low, soothing voice. "That's why I came tonight. Not so I could spy on you or torment you. I didn't mean to get mad." He stroked her hair and brushed the tears off her cheek with an infinitely gentle thumb. "Can't you trust me? I'm on your side."

"You're a cop. You're on their side," she said even as her hand crept up to cling to the lapel of his leather jacket. She also clung to the faint hope that she was wrong about him.

"I don't think you killed Terry Rodin," he said quietly. "That puts me closer to your camp than Clewis's."

She felt herself wavering. Oh, God, she wanted to believe in him. She reminded herself that Kyle Branson was a quick thinker and a smooth talker, and he had way too much persuasive power over her vulnerable mind. In no time he could have her eating out of his hand.

She thought out her next question carefully. "If you believe I'm innocent, why did you insinuate just now that I'm lying about the blood in the sink?"

"I wasn't insinuating anything." He continued stroking her the way he might try to calm a skittish cat. "You misread me, sweetheart. I am purely frustrated at the confusing evidence we're dealing with. Someone's hiding something. That's not the same as accusing *you* of lying."

Amazingly, she did relax. She had to force herself not to be too complacent. "What about when you followed me?"

"I have a job to do. Lieutenant Easley thinks you're guilty. Right now, he's my superior. I do what he tells me to do. Today he told me to follow you. I figured you were better off with me tailing you than someone else."

"So you're entirely altruistic in all this?" She tried to inject suspicion and skepticism into her voice, but instead the question came out sounding hopeful.

He sighed. "My number one priority is solving the case. I happen to believe finding out the truth—that Terry's still alive, or uncovering his murderer—will clear you. If that makes me altruistic, fine. I'm not some bleeding heart taking you on as a charity case, if that's what you think."

He sure knew how to say all the right things.

All at once she became excruciatingly aware of the myriad physical sensations brought on by her closeness to him—the feel of his smooth cotton shirt against her cheek, the smell of leather and faint aftershave, the sound of his heartbeat, oddly accelerated.

And his hands, one rubbing her back, the other sifting through her hair. Needing even closer contact, she reached up with her left hand to touch his face. It was warm and rough with a full day's growth of beard. She touched his stitched-up cut with one featherlight finger.

He enveloped her small hand in his and pulled it away from his face. "Honey, right now I'm confused and tired, running on caffeine and adrenaline. I'm trying like hell to fight a strong physical attraction to you, and you're not helping a whole lot. I'm not that strong."

The atmosphere inside the car altered dramatically. An electricity filled the air, making Jess's skin prickle with awareness. Her heartbeat doubled in tempo and her mouth went dry.

She knew what she ought to say, what she ought to feel. She should pull away, disengage before things really did get out of hand. She should politely thank him for looking after her, then ask him to get out of her car so she could get home.

She didn't. The plain truth was that her body craved the simple comfort of touch—Kyle's touch. His hands had already tangled themselves in her hair. She could so easily imagine what those hands would feel like caressing her breasts or stroking bare flesh. She sensed his readiness, the thin thread of control threatening to snap. All it would take was for her to turn her face toward his....

But that would be insanity. If it became known that she'd involved herself with a cop investigating her case, the D.A.'s office would have a field day. So when she felt the urge to take that next step, she instead imagined Marva's disapproving scowl.

"I think it would be best if we said good-night." She tried to keep her tone casual, as if the possibility of sex didn't concern her much. But her voice quavered, which irritated her. At least she'd stopped crying.

"Jess. You're not afraid of me, are you?"

"Shouldn't I be? You just admitted you're close to losing control." She'd be crazy not to fear him. He was so damn powerful, and at the moment she felt weak. She hated to be at the mercy of her fears and her hormones. But her free will, her intelligent decision-making powers, seemed to have taken a hike to another planet. Some men, like Kyle, simply turned her to mush.

"I may want you, but I've never pushed myself on a woman who didn't want me."

Should she have been reassured? Part of her wished the decision could be taken out of her hands. "Regardless of who wants whom, it would be crazy for us to give in to lust," she said sensibly, though she felt anything but sensible right now. "What if the press found out? The district attorney?"

"If we were stupid enough to sleep together, we would both deserve the consequences. I wouldn't take it that far. I know better."

"Oh." She should have been overwhelmed with relief. She wasn't.

"How about you? How far were you willing to take it?" The slight note of amusement in his voice somehow broke the tension.

"I don't dare answer that question." She almost laughed, but she couldn't, not when laughter could so easily turn into hysteria.

"What about when the charges are dropped?" He threw the question out casually. It hung in the air between them, glittering, inviting.

She grabbed on to the first easy answer that came to mind. "I can't think that far ahead." Then she forced herself to pull away from him. Her tears were dried. She didn't need his comforting anymore.

"I'll take that as a maybe." He released her, reluctantly it seemed. He reached for the door handle, then paused. "Sure you're okay? Not too shaky to drive home?"

"No, I'm fine." Please, she thought, don't leave me alone. Surprised by the errant thought, she grabbed on to the steering wheel to keep her hands from reaching for him. She was nuts, crazy, bonkers, to want a man whom she didn't completely trust. A man who, if he turned on her, could send her to jail with a few well-placed words.

She was proving, once again, that she had appalling judgment when it came to men.

Although she thought she should have been immune to surprises by then, when he leaned over to kiss her cheek, she jumped. This wasn't like the other night, when he'd merely brushed her lips with his. This time she turned her head and he took full possession of her mouth. He didn't try to hold her. In fact, he didn't even touch her with his hands, giving her every opportunity to pull back.

She didn't. She leaned into the kiss, opening her mouth against his, meeting his tongue with hers.

He abruptly broke the kiss. "Something to think about, for later," he said with a wicked smile. He was gone, the car door slamming behind him, before she could formulate a suitable response.

Kyle thought about that kiss all during the drive home. And even though he desperately needed sleep, images of Jess's welcoming mouth kept him awake even later.

What had he been thinking? He was reasonably sure no one had been watching them. But what if he was wrong? She was right about the D.A.'s office going nuts if they caught her sleeping with a cop. If they saw her even kissing a cop, they would assume the rest.

She would land in jail. And Easley would probably give him a pat on the back for orchestrating the whole thing— after he was brought up on disciplinary charges.

He had to forestall that chain of events at any cost. And that meant no more kissing—no more touching, period, no matter how bad he had it for her. No matter how receptive she appeared to be. To let it go any further could seriously damage Jess's standing.

Again after catching only a few hours' sleep, he stumbled into work, feeling like a zombie. The first thing he had to do was report the results of his unsanctioned stake-out. Even though Jess hadn't caught Terry in the act, the fact that there really was a crank caller, and that he was someone connected to the case, was intriguing information.

Not that Clewis, the Neanderthal, would do anything with it.

Clewis, sitting behind his desk with his attention focused on a ham-and-cheese breakfast sandwich from 7-Eleven, seemed to pay scant attention to Kyle's report. Eventually, however, he did look up. "So the babe didn't press charges?"

"What for? Even if he was found guilty, Gilpatrick would get a little slap on the wrist at most. She didn't want to mess with that."

"Or," Clewis said thoughtfully, "she and Gilpatrick are in cahoots somehow. I hadn't thought of that. You know, maybe they had a little thing going on the side, and Rodin was in the way?"

It was the most moronic conclusion Kyle had ever heard anyone draw, but he resisted the temptation to say so. "Gilpatrick's statement was very damaging to Jess's case. If he was in cahoots with her, he would have tried to draw suspicion away from her."

Clewis thought for a minute. "Yeah, I hate to say it, but I think you're right."

"On the other hand," Kyle said, taking advantage of this rare open-mindedness on Clewis's part, "what's to say Gilpatrick didn't kill Rodin on his own and try to frame Jess? Have we even considered him as a bona fide suspect? He *is* the one who first reported his friend missing, and you know the statistics as well as I do."

Clewis threw down his sandwich. "Oh, for God's sake, Branson, will you stop thinking with your private parts? Jess Robinson is guilty. How much evidence do you need?"

"A body and a murder weapon, for starters." Kyle fought for control, won it. "I want to do some more checking on Gilpatrick."

"Already done. He's clean," Clewis said, showing renewed interest in his sandwich. He took another bite and washed it down with coffee. "Unless you want to count parking tickets."

"I want to stake out his house."

"No way. Jeez, you and your stakeouts."

"I think he might be hiding Terry Rodin there."

Clewis's only response was to roll his eyes.

"Dammit, Clewis, are you doing anything on this case?"

"The D.A. is happy with what I've turned over so far. They can try her without a body, you know. It's been done."

"Have you even tried to find a body?"

"Chances are she put it in a Dumpster and it's at the landfill by now. No way to find a body in that mess. Or she dumped it in the river, and it's hundreds of miles downstream by now. The body won't be found," Clewis said with annoying confidence.

"Have you made any phone calls to see if a body *has* been found?" Kyle asked, thinking of how he would run the investigation if it were his.

"Bodies are found all the time in the river," Clewis said boredly.

"So maybe one of them is our guy."

Clewis flashed an evil grin. "Then why don't *you* make the phone calls?"

"I thought I was supposed to tail Jess today."

"I'm canceling the surveillance," Clewis flatly announced. "She knows we're there and she's not about to do anything incriminating. After a few days, when she's convinced we've given up, we'll try again. Meanwhile, you're back in missing persons.'' Where you belong, his hostile gaze seemed to add.

"Fine." Kyle spun around on the toes of his boots, intending to get as far from Clewis as possible—before he resorted to violence. The sound of the other detective's phone ringing stopped him in his tracks.

"Clewis here…yeah? Who is this? Look, buddy, I don't take no statements without a name…yeah, no foolin'? She as good as she looks?"

At that, Kyle drew closer, blatantly eavesdropping. Clewis swiveled in his chair so that his back was to Kyle, but the man apparently didn't know how to talk in an undertone, because the one-sided conversation continued in perfect clarity.

"Uh-huh. Under the front-porch steps. Yeah, we'll check it out, all right. Although, you know, it's kinda hard to get a search warrant on the basis of an anonymous tip.…" Clewis cursed and slammed down the receiver. "Jerk." Then he shook off his momentary anger, swiveled in his chair again to face Kyle and grinned that awful, evil grin that made Kyle's skin crawl.

"You wanted a murder weapon?" he said to Kyle. "Well, I think we're about to get one. That was a man claiming to be—oh, how shall I put it delicately?—*intimate* with Jess Robinson. She told him where she stashed the bloody knife."

Kyle was dumfounded for a moment. Jess had been recently intimate with another man? She'd confided in him, shared her secrets—

Then reason took over. "An anonymous tip, Clewis? You buy that?"

"Not entirely, but it's worth checking out. I may not even need a warrant, if the old one hasn't expired. You remember what day that other one was issued?"

The fifth. "Not offhand. Don't you think this is just a bit too convenient?"

"I'll take convenient, if it gets me a murder weapon."

"But under the front-porch steps? In the first place, why there? That's utterly stupid, and we both know she isn't that. In the second place, our evidence guys went over the exterior of the house with a microscope. They wouldn't have missed a knife under the front steps."

"Evidence guys miss all kinds of things. You never know." He picked up the phone and began making preparations for the search, making sure everything was legal.

Kyle left. He returned to his own desk in missing persons and dialed Jess's number.

He hung up before the connection was made. For God's sake, he couldn't warn Jess about an impending search. He couldn't give her time to move or dispose of evidence before the search team got there.

Not that he believed, for one minute, that she knew about any knife under her porch steps. But suppose the evidence had been planted? If he told her where to look, she might remove it, hide it, out of sheer fear. If someone saw her do it, that would be more evidence against her.

And if the department found out he'd called her—an easy chore with that caller-ID box he'd installed on her phone—he'd be hit with an internal-affairs investigation so fast his head would spin.

So he couldn't call her. But he could sure as hell be there when the search team arrived. He would watch those guys, make sure the search was conducted fairly and that nothing was "discovered" that hadn't previously been there.

The doorbell was insistent. Jess, not at her best from the hectic schedule she'd been keeping, was positive it was another reporter. She jerked open the door. "What do you people *want* from me?"

"Police, ma'am," a stone-faced young man on her front porch said. He wore the now-familiar black-and-white jacket of an evidence tech. "We have a warrant to search the exterior grounds of your home for evidence related to the disappearance—"

"Yes, I know the routine by now. You already dug up my whole yard. What more could you want?" Then she noticed the crowbars. Another man and a woman carried crowbars and hammers. Behind them stood Detective Clewis, his self-satisfied smirk almost nauseating. Behind them stood the press—two minicams and a still photographer from the *Star*. And behind them…Kyle. His gaze was glued to her, his dark eyes almost apologetic.

"The porch steps, ma'am," the lead cop said.

She wanted to run inside and slam the door against the inquisitive, accusing stares and the bright lights. But she and Marva had agreed that she would not shy away from the press as if she was guilty. All she could think of to do was shrug.

"Do what you have to do," she said.

"Ms. Robinson, could you tell us—"

"I'm sorry," she interrupted, forcing a smile, "you guys know by now that I can't make statements to the press." She shrugged again. "Lawyer's orders." Her gaze slid toward Kyle.

He looked away. Was this his doing? she wondered. Why was he here, if he really wasn't a prominent member of the investigation team?

By now the evidence techs had cleared the steps, and the cameras refocused their attention on the matter at hand. Should she go inside? she wondered. Or stand here and watch?

She would watch, she decided, curious as hell to know why they'd suddenly zeroed in on her porch. It didn't bode well.

She saw movement behind the uniforms who were keeping the too-curious at bay. It was Kyle. He'd moved forward, and he was flashing his badge. The blue uniforms parted to let him through. Carefully skirting the activity on her steps, he vaulted up to the porch.

She didn't quite know how to greet him.

"I wanted to warn you about this," he said, his back to the cameras. "But to do so would have seriously violated ethics."

"What the hell are they—" she started to reply, but he hushed her with a furtive hand gesture.

"Be careful what you say. Cameras are rolling. They can go over the tapes and read lips."

She felt suddenly paranoid. "Okay," she mumbled. "Why are they doing this?"

"Anonymous tip." The shriek of splitting wood punctuated his sentence. "Man said he was intimate with you. You confessed to him and told him where you'd hidden the knife. I shouldn't even be telling you this."

Jess's insides were cold. She looked into Kyle's eyes, saw the doubt written there and went even colder. He actually thought it could be true.

"Do you have a lover?" he asked, almost defiantly, daring her to answer yes.

If she hadn't been concerned about a murder conviction, she might have answered yes just to needle him. But this wasn't about mind games, she reminded herself. Not on her part. She had to be scrupulously honest...about this, anyway.

"No lovers," she said, staring down at her toes. "I don't suppose this phone call was recorded?" She'd bet her bloomers it was Terry himself.

"No."

"He's playing hardball. I wonder when he intends to stop—when I'm on my way to the electric chair?" She turned her head to the side so the cameras couldn't catch her words. "Kyle, you don't take this seriously, do you? An anonymous tip? Conveniently timed to heat things up when the investigation was slowing down?"

"I think it's a crock," Kyle said. "I also think Clewis alerted the press so he could showboat when the murder weapon is found."

"They won't find anything," Jess said flatly. "He'll look like a fool."

"Think about it, Jess. Would Terry have made this gesture without preparing for it?"

Jess felt sick to her stomach. Of course. Terry had planted the knife there. And when the evidence techs had overlooked it, he'd been forced to draw their attention to it.

"Looks like we found something," the female tech said. A hush fell over the crowd. Cameras whirred and clicked. Reporters jockeyed for position. With a pair of forceps, she withdrew a knife. A large butcher knife, its blade rusted or dirtied or both.

Jess recognized it instantly, even from a distance. It belonged to the cutlery set the police had confiscated earlier. It was her knife, probably loaded with her fingerprints.

"Go inside—now!" Kyle hissed.

That was exactly what she wanted to do. But her feet wouldn't cooperate. Everything was spinning. A collective gasp issued from the onlookers as she went down. Kyle caught her before she hit the ground.

What priceless footage this stunt would make for the evening news, she thought fuzzily. Marva would be furious!

Her last thought, before everything went black, was how nice Kyle's arms felt around her.

Chapter 9

She woke up inside her duplex, sprawled on her sofa, to find Kyle bathing her face with a wet towel.

"There you are," he said when she opened her eyes, his voice a caress. "You okay?"

"That depends." She cleared her throat so she wouldn't sound like a sick sparrow. "Where's everybody else?"

"Stalled, for the time being. Clewis is out there smiling for the cameras. But he'll be coming after you before long."

"I'm counting on it. Damn, I can't believe I blacked out. I've never done that before." Well, maybe once, after she'd stabbed Phil Cattrone. She'd awakened to find herself lying next to his inert body, his blood all over her. She shivered at the memory.

"If you're not up to questioning, I can call in the paramedics," Kyle said, all full of concern as he stroked hair off her damp forehead. "A night in the hospital will buy you some time."

"I don't need time," she said indignantly, trying to sit

up. But her woozy head forced her down again. "The questions shouldn't last long. I don't know anything."

"Yeah, well, it'll take Clewis a couple of hours to convince himself he can't worm any answers out of you. By now you know how that goes."

She nodded miserably. "I should call Marva. She's going to hit the roof."

"This isn't exactly your doing."

"True, I can't do anything about planted evidence. But I should have at least stayed inside the house, away from the cameras."

"Maybe. Maybe not. They say a picture paints a thousand words. And the look of shock on your face when they pulled that knife out from under your steps was as genuine as they come."

"If you say so."

"Every camera out there captured it. You could use it at the trial"

"Please, let's not talk about trials. Surely Terry won't put me through that."

"Whoever's framing you might not stop at anything." He paused to let that sink in. "I'll call Marva for you."

"Her number's by the phone in the kitchen."

While Kyle made the call, Jess tried to collect herself. God, this was insanity. She had to put a stop to it. She had to find Terry. As she lay there on the couch, her head spinning, her stomach churning, she thought of a plan.

She couldn't tell anyone about it, though, not even Lynn. Not Marva. Especially not Kyle, who would try to stop her. And if he couldn't, he would follow her, and possibly end up in trouble himself. He could lose his job if he got caught breaking and entering.

Detective Clewis made an appearance a few minutes later. He banged on the door. And when Kyle let him in, he swaggered and stared down his nose at Jess, still supine on the couch. He almost crowed.

"Her attorney's on the way," Kyle said.

Clewis rolled his eyes, the wind momentarily out of his sails. "I'll wait."

The female evidence tech, who'd followed Clewis inside, sat gingerly on the edge of a chair, looking nervous. She held a paper sack.

Jess knew what was in the sack. They were going to make her look at it. As if she needed to see it.

Marva showed up in record time. Her wig was on a little crooked, as was her lipstick. But her presence was commanding nonetheless. Even Clewis sat up a little straighter as she swept into the room, and Jess was once again pleased with Lynn's choice of lawyer.

"Are you up to this, honey?" she asked Jess first thing. "'Cause if you're not—"

"Yes. I want to get it over with."

"All right, then." She pulled a chair over from the dining room and sat in it like a queen taking her throne. She nodded at Clewis. "Go ahead."

Things went predictably from there. Clewis asked Jess what she knew about the knife. She replied that she knew nothing more than anyone else. Yes, she recognized it as her knife. She didn't know how it had gotten under the porch. Whenever she mentioned the possibility that someone had framed her, Clewis ignored her.

They went round and round. The nausea worked in Jess's favor. Her stomach hurt so badly that she couldn't spare any energy to fuel emotions. Her answers to Clewis's questions were sedate, calm, matter-of-fact.

He gave up more quickly than she would have guessed possible.

The moment Clewis was gone, Marva turned a jaundiced eye toward Kyle. "You can go, too, you know."

Jess longed to defend Kyle. He'd been kind to her this afternoon—warning her about the TV cameras, catching her when she fell, protecting her from the press vultures.

But Marva would be horrified if she knew exactly how close she'd gotten to Kyle Branson. The best she could do for Kyle was to give him an apologetic shrug.

"I'm gone," Kyle said, putting on his jacket. "Call if you need anything."

When he'd left, Marva stared suspiciously at the closed door for several seconds. Finally she asked, "What's going on with him?"

"He's been nice to me, some of the time, anyway," Jess answered, finding it impossible to fib to Marva. "He's the only one who even halfway believes my theory that Terry framed me."

Marva clicked her tongue and shook her head. "Girl, you ever heard of good cop, bad cop? Your fine-looking detective there is playing good cop. And don't you fall for it. He's after something, and it's not your sweet behind, although he'd probably take that with a smile."

Jess shifted uncomfortably on the sofa. Marva was only voicing the same doubts Jess had experienced about Kyle from time to time. She said cautiously, "I think he's on the level."

Marva used the scowl she reserved for when she really wanted to make an impression. "You get this through your head. With the police, *nothing* is on the level. You don't tell that man a thing, you got me?"

Jess nodded numbly. Marva didn't understand. Just the same, she was obliged to follow her attorney's advice. Marva knew what was best for Jess's case. But did anyone know what was best for Jess's soul? For reasons that were beyond her understanding, she was beginning to need Kyle.

Kyle tried to watch TV, but on every channel they kept showing news updates. Short film clips of the knife and Jess's pale face dominated the screen, along with some not-so-clever sound bites from Clewis. Kyle couldn't get away from them. So he turned off the box. It was after midnight, anyway.

He needed sleep, but he knew it would elude him. His right leg ached, the vestiges of an old injury he'd incurred when he was a street cop. Some doped-up drug dealer had run Kyle down with his car. When the pain kicked in, the only way he could sleep was to achieve total exhaustion.

He was close to that now. He thought longingly of the prescription pain reliever tucked away in his medicine chest, then shook his head. His old man had long been addicted to prescription narcotics. The drugs ruled his life. Kyle had vowed not to make that mistake. The bottle of pills remained untouched.

He lay down on his butt-sprung couch, his leg propped up by a couple of cushions, and listened to the traffic outside. Someone down the street was having a party. The cars came and went. He'd almost drifted off when the phone rang.

He pounced on it, hoping it might be good news for Jess. Or Jess herself. "Branson."

"Kyle?"

At first he thought it was Jess, then realized the voice wasn't quite right. "Lynn?"

"Yes. I'm sorry to bother you, but something's wrong and I don't know who else to call. Jess is missing."

"What?" Alarming pictures flashed through Kyle's mind.

"She wasn't kidnapped or anything," Lynn said hastily. "She went off someplace. She said she was going to bed a couple of hours ago, but just now I got a funny feeling and I went to check on her. She's gone, her car's gone, her bed's made. She sneaked out."

That news was only slightly more welcome than a kidnapping would have been. He sighed and rubbed his eyes with thumb and forefinger. "Any idea where she went?"

Lynn hesitated, then plunged ahead. "I think I know.

Earlier, she kept talking about how finding Terry was the only way she could get out of this mess. She's convinced Kevin is hiding Terry. Ergo..."

"I get it." Oh, Jess, how could you do something this dumb? "We have to stop her."

"What if we're too late?" Lynn wailed.

He didn't even want to consider the possibilities. "I'll do what I can." He was already shoving his arms into the sleeves of his leather jacket. "Thanks for calling, Lynn. You did the right thing." Although Jess wouldn't think so, not after he got done with her. If he caught her before Kevin did.

Jess was freezing. This stakeout was by far more uncomfortable than her last one. At least last time she'd had a car to block the wind. Now, all that protected her were the scraggly bushes Kevin had planted around his garbage-can rack in the alley.

After observing the house from all angles, Jess had decided the view from the back was best. She'd removed one of the garbage cans from the rack, replacing it with herself. The position afforded her a nice knothole in the stockade fence to peer through, and although she was scrunched up and the place smelled of bad meat, it wasn't terribly uncomfortable.

Just cold.

She consulted her watch. It was after midnight. The lights had been off for more than an hour and all was quiet. Time to move in.

She'd thought out her plan and it was a good one, though not without its risks. The worst-case scenario was that Kevin would catch her and call the cops. She would be arrested and charged with breaking and entering. Next to a murder charge, big deal.

Best-case scenario, she would get into the house and find evidence that Terry had been living there. His razor, for one thing. When Jess had packed up the stuff from his bathroom, his gold designer razor was the one personal item that had been missing. Jess figured he just couldn't stand the thought of using a disposable. When she'd found what she wanted, she would get out. And tomorrow, *she* would be the one to make an anonymous call. She would pose as Kevin's girlfriend and describe the evidence she'd seen in Kevin's house. The police would have to check out her story.

She quietly opened the zippered case she'd brought with her and extracted her burglar's tools—a crowbar and a towel. She had a tiny penlight in one jacket pocket, and an old Kodak disk camera in the other. She was able to slip the tools through a loose board. She herself, however, would have to go over the top of the six-foot wooden fence. With one final look around to be sure no one was watching, she climbed up on top of the garbage can, grasped two of the pointed slats of the fence and heaved herself over.

She landed in a great heap on the other side, jarred but unhurt. She grabbed up her tools and sprinted for the first window well she saw, which would lead into the basement.

So far so good. All was quiet. No lights came on.

She would have to break the glass. She wrapped her towel around the crowbar and, lying on her stomach to reach the low window, gave it an experimental tap, then a harder one. With her third attempt, the glass cracked with very little sound.

Piece of cake. She pushed and tapped a little more until she'd punched out a piece large enough for her arm. She reached inside, unlocked the window and opened it. It was a tight fit, but she managed to wiggle through feetfirst. Her sneakers hit the concrete floor with a thud.

A momentary panic seized her. She'd crossed the line. She was committing a crime. But she swallowed back the fear. There was no turning back now. She switched on the miniature flashlight and had a look around.

Typical basement. Dusty boxes, old exercise equipment, rakes and garden hoses, paint cans, lumber. A pile of carpet remnants caught her eye. Moving closer, she noticed a larger than average "remnant" tightly rolled and wrapped in plastic. She couldn't easily unwrap it, either—the thing was sealed with duct tape. But she noted with a surge of satisfaction that the rug had fringe. It was an Oriental, about the right size to be hers.

Elation emboldened her. She snapped a quick picture of it, put the camera away, then made her way up the stairs, cringing with every creak. She hoped Kevin was a sound sleeper.

The door at the top of the stairs opened onto a kitchen. A filthy kitchen. Two dirty plates sat on the table. Two. Good sign. But it wasn't conclusive enough evidence for her to risk the camera flash.

She moved on to the dining room. The table was piled so high with junk that she guessed no one had actually eaten off it in months. In the living room, she found clothing scattered about, including a UMKC sweatshirt. Now *that* looked familiar. Still, she was afraid to use the camera. If she was discovered, she planned to simply bolt out the front door. She was a pretty fast runner.

A hallway led to the bedrooms. Did she dare? Why not? she thought brazenly. She'd come this far. Might as well get what she came for. She tiptoed down the hallway.

The first door opened into a bathroom. Jess shined the flashlight. Only one toothbrush. No gold razor. She even checked the medicine cabinet. Nothing she could identify as peculiar to Terry. Damn.

Her own breathing reverberated in her ears. Concentrating on gasping quietly, she left the bathroom and came to another bedroom, empty. Not even any furniture.

The last door had to be Kevin's. It was closed. She

pressed her ear up against the cheap particle board. She could hear snoring. Unfamiliar snoring. Kevin's. Damn, damn.

There was no one else here with Kevin. If Terry had ever been here, he was gone now.

With that realization, the fear returned. What the hell was she doing here? She had to get out before someone caught her. She moved quickly and quietly back toward the kitchen. She had almost reached the basement door, which she'd left open, when a draft of cold air gusted up the stairs. The door slammed with the force of an explosion. The whole house shook.

"Oh, no!" She opened the door and ran headlong down the stairs, then banged her shin on something in the dark basement. Squelching her cry of pain, she hop-skipped to the broken window. It was higher up than she remembered. It took her several precious seconds to find a broken chair to climb up on so she could hoist herself up and halfway out.

"Who's out there!" an angry male voice yelled from upstairs. "I have a gun, and I shoot to kill on my property!"

Oh, great. She might not have to worry about the damn murder charge. She'd be dead.

As she wiggled her way out the window, a piece of her hair caught on the latch. Panicked, impatient, she yanked it loose, though she left some behind. At least she was free.

She didn't bother with the crowbar or the towel. Neither could be traced to her. She just ran for the fence. Adrenaline pushed her beyond her normal limits. She clambered over the fence like a pro—and landed squarely in a pair of strong male arms.

Reflexively she started to scream. A hand clamped over her mouth.

"It's me, dammit, shut up," Kyle hissed in her ear.

"Who's out there?" came Kevin's voice from the other side of the fence. "You better freeze or I'll shoot your ass."

Kyle issued a pithy curse. "Run. My car's at the other end of the alley. I'm right behind you."

She didn't have to be told twice. She took off like a shot. She heard Kyle's footsteps thumping reassuringly behind her. Then she heard an "oomph" that wasn't so reassuring. She screeched to a stop and spun around.

He'd fallen.

"Kyle?"

"Keep going," he ordered her, urgently gesturing with his hand. "I'm okay. I can talk my way out of this one, no problem."

She hesitated. "But…"

"Go!"

Operating on sheer instinct, she did what he'd told her, running hell-bent toward the opening at the end of the alley. Tears blinded her by the time she reached his car, parked at the curb. It wasn't locked. She jumped into the passenger seat, slammed the door and huddled there, sobbing and waiting.

Oh, God, what had she done? What if he was seriously hurt? What if Kevin shot him? Never mind that she hadn't asked Kyle to get involved in her escapade. He'd done it, and it was her fault if anything happened to him. She would never forgive herself.

He lay in the alley, clutching his leg. Damn knee. It chose the worst times to act up. He heard Kevin's gate creak open. Preparing for the confrontation, Kyle pulled his shield out of his pocket and held it up.

"Don't shoot. I'm police," he said, pushing himself into a sitting position.

Kevin Gilpatrick peered around the gate. He held a shotgun, the barrel pointed up. "Police? Breaking into my house?"

Kyle motioned him closer so he didn't have to shout. A neighbor's dog was already barking. "*I* wasn't breaking in. I was doing routine surveillance."

"On me?"

"On you," he confirmed. "Just routine. We're keeping an eye on everyone associated with Terry Rodin, hoping to get a break. You're not under suspicion—don't worry," he lied.

"Then who was in my house?" Kevin asked suspiciously.

"A garden-variety burglar, I'm afraid. I was watching the front of the house, and he broke in the back. But I caught him coming over the fence on his way out. I almost had him, too, but he slipped away. Then this bum knee of mine gave out." Kyle managed to stand, though the knee was screaming.

"Can we go inside?" Kyle asked. "I'll need to file a report. We'll bring some evidence guys over—"

"Oh, I don't think that's necessary," Kevin said quickly. "Nothing was taken."

"Are you sure? Maybe we better call in the crime-scene unit—"

"No. He's gone now. He won't be back. It's too much hassle to file a complaint."

"There's been a lot of burglaries in this area," Kyle improvised. "Our man might have left some clues behind that could help us catch him. You know, the tiniest bit of physical evidence—"

"I said no. I've had it with you cops and your bungling. Why are you wasting your time watching me when the real murderer is sleeping soundly in her own bed? She's the one you ought to be hassling."

"Trust me, she's being hassled. Or didn't you see the news tonight?"

Kevin's teeth glittered in the pale moonlight. "Oh, yeah, I saw it. That was nice work. But where do you guys get off claiming Jess has a clean record? Have you checked back in Massachusetts where she went to school?"

"Boston police say she's clean."

"Oh, well, no wonder. You didn't check in the right place. Look her up in Barnstable County. It'll open your eyes, lemme tell ya."

"What the hell are you talking about?"

"I don't know the details. Maybe it's just rumor. Anyway, you ought to check with the police in Barnstable County." With that, Kevin sauntered away and disappeared through the gate.

Kyle limped down the alley toward his car. Barnstable County, huh? Interesting. Maybe he'd look into it. But he'd look into Kevin Gilpatrick's background first. The man was hiding something. Fear had rolled off him in waves at the mention of an evidence team combing his house. Kyle had smelled it.

The moment he emerged from the alley in view of his car, Jess burst out the passenger door. She ran toward him and flung her arms around his neck. "You're okay. I'm so sorry, really I am. I didn't think Kevin would have a gun."

Reflexively Kyle's arms went around Jess, and for a moment he forgot all about his swelling knee and the disaster he'd just avoided. He even forgot how angry he was at Jess. All he could think about was how good she smelled, how soft her hair was, how warm her body felt against his in the numbing wind—and how relieved he was she was safe. He'd almost blown her getaway.

He stroked her hair with one hand and slid his other beneath her jacket. "Shh, it's okay," he soothed. "We're both safe. He doesn't know it was you, and I made him believe I had a legitimate reason for being there." And now he was guilty of aiding and abetting.

"You shouldn't have come," she said. "I know what I

did was crazy. I knew I could've been caught. I didn't intend to get anyone else in trouble.''

"I couldn't *not* come," he explained simply.

"How did you know where I was?" she thought to ask, a note of suspicion entering her voice. "I'm beginning to think you're psychic, the way you always show up at opportune moments."

"Not me. Lynn figured it out. C'mon, we have to get out of here." Reluctantly he released her and limped to the driver's side of the car.

She returned to the passenger seat, rubbing her upper arms. "You're hurt," she accused, the moment he was inside the car.

"It's nothing. A trick knee. Couple of days, it'll be fine. Happens all the time." He started the car. The heater blasted to life and was blowing warm air in seconds. He realized he hadn't been gone from the car longer than five or six minutes. It had just seemed a lot longer.

They took a brief break to call Lynn on the car phone and let her know that Jess was safe. Then Kyle asked, "Where's your car?"

"Parked about a mile away. I didn't want to take any chances of some neighbor spotting it and tying me to the break-in, if it came to that. I wore gloves, and I used an old crowbar and a towel that couldn't possibly be traced to me."

"You did think this out." He felt a sudden, odd respect for her, for her cunning, even if she had been breaking the law. Funny, until he'd met Jess, he'd considered himself a real straight arrow. Now she had him lying to his associates and his superiors, protecting murder suspects, sneaking around in dark alleys.

And he was enjoying it.

"I didn't think you could be that devious," he said. "Is there some criminal bent you've been hiding from me?"

He'd meant the question as a tease, but when she greeted

it with silence, he thought once again of Barnstable County. Was it possible Gilpatrick was right? That she had some kind of record? Counties and municipalities often didn't share their files. It was entirely possible that the Boston police would be ignorant of what went on across the county line.

"I thought of everything," Jess said, now perfectly composed. "And then I blew it. I left a big hunk of my hair behind, caught on the window latch. I might as well have dropped a business card."

She was right. With DNA testing, hair could be positively linked with the person it belonged to. "You probably don't have to worry about that. Even if Kevin figures out it was you, he's not anxious to bring the police in. He went white when I mentioned the words 'crime-scene unit.'"

"Really?"

"He's hiding something. What did you find in there, anyway?"

"My rug. At least, it looked like my rug in the dark. I took a picture of it…" She reached into her jacket pocket. It was empty. "Damnation! I must've dropped my camera when I went back over the fence," she said, dejected.

"You really think it was your rug?"

She hesitated. "Yes. It looked like it had been purposely hidden, too. Oh, turn right here. I think. Anyway, if Terry was there earlier, he's gone now. I was so positive…."

She sounded so forlorn that Kyle would have said anything, done anything, to make her feel better. "Hey, take it from one who knows. Hunches don't always pay off. But I follow them, anyway. When you're right, it can make all the difference in a case—sometimes between life or death."

"I hope you're right, because I still have that feeling about Kevin. He's hiding Terry somewhere. Maybe he has another house somewhere that Terry's using. Yeah, that's it! I seem to remember the two of them going fishing around here, staying in some cabin.''

"Do you remember which lake?''

"No. Oh, turn left here. I think. This is looking familiar.''

"Do you know where your car is or not?''

"Well, I thought I did. Try this street. Hmm, it's darker than I remember.''

There were a couple dozen cars parked on the street. Kyle drove slowly, peering at every one. None appeared to be Jess's anonymous sedan.

"Another block over, then.''

With a shrug, he followed her directions. For the next fifteen minutes. She was starting to act panicky. "What if I can't find it? I can't get home without a car. I can't have you bring me home at this hour. What if someone's watching the house?''

"The police aren't, I'm pretty sure.''

"But the press? I'm almost more afraid of them than the police.''

She had a point. It was a small risk, but something to think about nonetheless. "We could find the car more easily in the daylight.''

"Maybe if I approached the neighborhood from the same direction I did earlier—''

"And in daylight,'' he added. He was too tired and too sore to keep roaming the streets in this haphazard fashion. "My house is closer than yours. We can grab a few hours' sleep and come back here at dawn.''

He didn't wait for her assent but turned onto the first main street he came to, got his bearings and headed home. He tried not to think about the fact that he wasn't planning to tell Easley or Clewis about the break-in. He tried not to think about the fact that he'd just invited a murder suspect to spend what was left of the night in his house. He especially tried not to think of the woman in black sitting in the seat next to him, or what he wanted to do with her when he got her home.

Chapter 10

Sometime during the past few days, Jess had lost control of her life. She'd suspected it before, but as she allowed Kyle Branson to lead her into his house through the garage door, she knew for sure. She'd never made a conscious decision to spend the night with him, yet she hadn't offered a single word of protest when he'd suggested they sleep here.

Nor did she want to now.

Kyle was both persecutor and savior, accuser and defender, dark and light. She was drawn to him even as she feared him. He stood for avenging justice, cruel and blind, yet he was also her hope, her ally, even her friend.

Perhaps soon to be her lover.

The idea had been planted in her head long ago, maybe even that first afternoon when he'd come to her house. But the seed was only now germinating into something vigorous and green, with thirsty roots and leaves reaching for the warmth of the sun.

Whether the same species of fantasy had taken root in

Kyle's mind was unknown to her. He'd certainly kissed her as if he'd meant it. But he was a guy, after all, and her experience had shown her that the whole male gender was a little weak when it came to resisting sex. Most men would take it if offered, even if they hadn't been considering the possibility before.

So by placidly agreeing to sleep in his house, was she offering? Did he read it that way? And would he play true to his sex and take advantage of the offer?

Even as these thoughts chased their own tails around in her mind, she recognized that she wasn't thinking any too clearly. The lack of sleep over the past few days, combined with the rush of adrenaline and the sudden letdown, had left her totally spent.

Her dementia was confirmed a few minutes later, when, after sitting her in a chair and making her a cup of hot chocolate to stop her from shivering, Kyle began folding out the futon in the living room. He spread a sheet over it, then a blanket, then disappeared for a minute or so and returned with two pillows bearing mismatched cases.

"It's pretty comfortable," he said, breaking the silence. "But if you'd rather have my bed, I can sleep out here."

I'd rather have your bed with you in it. The thought was so vivid that she believed for a moment she'd spoken it aloud. When he continued to gaze at her, awaiting her decision, she knew she hadn't. "Um, the futon will be fine."

The fatigue had scrambled her brains and her hormones, not to mention her perceptions.

"Oh, the bathroom," he said, as if he thought that was the explanation she was waiting for. "We'll have to share, I'm afraid. The second bath is undergoing some do-it-yourself renovations—the slow kind. The master bath is this way."

She followed him like a zombie down a dark hallway and into his bedroom. It was a typical guy room, with the bed a little rumpled, looking as if it was made in haste, and some shirts hanging over the corner of the closet door.

Yet it was inviting, somehow. Warm. Imbued with his subtle scent, his imprint.

"Jess?"

"Oh. Sorry. I was zoning out."

He smiled. "No kidding. You must be wiped out. I don't have an extra toothbrush...."

"I'll survive."

She went into the bathroom, which was clean but comfortably cluttered with male stuff—including a disposable razor, she noted with a smile. Not a designer fragrance in sight, just Crest toothpaste, VO5 shampoo, and Old Spice aftershave. Maybe he'd thrown out that stuff that smelled like Terry. She hoped so. She splashed her face, swished some Scope around in her mouth, used some dental floss and called it good.

She was thinking about the comfy-looking futon as she exited the bathroom, not paying attention, and she all but stumbled into Kyle's arms when she left the bathroom— the third time that day she'd found herself in that pleasant circumstance.

Rather than fight it, she gave in. She didn't have the energy to do otherwise. His arms went around her, keeping her from flowing right to the floor.

"Hey, you okay?"

"I don't know anymore." But she needed this. She knew that. Did she dare tell him?

He swung her up in his arms and carried her the few feet to his bed, laying her down so gently that she hardly felt the contact of the mattress. She lay still as he pulled off her black Reeboks with almost clinical detachment. Oh, hell, she thought in a flash of clarity, this isn't about sex at all.

"I'm worried about you, Jess," he said, sitting on the

edge of the bed. "You fainted earlier, and you almost did it again just now. Are you sure you don't need a doctor?"

"I need rest. I haven't been sleeping."

"You can sleep here. I'll unplug the phone." He reached toward the nightstand and made good his word.

"Could you stay with me?"

His eyebrows flew up, and his chest noticeably rose and fell.

"I don't mean anything," she added hastily, "just that I'd feel safer with someone...with you close by." That, at least, was true.

The expression on his face was impossible to read. Was he disgusted? Had she just proved she was the opportunistic slut the papers had painted her as? Lord help her, maybe she was. But this was different, she reasoned. Extraordinary circumstances. She wasn't the type to fall into bed with any handsome guy she met. But would he know that?

Did it matter?

She was drifting off. The next time she became aware, she knew she was sleeping curled up next to Kyle's bare chest. An incredible feeling of peacefulness and safety washed over her as she listened to his slow, rhythmic breathing, inhaled his scent, felt the warmth radiating from him. She slipped back to sleep, falling into a soft cloud of dreamless comfort.

The next time she woke up she was alone in the bed, and the sun was shining with obnoxious cheerfulness through Kyle's bedroom window. How long had she slept?

She jumped out of bed in a near panic. She had to go get her car. Where were her shoes? Where was Kyle?

She jerked the bedroom door open and was immediately assailed by the scent of coffee and bacon, and the unmistakable sound of cooking noises...and whistling. Cheerful whistling.

What in the hell was there to be cheerful about? she

thought, annoyed, as she padded down the hall in bare feet. As she passed through the living room, she noticed things she'd missed last night—the group of family photos arranged haphazardly on a shelf in the living room, the mismatched furniture that somehow managed to look cozy, the huge stereo system and a floor-to-ceiling collection of CDs. She had an impulse to check out the titles, but then she remembered the urgency of her situation and resisted.

She found Kyle in the kitchen, busily tending to a skillet full of bacon and another pan with scrambled eggs. He was shirtless, barefoot, wearing only jeans, and the sight of that awesome bare chest made her suddenly remember her behavior last night.

Her face grew warm, and she couldn't seem to find any words to explain herself or apologize.

He noticed her and smiled. "Hi. Feel better?"

"What time is it?" she demanded.

Unruffled by her lack of civility, he checked his watch. "Almost ten."

"What? Oh, heavens, what about my car? I have to—"

"It's done. I tried to wake you up earlier, but you were about as responsive as a hibernating bear. So I called Lynn, and she and I went and picked up your car."

"How did you find it?"

"I knew the approximate location. In daylight it wasn't so hard to spot."

She was unutterably relieved to have that problem solved. "I feel so stupid…"

"You were exhausted." Kyle dumped the scrambled eggs onto two plates. "I hope you're hungry."

"I really should get home…"

"Not until you eat."

She *was* suddenly hungry. She hadn't been eating well, and the mountain of eggs and bacon and toast Kyle piled onto her plate was too tempting to turn down. "All right, twist my arm. I'll eat. Don't you have to be at work or something?''

"It's my day off."

"Oh." She hadn't kept track of such things. She had no idea what day it was. She sat obediently at the kitchen table, and he placed the food in front of her, then sat across from her with his own plate. Her attention was torn between the delicious-smelling food under her nose, and the delectable man slightly farther away.

"I should put on a shirt," he said, though he made no move to do so. "I always get half-naked to cook because I hate getting grease on my clothes. My mother would be horrified if she saw me sitting at the table like this."

"You're not offending me," she said, trying not to stare at that broad, muscular chest as she took her first bite of eggs. They were the best eggs she'd ever tasted. "I mean, we slept in the same bed. At least, I think we did. My memory is a little fuzzy."

She'd been trying to make light of her needy behavior from the night before. She could see what had happened much more clearly now, and she cringed at the memory of her own wantonness. Her fatigue had somehow knocked down her normal barriers of caution, her inhibitions.

Kyle wasn't smiling. Of course he wasn't, she thought, staring down at her food. He probably considered her behavior last night a major annoyance. He'd only wanted to help her out of a jam, not serve as her emotional crutch.

"Oh, we slept together, all right," he said, "for a few hours, anyway. I wouldn't forget something like that."

"I wish I'd been awake to enjoy it," she quipped.

Finally she won a smile from him. "I'm sorry you missed it, too. It wasn't half-bad."

She relaxed slightly and took another bite of toast. It was going to be all right. Maybe she could survive the humiliation of throwing herself at a man who simply wasn't all that interested, steamy kisses notwithstanding.

"I really wasn't myself last night."

He grew serious again. "I understand."

"Do you? I hope so. I feel like I've taken advantage of you. You offer help and I'm all over you like a rash."

"Taken advantage? Honey, there's something you ought to know about men. When you ask them to sleep with you, it's not taking advantage. When *they* get in bed with you when you're half-unconscious, *that's* taking advantage. You have nothing to apologize for, okay?"

"Neither do you," she said quickly. Did he think *he'd* done something wrong, for heaven's sake? She looked him in the eye so he couldn't mistake her sincerity. "It helped me sleep, to have you there, because I knew I was safe."

Kyle took a long draw of coffee. "You weren't *that* safe."

Ah. So she'd once again misread the situation. And she realized now that they were in a very dangerous gray area. She couldn't trust herself; he'd just told her she couldn't completely trust him. They ought not to be spending this much time together. If they continued, the consequences were almost inevitable.

She concentrated on her meal, shoveling down the food as fast as she dared without calling attention to the fact that she was anxious for breakfast to be over.

"So where's my car?"

"Back at your house."

"You'll have to take me home, then."

"Eventually. When you're ready to face the world again. I should warn you, the reporters and photographers were hanging out at your place early this morning."

"But I can't stay here!" she blurted out.

"Why not? It's the last place anyone would think to look."

"I'm afraid it'll get us both in trouble. What if your boss finds out? Marva's going to freak out as it is."

He toyed with a piece of bacon. "I won't get in trouble.

I'm not officially on the investigation anymore. Even if someone found out you're here—which they won't—what I do on my own time is my business.''

She wasn't sure she bought his unconcerned act. Surely cops weren't encouraged to fraternize with criminal suspects, whether they were connected with the case or not.

"Just the same," she said, "I should get home. Think you could loan me cab fare?"

"I'll take you."

She shook her head. "Someone could see you. I'm not being paranoid about this. Have you ever been harassed by the press?"

He shrugged.

"You will be, if some smart-ass reporter connects you to me in any way but a professional one. It could hurt my case, and it wouldn't do you any good, either."

He looked at her, indecision playing about his face, then set his coffee cup down with a clunk. "All right, you've convinced me. How about I drop you off at that library close to your house, and you can call a cab from there?"

It was a good plan. "I can live with that." But, she had to admit, the idea of hanging out here with Kyle was much more appealing than the thought of facing her home, with all its little reminders of the trouble she was in—the cut-up hall carpet, the missing kitchen knives, and Lynn with her law books.

"You can stay if you want," he said, reading her mind. "It's okay."

"Maybe just for a little while." It was so quiet here.

They were silent for a few minutes. Jess sipped black coffee and flipped disinterestedly through the entertainment pages of the newspaper, carefully avoiding any section that might contain news of her case. Marva, she knew, was keeping track of news coverage so Jess wouldn't have to torture herself by reading and hearing about the half-truths, speculation and innuendo.

"I'm not scheduled to work today," Kyle said, "but I do have to go to the station and catch up on some of the stuff I've been neglecting—writing up reports, returning phone calls. It'll take a few hours. You can hang out here, watch TV, relax. I'll grab some take-out on my way home, we can have lunch here, then I'll run you over to the library. How does that sound?"

Being alone here didn't sound half as nice as being with him. "Sure, that'll be fine. Say, as long as you'll be working, maybe you could do some kind of background check on Kevin Gilpatrick."

"It's been done. Except for a few minor brushes with the law—no convictions—he's clean."

"I was thinking you could check out some other things—like if he owns any property somewhere else, someplace he could stash Terry."

"Mmm," Kyle said noncommittally. He was studying the sports section.

"I'm serious. I know Kevin's involved—I could see it in his eyes that night we caught him making the phone calls. I'll bet you Terry was staying at Kevin's house until then. Then they probably thought things were heating up too much, so they moved him to a safer place."

"That's pure speculation, Jess."

"Haven't you ever followed a hunch?"

He acknowledged her point with a nod. "I'll see what I can do."

That was the best she could expect, she supposed. His lack of enthusiasm served as a gentle reminder that though Kyle was concerned and helpful, he was still a cop. He had his responsibilities, his loyalties, his own convictions about her case that fell somewhere between Clewis's and her own. He was not completely her ally.

Kyle had almost cleared his desk and was thinking about how best to check on Kevin Gilpatrick's property holdings when Bill Clewis made a rare appearance in missing persons. "Branson. Thought I might find you here, nose to the grindstone. Track down any runaway teenagers today?"

He said it as if Kyle's job was insignificant. But that didn't bother Kyle. He liked his work. He would be really happy to get back to it and leave murder cases to his more cynical colleagues.

"Yeah, I did track down a runaway. Her father beat her up, and she was hiding out in a homeless shelter. She's now safely with family services and her dad's been arrested. How about you? You catch any murderers today?"

"Nope," Clewis replied with a self-satisfied smirk. "As a matter of fact, I lost one. Your innocent little angel flew the coop." He threw this out casually.

While his heart started up a staccato rhythm inside his chest, Kyle carefully schooled his features to reflect only mild surprise. "Jess Robinson?"

"Who else? I called her this morning to get her in here for some more questions. I thought a good night's sleep might have improved her memory about that knife. But you know what? She wasn't there. Her kid sister's voice was shaking when she told me Jess was staying at a friend's house.

"Which friend's house, I ask. She says she doesn't know. I remind the sister that Jess is supposed to be available for questioning at all times. The sister says not to worry, Jess'll call in. I say, my aunt Fanny. She don't call in by noon I'm calling the judge to get her bail revoked, and then I'm putting an APB out on her."

Kyle tried his best to hide his growing alarm. If Jess went back to jail it would crush her, destroy what little resilience she'd managed to hold on to.

"It's twelve-thirty." Clewis tapped his watch. "No call. You wouldn't happen to have any ideas where to look, would you?"

Kyle took a deep breath. "I know where she is. She hasn't flown the coop."

Clewis's eyebrows flew up. "Where might that be?"

"She's staying with a friend, like her sister said. Trying to get some relief from the press. They're harassing her. Oh, speaking of harassment," Kyle said, deftly changing the subject, "I caught the crank phone caller red-handed. It was Kevin Gilpatrick. He's in this thing up to his eyeballs, and I think you should haul him in for questioning." If Jess was right—that Kevin was hiding Terry—a friendly little encounter with Clewis ought to convince him to bail out of Terry's practical joke.

"I got better things to do than chase my tail with that one," Clewis said dismissively. "So you gonna tell me where the babe is, or what?"

"I'll have her call you," Kyle said casually, as if it was no big deal. He returned his attention to his paperwork, hoping Clewis would go away.

Clewis crowed. "She's at your house!" he concluded, clapping his hands like a demented preschooler. "I shoulda known you were protecting her. So you're not making any headway with her, huh?"

Kyle didn't know how to answer that. On the one hand, their original good cop–bad cop plan was working nicely. Jess was warming up to him, confiding in him. Getting intimate, even. But the thought of telling Clewis any of that made his stomach turn. Jess was growing to trust him. It seemed heinous to violate that trust.

But wasn't that what he'd set out to do in the first place?

She hadn't told him anything the least bit incriminating, he reminded himself. Until she did, Clewis didn't have any right to know the details.

"When I caught her crank caller, she was grateful," Kyle said. "She warmed up to me a little."

"A little? She spent the night at your house! Wait'll I tell Easley—"

"You've got it all wrong, Clewis. She went to a friend's house last night." That was the story they'd agreed on.

"You trying to tell me nothing happened? You got a babe like that warming up to you, and *nothing happens?* Branson, you're a pathetic excuse for a man. I'd have had her ten times over."

Kyle straightened the papers on his desk while he got control of his temper. When he spoke, his voice was low and deadly. "Nothing happened," he said, enunciating each word. "That's the difference between you and me, Clewis. I have self-control. I have ethics. And I don't sleep with a woman just because she's there."

"I do," said Blayney Cook, Kyle's partner, who'd entered the room just in time to hear the last sentence of the exchange.

Kyle shot him a withering look that sent the younger man skulking to his desk to sharpen pencils. He wasn't in the mood for Blayney's peculiar sense of humor just now.

Clewis stared at him, sizing him up like a prize-fighter about to enter the ring. Kyle had the fleeting impression that Clewis would throw a punch if there weren't a dozen witnesses around in the bull pen. Then suddenly he relaxed, and a wholly unpleasant smile spread across his face.

"Okay, we'll play it your way," he said. "Nothing happened." Clewis turned and strolled from the room. Had he swallowed Kyle's story about Jess staying at a "friend's" house?

"What the hell was that all about?" Blayney asked in a less than confidential whisper. The room went quiet, as if E. F. Hutton was about to talk.

"Just Clewis being an ass, as usual," Kyle said, trying to dismiss the conversation from his mind. But the fact that Clewis had backed down so suddenly bothered him.

Blayney scooted his chair over closer to Kyle's desk. "Hey, there's something you ought to know," he said in a low voice. "There's a rumor making its way along the department grapevine. Pure speculation, mind you—"

"Then why do I need to hear it?" Kyle snapped. He was being more short-tempered than usual with his affable partner, but Clewis had crushed what little goodwill he'd started with that morning.

"Because it directly concerns you, and it could mean your career, buddy."

That caught Kyle's attention. "Okay, you got me. What's the rumor?"

"Well, I guess everybody knows you're sort of on loan to homicide in the Jess Robinson investigation. Officially the reason is for continuity—you initiated the original missing-persons investigation, you've spent time with the babe—"

"Her name's Jess," Kyle said between clenched teeth.

"Oh, yeah, I forgot," Blayney murmured. "Anyway, it all sounds kosher on the surface. You have an in with her, so your assignment is to cozy up to her and see what you can pick up that would help the investigation. Only so far—"

"I've come up with zilch," Kyle said, resigned. "What can I say? She hasn't spontaneously confessed where she put the body. I can't report evidence I haven't found."

"Yeah, but you're doing just the opposite of what Easley originally wanted. Everything you pick up is pointing to her innocence."

"Did it ever occur to any of these yo-yos that she might *be* innocent?"

Blayney looked at him speculatively. "You really believe that."

"I do. Don't look at me like that. I'm not some naive bumpkin taken in by a pretty face. She didn't kill Terry Rodin. Someone framed her. I'm not making things up.

I'm reporting evidence as I come across it. I can't help it if it all points to Jess's innocence." He winced inwardly as he thought of some of the things he *hadn't* reported. Like the fact that she'd broken into Kevin's house. And the tip Kevin had given him—to check with the police in Barnstable County, Massachusetts. He hadn't decided what to do with that just yet.

"Regardless, you're still not doing what Easley wanted you to do. Which brings us to the speculation part. Some people think you're being set up for a fall."

"How so?" Kyle shot back, full of skepticism. The Kansas City Police Department had its share of problems, but it protected its own.

"They want you to sleep with her. When the press finds out, it'll be all over the front page. It'll destroy her credibility when everybody learns she was sleeping with a cop. You'll be out of a job because Easley will deny any knowledge of your actions."

"He sanctioned this whole thing," Kyle said. "He practically told me in so many words to sleep with her. Not that I'm planning to—"

"But she's at your house now?"

"Yeah," Kyle admitted.

"Hell, man, Clewis is probably calling the papers right now. You saw how he used the press when he found the murder weapon. If I were you, I would get that woman out of my house and keep her out."

Kyle finally got it, and he mentally kicked himself in the butt for being so dense. Easley and Clewis wouldn't hesitate to sacrifice him for the sake of adding fuel to the fire that was going to burn Jess at the stake. A conviction would make them both look good. Finding Terry Rodin alive would make the whole department a laughingstock. Under no circumstances could they risk the latter possibility actually coming to pass.

Kyle snatched up the phone, talking as he dialed. "Thanks, Blayney. Sorry I yelled at you. I owe you one."

"S'okay, man. You'd do the same for me."

Kyle heard his own voice on the answering machine tape, then the beep. "Jess, are you there?" he said. "It's me, Kyle. I need you to pick up. This is an emergency."

She didn't pick up the phone.

Kyle issued a pithy curse and hung up. Without a word of explanation to anyone, he left the office, hoping against hope that he wasn't too late. If his indiscreet behavior cost Jess her freedom, he would never forgive himself.

And if, by some miracle, he made it home before the reporters got there, he still had to find some way to get her out of his house and then let her go. Forever this time. He could be of no more help to her.

Chapter 11

Jess cowered in the bathroom with the lights off. They were outside—reporters, photographers, even a TV news van. The one who'd arrived first had brazenly rung the doorbell. And when she hadn't answered, he'd started peeking through windows, no doubt trying to get a glimpse of her so he could report, with complete authority, that she was intimate with an investigator working on her case.

She'd retreated in time to avoid detection, she hoped. Now all she could do was wait until Kyle—the rat—returned and got her out of this mess. He'd sworn no one would know she was here, and she believed him. Then where had these carrion eaters come from?

She was afraid to discover the answer to that question. If no one had followed them here, the press could have found out her whereabouts from only two sources—Lynn, or Kyle. A clever reporter might have weaseled the information out of Lynn, somehow—posing as a cop or something, intimidating her. That was a reasonable theory.

She tried not to consider the other alternative. She

wouldn't jump to conclusions, she told herself. She would wait for an explanation.

She didn't have to wait long. She heard the garage door opening, Kyle's car roaring inside, then the door closing again. Soon she heard Kyle's voice calling softly.

"Jess? Are you here?"

She waited until she heard him enter the bedroom. Then she opened the bathroom door a crack. "I'm here."

He swiveled around, looking surprised, then concerned. "Jess? You okay?"

"Depends. Is the coast clear?"

"If you mean are the reporters still outside, then no, the coast isn't clear. But they're not in the bedroom."

"They were looking in windows earlier," Jess explained, emerging from her hiding place like a rabbit from its hole. She felt foolish. "What are they doing here? How did they know?"

"It's my fault, I'm afraid."

Her heart sank. But as she listened to Kyle's explanation of how Clewis had cornered him and jumped to an unfortunately correct conclusion, Jess almost felt sorry for him.

"Not much fun being in the hot seat with that jerk trying to worm information out of you," she said with a wry smile. "I can vouch for that."

Although they were still in a jam, she felt relieved that Kyle had provided a reasonable explanation for how the reporters had found her. Now she was ashamed to admit that she'd been afraid her on-again, off-again white knight had betrayed her.

"Did you talk to them?" she asked, keeping her voice almost to a whisper for fear the rat finks outside might pick her up with some supersensitive microphone.

"Yeah. I rolled down my window and asked what the hell they were doing camped out on my front lawn. They asked me if you were here, and I just acted bewildered."

"Are you a good actor?" she asked.

"I don't have any idea." He walked over to the window and peeked out the curtain. "They're not going anywhere."

"What do we do now?"

"We wait, I guess. I brought home a pizza."

Jess was still stuffed from breakfast. "I can't stay here. I need to be at home."

"I agree. It's probably best if we part company before we do any real damage to each other."

She felt vaguely disappointed that he'd agreed with her so readily, although she knew that was stupid. Had she expected him to declare his undying loyalty to her, that he intended to protect and shelter her even at the expense of his job? What hogwash.

"We could smuggle you out," Kyle suggested.

"How?" She was picturing herself in a disguise. A hat and Groucho Marx glasses wouldn't fool that bunch outside, but at least the photographs wouldn't be easily recognizable.

"In my car," Kyle answered. "In the trunk."

"No, no, no, no, no," was Jess's immediate response. "I'm claustrophobic."

"It would only be for a little while," Kyle reasoned. "Just long enough that I could drive away and make sure no one was following. Then I'd let you out, and I'll drop you off at the library like we'd originally planned."

His plan made sense, she conceded. Still, the mere thought of being closed up in a dark automobile trunk, unable to release herself, made her palms clammy and her stomach clench. It made her think of coffins, and being buried alive. She shook her head. "I just don't think—"

"Then we'll have to wait them out," he said easily, as if it didn't make much difference to him which choice she made. Sure, of course he didn't care. He wasn't a virtual prisoner. He could come and go as he pleased. And *he* didn't have to contemplate being folded up into a car trunk like someone's dirty laundry...

Oh, stop it, she chastised herself. She was being melodramatic and self-pitying again. Kyle's plan for smuggling her out of this mess made perfect sense. "Could I have a flashlight in the trunk with me?"

He smiled. "Of course. You'll be in there five minutes, no more. Promise."

She found herself smiling back. She trusted him. Then she felt something else, that insidious, uncontrollable longing for his closeness that took over her body during unguarded moments. His gaze caught and held hers, and she felt for a moment that his thoughts had to be echoing hers, that he would take a step forward and reach for her, hold her in the comfort of his arms...and more.

Then, without warning, he turned away from her and headed out of the bedroom.

She had to fight the irrational urge to burst into tears of pure frustration. What was it about this man? Was it just that circumstances had forced them into a peculiar intimacy, or did she really feel something for him?

"Pizza's in here," he said, leading the way to the kitchen. "I don't know about you, but I'm starved."

Yeah—starved for him. She felt something for him, all right, pure and hot and undeniable. She also knew she'd set herself up for disappointment with Kyle. Whether he felt the same way about her was a moot point by now. He was off-limits. After today, they wouldn't see each other. He'd said so. She agreed it was for the best.

That thought didn't help the lump that had formed in her throat, making normal breathing nearly impossible.

She could only pick at the pizza. Kyle kept glancing up at her from across the kitchen table, appearing concerned, and he finally asked her, "You okay? You sound funny."

"Just nerves," she said. "About the trunk."

"I won't let anything happen to you. I promise."

"I know. I trust you, Kyle. I'm lucky you don't just turn me over to the wolves. My being here would look worse for me than for you."

"I would never do that. Having you sleep here was my idea, after all."

"And I'm the idiot who mislaid her car."

"I think there's plenty of blame for us both to feel guilty and stupid," he said with a grin. He grasped her hand. "Let's just move forward, okay?"

She nodded, determinedly swallowing the lump in her throat. If only she *could* move forward, and forget that the past nine days had ever happened. If only she'd met Kyle under different circumstances.

Quickly she released his hand and stood before he could see the moisture gathering in her eyes. "Let's get this show on the road."

Kyle nodded solemnly. He then led her out to the garage, where the red Mustang awaited them. He found a flashlight in a cupboard, tested it, handed it to her. "I just put new batteries in last month. Should be good to go."

Jess tested the device, assuring herself it worked.

The trunk was minuscule, much smaller than she'd imagined, and for a moment her courage waned.

Probably sensing her fear, Kyle put a reassuring arm around her. "It'll be okay."

"I won't suffocate?"

"There's air enough in there to last for hours. Think of it as a cozy little cocoon."

She gave him a dubious look. "If you say so." She started to climb in, but abruptly he pulled her to him. She was so surprised to find herself pressed against his chest, her head nestled under his chin, that for several moments all she could do was gasp for air.

"Jess, I'm sorry for all this. I never dreamed it would end up like this. I was only trying to help."

"I know that," she murmured, enduring the exquisite

torture of his nearness with saintly restraint. She freed the arm that was pinned between them and slipped it around his waist. Very saintly, almost like a sister.

He wasn't satisfied with that. He placed a hand along her jaw and tilted her face up to his. "If I don't do this now, I won't get another chance." He captured her unprotesting lips in his and kissed her deeply, as if it was a matter of life and death.

She responded eagerly. Her body tingled as she pressed closer to him, aching for more than this single, soul-shattering kiss. She prolonged the embrace for as long as she could, until both of them needed to breathe. Then they parted mouths jerkily, gasping for air. He pressed her cheek against his neck, and she could actually hear his pulse pounding, matching hers in its rhythm.

"Life's not really fair," she said in a faint voice. "But I guess I already knew that."

"It has its moments." Then, as if the past couple of minutes hadn't happened, he added, "C'mon, in you go."

Like a diver about to go under, Jess took a deep breath and climbed into the trunk. There was a folded blanket to pillow her head, and if she arranged her legs around the spare tire just right, it was almost comfortable.

"Okay?" he asked.

"Okay." He gave her the thumbs-up sign. She flipped on the flashlight, and he slammed the lid.

This isn't so bad, she told herself. She could breathe fine, and there was plenty of light. She looked at her watch. Five minutes to two. At two o'clock Kyle would let her out. She would count the seconds.

The Mustang's engine rumbled to life. The garage door opened, and the car reversed down the driveway. There it stopped. She could hear muffled voices but couldn't understand the words.

After a few moments, the car was in motion again. It accelerated, and although she couldn't see out, Jess knew they were going fast. Kyle turned a corner, and she slid across the carpeted trunk, burning her elbow. There was nothing to hang on to! Now they were traveling over some kind of rough terrain, and she bounced around like a marble in a shaking jar. Was that a curb he just hit? She bounced and banged her head on the trunk lid.

What the hell did he think he was doing?

The car came to an abrupt stop. A door opened. Jess waited. Her breathing sounded as if she was in a wind tunnel. The trunk lid popped open, and Kyle stood grinning in at her. They were in a deserted alley overgrown with hackberry trees and forsythia bushes.

"Three and a half minutes," he said triumphantly. "See, I didn't keep you in there for long."

"Yeah? Well, you didn't tell me you were going to drive through a field of boulders at seventy miles an hour, either."

Immediately his smile faded. "Are you all right? You're not hurt, are you?"

She ignored his proffered hand and climbed awkwardly out of the trunk by herself. "I hit my head," she huffed, though now that she could see the light of day and breathe fresh air, the experience was starting to seem funny. "And I have a carpet burn on my arm." She showed him the faint pink spot on her elbow.

"Here, I can make it better." He grasped her arm and, before she could guess his intentions, had pressed his lips to the injury. The contact stung slightly, but that was nothing compared to the zing that went through the rest of her body.

"And where did you bump your head?"

He had better not kiss her there, not here in broad daylight, not when his slightest touch made her melt into his arms. "It's fine," she said sharply, ducking away from him. She slammed the trunk. "Are we in the clear?"

"Yeah, I lost the guy who was following us a couple of miles ago. We're safe now."

"Then we'd better get to the library." She skittered around to the passenger door and let herself inside the car.

Moments later Kyle slid behind the wheel. "Sorry," he mumbled as he kicked the car into gear. "I can't seem to stop kissing you."

"I feel the same way," she said, then added with an air of practicality, "must be all the adrenaline. I like to blame everything on adrenaline, sleep depravation and poor eating habits."

"Don't forget hormones. They're to blame somehow."

"Definitely. The only thing missing in this combination is common sense."

"Amen to that. I think we see things the same way."

Kyle knew that if he returned home, he risked losing his temper and decking one of those reporters. So instead he went back to the office. There was something he'd been meaning to check out, and he needed to consult his notes on Jess and get the name and number of his contact from Boston to do it.

Better that he make the call now, before Kevin Gilpatrick put that bug about Barnstable County in someone else's ear. Kyle figured he would discover Jess had had a minor brush with the law—traffic tickets, marijuana, underage drinking. Then he could report it to Clewis and Easley. They would see that he was being thorough. He might have the hots for Jess Robinson, but that didn't mean he'd suddenly turned into a lousy cop.

It was a damn shame he wouldn't see her again. But she'd been right that they lacked common sense—he especially. They were living in a fishbowl now. One wrong move and the consequences could affect them for the rest of their lives.

The memory of her kisses, her touch, her smell, would

haunt him, he knew, especially knowing that they *could* have made love and hadn't. Last night she'd been willing, and he'd been tempted. But she'd also been half out of her mind with exhaustion. So he'd settled for sleeping with his body curved around hers, his arousal nestled against her bottom. Even the way she'd breathed had turned him on.

He still didn't know how he'd managed to get any sleep at all under those circumstances.

He stopped by the break room to get coffee before tackling his tasks. He'd just filled his mug when Clewis's grating voice reached him, along with the slap of crepe-soled shoes on linoleum heading closer.

Kyle gripped his mug tightly enough that he was sure it would break. In focusing on Jess, he'd forgotten for a few minutes that their misadventures this morning were Clewis's fault. Now Kyle had to apply all of his willpower not to turn around and punch his fellow detective right in his paunchy stomach.

He waited, biding his time, until Clewis was close behind him, apparently waiting for access to the coffee machine. Kyle abruptly turned, ran smack into Clewis and dumped most of his hot coffee down the front of the other man's shirt.

Clewis screeched and jumped back, plucking at his soaked shirtfront. "You clumsy idiot!" Then he looked up and saw who'd assaulted him. A look of consternation froze on his face.

Kyle smiled blandly and shrugged. "Sorry. Didn't know you were there."

"You son of a bitch! You did that on purpose."

Kyle remained unruffled by the perfectly justified accusation. He grabbed a wad of paper napkins from the counter and handed them to Clewis. "Now, Bill, why would you think that? Is there some reason you believe I should be angry with you?"

Clewis snatched the napkins away from Kyle and began

sopping up the brown mess that had stained his white shirt. It struck Kyle as odd that Clewis was so dressed up.

"Nice suit, Bill. I don't recall that you were wearing it earlier. Did you have plans for something…important? A meeting with the press, perhaps?"

"Does a guy have to have a reason to wear a suit?"

"On an ordinary day around here, he does."

"What are you doing back here, anyway? I heard you flew out of here a couple of hours ago like a bat out of hell." Clewis tossed the sodden napkins toward the garbage can, missed and didn't bother to pick up the misdirected trash.

"It was…too quiet at home," Kyle answered. "Lonely. No one around."

Clewis stared at him, too dense to catch Kyle's sarcasm.

"What's the matter, Bill? Are you puzzled by the fact that I'm not, even now, trying to explain to the press why I'm sheltering a murder suspect at my house? Well, I did speak to one or two reporters. Seems they got a bad anonymous tip, some completely off-the-wall jerk who claimed I was sleeping with Jess Robinson. I can't imagine who would tell them such a thing."

Kyle actually enjoyed the play of emotions on Clewis's face. The other man's train of thought was as clear as if he'd written it down on paper. He was thinking "How did I get this wrong?" and he was wanting to confront Kyle, accuse him of dropping misleading information on purpose. But to do so would have been admitting he was the one who'd called the newspaper and TV stations.

"Well, I've got things to do," Kyle said. "Sorry again about the coffee."

Without warning, Clewis delivered a sucker punch to Kyle's gut. Kyle bent over, clutching his middle, surprised as hell.

"Don't mess with me, Branson," he said. "Just a friendly little warning."

Kyle, once again alone in the coffee room, eased himself into a chair and sat there, unmoving, until he could breathe again. He couldn't believe Clewis had just assaulted him. The idiot could get fired for such conduct. Then again, he had to know Kyle wouldn't go running to his superiors about this. Even if he did, Clewis would deny it. There were no witnesses. It would be Clewis's word against Kyle's.

There was nothing Kyle could do, he decided, except look forward to the day when Clewis fried his own butt by doing something else stupid—and getting caught. It was only a matter of time. Meanwhile, Kyle would think twice about baiting the man. He was dangerous.

Back at his desk, he dug out the phone number for Detective Joe Schank of the Boston Police Department, who had checked up on Jess for him earlier. He was in luck; Joe was at his desk.

"What can I do for you?" he asked amiably.

"When you were checking for an arrest record for Jess Robinson, did you include any surrounding areas, or just Boston proper?"

"Lessee, I checked with Suffolk, Norfolk, Plymouth, Bristol, Middlesex, Essex—"

"What about Barnstable County?"

"Uh, no, actually. That's Martha's Vineyard and Nantucket and Cape Cod. Not the usual hangout for a college student. She was a college student at the time, right?"

"Yeah. But I have reason to believe she might have been living in Barnstable County at one time. Could you check it out?"

"Sure, I know a guy over there. Probably have to wait a couple of days, though."

"That's okay. I'm not really expecting anything earth-shattering. Just want to be thorough."

"Sure thing. I've got your number right here. And if you're not around, I should speak to Bill Clewis, right?"

"No," Kyle answered hastily. "For reasons I'd rather not get into, I'd prefer it if you'd relay what you find to me and only me."

"Whatever."

Kyle concluded the conversation, secure in the knowledge that he was not ignoring leads that were potentially damaging to Jess's case. If Schank actually did turn up anything incriminating, *then* Kyle would have to wrestle with his conscience. The chances of that eventuality, he figured, were pretty remote.

Kyle spent the next couple of hours over at the records office, going over birth records and tax rolls. He established fairly quickly that Terry Rodin wasn't documented in Kansas City. There was no birth certificate, tax records, or driver's license. That wasn't a big surprise, though. It was common knowledge that Rodin wasn't from around here originally, although no one could say exactly where he'd come from.

Kevin Gilpatrick was another story. He was a local boy, born at Trinity Lutheran Hospital. His parents lived in Blue Springs, a fairly well-to-do suburb, where they'd lived for at least twenty years. Kyle made a note of the address. Not that he expected the elder Gilpatricks to be hiding Terry— this was the prank of a couple of overgrown college boys, not a wealthy middle-aged couple. Still, it wouldn't hurt to check.

Some more industrious digging yielded something a little more promising. The Gilpatricks owned a house on Lake Weatherby, a small, affluent municipality on a picturesque lake north of the city. The area was quiet, secluded—just the place for a fugitive to hide. Mr. and Mrs. Gilpatrick probably wouldn't be visiting their lake house this time of year. Terry could stay there in relative comfort while his practical joke spread its damaging tentacles.

Kyle went to Clewis first, even though he knew what the answer would be. He made sure there were witnesses around when he asked, as pleasantly as if the incident in the break room had never taken place, "Bill, I want to get a search warrant for a lake house at Weatherby. I have reason to believe Terry Rodin might be hiding out there."

Clewis looked at him as if he was crazy—and maybe he was. "Go play in traffic, huh, Branson? As I recall, you aren't the primary investigator on this case. You were called in to help with a couple of specific details, and you're done with those now. I don't want or need your help."

Kyle shrugged, acknowledging a look of silent sympathy from another homicide detective at the desk next to Clewis's. "Okay, fine." He'd expected as much, but he didn't want anyone claiming he hadn't at least tried the appropriate channels first. "Did you get hold of Jess Robinson yet?"

"Yeah, as if it's any of your business. She got the message from her sister a few minutes ago and she's on her way here."

"Where did she say she'd been?" Kyle asked, as if only mildly curious.

"A friend's house. Some babe from her hometown. I already checked it out. The babe verified the story."

Good work, Jess, Kyle thought. He'd wondered if she'd be quick enough to manufacture an alibi for the past few hours. Apparently she could lie when she had to. That didn't make him all that happy, but her deceit was no worse than his, he supposed. They'd both lied to get themselves out of hot water, and they'd succeeded.

Kyle walked away from Clewis without further comment.

His next target was Jon Easley. The lieutenant wasn't on duty today, so Kyle called him at home.

Easley sighed deeply. "What is it, Branson?"

He repeated his request and the reasoning behind it.

Easley sighed again. "You know, Branson, you're getting to be a real pain in the butt."

"I realize that, sir. Sometimes being a real pain in the butt is the only way to get things done. This is something I believe in. Call it a gut feeling, instinct—"

"Lust?" Easley put in.

Kyle answered carefully. "Sure I feel lust. Who wouldn't? But I'm not crazy enough to put my professional reputation on the line because of a few hormones." Or was he? "I know my reputation *is* on the line. If Rodin's body turns up with her fingerprints all over it, I can forget getting any kind of promotion for the next twenty years." A sobering thought.

"You got that right," Easley said. "Look, I don't like you going over Clewis's head. He's the primary investigator—"

"He's an idiot, he hates my guts and he's worried sick that Terry Rodin will turn up alive and make him look like a fool. He wouldn't cut me slack about this, even if I had the mayor himself by my side, claiming to have seen Rodin alive. You know that, Jon."

Easley paused, as if digesting what Kyle had said. Kyle waited. Easley was a fair man. He would see the truth in Kyle's words, and if he okayed getting a search warrant, he wouldn't later deny it to avoid looking bad.

Finally he replied, though cautiously. "Okay. If you can get a judge to issue a search warrant based on your gut, go right ahead, with my blessings. But I don't think you stand a chance."

Maybe Easley was right, Kyle thought as he hung up. But that didn't stop him from trying. He went to the courthouse and sought out Wendy Paxton, a young judge who'd proved sympathetic to him on several occasions in the past.

She laughed in his face. "You don't have even the thinnest of evidence to support probable cause, Detective."

"It's a gut feeling," he said. "You know I'm often right

about these things." And he was. Paxton had given him warrants against her better judgment more than once, and they'd paid off. But not even his respectable track record would sway the judge this time.

"Sorry, Kyle, but the press is hot on this case and I can't afford to look like a jenny-ass. Your request is denied."

Kyle walked away from the courthouse, dejected. What other recourse did he have now? He felt helpless, ineffectual. Jess would go to trial with a mess of evidence against her—including a bloody knife with her prints all over it. Unless Kyle could uncover something useful in the next few weeks, she was toast. Clewis wouldn't lift a finger to follow any leads that didn't point directly to Jess's guilt.

During the walk back to the station, he made a decision. He had some vacation coming. He would take it and use the time to stake out that lake house on his own. Maybe it was a long shot, but it was all he had to go on for now.

When he got back to the station he headed straight for the interview rooms. Jess was already there, he discovered, and Clewis was hammering away at her. Kyle entered the observation room. An assistant district attorney was there, one Kyle knew only slightly. He was watching intently, and he hardly spared a greeting for the newcomer.

Jess was holding her own, Kyle thought as he took a chair. This was becoming old hat to her by now. She was composed, calm. She wasn't letting Clewis get to her. Marva sat next to her, looking sullen. Who could blame her? Helluva way to spend a Saturday afternoon.

After a few minutes the A.D.A. glanced over, then did a double take. "Oh, it's you. Did you really go to bed with her?" He nodded toward the two-way mirror.

"That's Clewis's wishful thinking," Kyle said, barely holding on to his temper. "I do not have carnal knowledge of Jess Robinson. And if Clewis persists in spreading rumors about me, he'll be talking to my lawyer."

The other man coughed, trying to hide laughter, Kyle guessed.

On that note, Kyle stood and left the room. Jess was doing fine. He wasn't worried about her. She could stand up to a bag of hot air like Clewis anytime. When it came to the trial, he hoped Marva would let her testify on her own behalf. A jury would have a tough time convicting her once they got to know her, no matter what the evidence said.

He had to believe that. Otherwise, he would be tempted to kidnap her and take her someplace far, far away—where she would be safe. With him.

Chapter 12

The interview didn't last long. Clewis gave up in frustration long before Jess tired out. Her answers to his questions were boringly consistent and not the least bit helpful to his case. He slapped his notebook closed and stood up. "That'll be all for now, Ms. Robinson." He continued to stare at her, as if trying to figure out a great puzzle. "You know, if you were to be even a little cooperative, the D.A. might go easy on you."

"Even if I believed that, I don't know how I could be any more cooperative," Jess said earnestly. "I can't give you information I don't have, and I can't confess to a crime I didn't commit."

Clewis's face went red. He turned abruptly. The female officer at the door opened it, and Clewis stormed out.

Marva and Jess followed. Marva patted Jess reassuringly on the shoulder. "You're doing fine. I don't know who that man thinks he is, speaking for the D.A.'s office."

Clewis didn't bother to escort them out of the police station. It didn't matter. They knew the way out by now.

They walked through the sparsely populated squad room toward the exit. As Jess opened the door, another arm pushed from the other side. Suddenly she found herself face-to-face with Kyle.

For a split second she panicked, especially when she saw his eyes and the intimacy they promised. He quickly schooled his face into a pleasant smile. Amazingly, she was able to do the same. "Oh, hello, Detective Branson." They shook hands like two strangers on the street. "I think you've met my attorney."

"Yes. Nice to see you again, Ms. Babcock."

"Charmed," Marva said, never cracking a smile as she gave his hand a perfunctory shake.

"I want to thank you again for helping me catch that crank phone caller," Jess said. She noted that others in the room, including Clewis, were listening intently.

Kyle shrugged. "Just part of the job. I trust he hasn't called back?"

"Not that I know of," Jess replied. "I was away from home last night, but my sister said the phone didn't ring all night long."

"Good."

"I won't keep you," Jess said, struggling to maintain a pleasant but neutral expression. She wanted to touch him! This was torture, pretending they'd shared nothing but a few polite words. "I'm sure you have work to do. Good-bye."

She barely heard his answering "Bye now." She was already out the door.

"Now that," Marva said as soon as they were in the elevator, "was a masterful bit of theater. No one but the most trained observer—which I am—would have noticed the way Detective Branson's nostrils flared when he looked at you. Now, are you going to tell me what really happened last night?"

Jess had thought she could get by without Marva's knowing of her wild escapades.

"We made a deal, remember?" Marva reminded her gently. "You tell me the truth up front, all of it, if you want me to take your case."

"When we're in the car," Jess said, properly chastised. She should have known she couldn't hide anything from the observant attorney.

Once they were safely ensconced in Marva's white Cadillac, away from prying eyes and ears, Jess spilled it. She confessed about breaking into Kevin's house, finding the rug that might or might not be hers, her narrow escape from a fannyful of buckshot, losing her car, crashing at Kyle's house and escaping in the trunk of Kyle's car. The only thing she omitted was that she and Kyle had— briefly—shared his bed. She figured no one, not even Marva, would believe that nothing had happened between them besides a few delicious kisses.

Several times during her confession, Marva clutched at her chest as if a heart attack was imminent and murmured, "Oh, child."

When Jess finished, Marva was silent for a long while as her brain processed the new information. Finally she spoke. "That man could ruin you."

"But he won't," Jess said quickly. "He honestly believes I'm innocent. Besides, if he tells what really happened, he'll go down with me. After all, he aided and abetted a burglar, fraternized with a murder suspect, lied to his superiors."

"You don't think he has something up his sleeve?"

"I did at first. But now I believe he sincerely wants to help. He wants to find out the truth."

Marva clicked her tongue. "You're too trusting. He could be setting you up for something bigger."

"I don't think so."

"Just the same, I want you to stay away from him. No sense in taking unnecessary risks."

"But I think he can—"

"No buts. If he wants to investigate and dig up evidence that will help you, that's fine. But he's not going to come within a mile of you while he's doing it. Do I make myself clear?"

"Yes, ma'am," Jess couldn't help saying. Marva reminded her of her third-grade teacher.

"We understand each other, then. Now, how about some barbecue at Little Red's? You can tell me about the leads you've been following, and I can tell you about mine."

Jess nodded, although she wasn't the slightest bit hungry, and if she was, she wouldn't want to eat that greasy, fatty meat from Red's. But Marva loved it, and she wanted her attorney happy.

Ten minutes later, they pulled into the gravel parking lot of Little Red's, a place that could only be classified as a dump. Thick black smoke poured out of the chimney that came from the smoker. The smell was deceptively pleasant.

Little Red's was a cornerstone of Kansas City tradition, attracting tourists of all colors during peak hours, so Jess wasn't really out of place. Besides, she was with Marva, whom everybody seemed to know. She could hardly make her way to the counter for all the waves and winks and handshakes she got.

Jess limited herself to an iced tea; Marva ordered a plate of ribs and Diet Coke. They found a table in the corner.

"Now," Marva said, "tell me what you've found out from checking with Terry's friends."

"Absolutely nothing, I'm afraid, except that most of them hate my guts because they think I killed Terry. I'm a wash as a private investigator."

"You're not so bad," Marva said. She took a bite of

ribs, savored it while she chewed, then delicately wiped her hands on her napkin. "You did get a look inside Kevin Gilpatrick's house. Now tell me more about this rug."

"It was rolled up real tight, covered with plastic and buried under a bunch of carpet remnants. And I only had a tiny flashlight. But it was definitely an Oriental rug, and it was the right size. If we could get a search warrant—"

"In the first place, attorneys can't ask for search warrants. Only law-enforcement people do that. In the second, judges don't grant them on the basis of such slim evidence. Anyway, are you prepared to go to a judge and tell him how you came to see that rug?"

"No. But how about an anonymous phone call to the police? Detective Clewis has proved he'll listen to anything."

"Anything that incriminates you, from what I understand. He won't give the time of day to a tipster trying to clear you."

"You're probably right." Jess sighed and took a sip of tea.

"Don't look so glum, child. I think there's a good chance this Kevin Gilpatrick is hiding something—or someone. I'll go over to records on Monday and see what kind of property he owns, any other place he could be hiding Terry."

"Kyle said he would do that, too," Jess said.

"We can't depend on him, even if his intentions are honorable. He probably has other priorities."

Undoubtedly, Jess thought. After today's near-disaster, Kyle would be doubly careful about showing her any special favors. "So what leads have you followed?" she asked Marva, brightly changing the subject.

Marva proceeded to give Jess a dissertation on the legal parameters of blood evidence in the courtroom and a case-by-case rundown of precedent. She did it all from memory. Jess was impressed by her attorney's acuity and convinced that once they were in the courtroom, she would give those D.A.'s a run for their money. But the promise of future clever legal maneuvers didn't cheer her up. She wanted evidence that would clear her. She didn't want to go to trial at all. Being the defendant in one criminal trial had left her decidedly lukewarm to the prospect of repeating the experience—especially when the outcome could mean losing her freedom forever.

Kyle pulled up to the huge house at Lake Weatherby and whistled softly. Finding a rental house, even this time of year, had been tricky. Finding one with a clear view of the Gilpatricks' house had been even trickier. Finding one that didn't cost a month's salary had been impossible, because the shortest rental they would allow was two weeks.

So here he was, spending his vacation in a four-bedroom three-bath lake house by himself. Just him, a pair of binoculars, and a video camera. So much for that camping trip to Colorado he'd been planning for this summer.

The weather was horrible, too—thirty-six degrees and pouring rain. He sure hoped this place had a good furnace and plenty of blankets.

The rental agent had given him a key and a garage-door opener. The opener didn't work, so he was forced to run through the downpour to the front porch. The key, at least, did work. Fifteen minutes later, he had all his gear inside, along with three bags of groceries and a stack of firewood he'd brought in from the back porch. He cranked up the furnace, which emitted a stale, natural-gas odor but otherwise appeared to be functional.

While he waited for the place to heat up, he made a tour. He'd taken the house sight unseen, paid for it in advance, so this was his first good look at his new digs.

Even he was impressed.

Ultramodern in design, the living room featured a huge, two-sided fireplace that dominated everything else. The enclosed chimney rose at least thirty feet to the top of the vaulted ceiling. The plush carpets were snow white, the enormous leather couches jet black. The white walls were sparsely decorated with abstract oil paintings and textile hangings. The kitchen was large enough to accommodate several professional chefs and all of their equipment; Kyle's pitiful TV dinners, frozen pizzas and microwave popcorn seemed a travesty in such a facility.

The first floor was amazing enough, but upstairs he found the pièce de résistance—a loft bedroom with a bed that had to be bigger than king-size, custom-made for an orgy, perhaps. And a bathroom like something he would expect to find in a decadent Hollywood mansion, with bloodred tile and three—count 'em, three—shower heads feeding into a Roman-bath sort of thing.

And no one to share with.

Kyle couldn't help thinking about Jess. He would love to pamper her here, scrub her back, shampoo her hair, rub her body with scented lotions. And then he would carry her to that football field of a bed and make love to her, slowly, as if they had all the time in the world....

But time was the one thing neither of them had, he thought, shaking off the delicious fantasy. The D.A.'s office was pressing to get a date set for the trial. Rumor had it that they wouldn't seek the death penalty—that, at least, was a relief. But locking Jess up for the rest of her life in some windowless cubicle might be tantamount to killing her.

Terry simply had to turn up before then, Kyle reasoned. No question the guy was a sick puppy, but would he actually disappear forever and leave Jess to wither away in prison? He might, Kyle conceded. Exhaustive background checks had revealed nothing about Terry's past prior to four years ago, when he'd shown up in Kansas City. Kyle suspected the man had already been a fugitive from some

other crime when he and Jess had met. If he could invent
a new life that easily once, he could do it again.

So the pressure was back on Kyle. He had to produce
Rodin or lose Jess forever. Hell, even if they found Rodin
and cleared Jess, would she want anything to do with him?
She'd probably had her fill of cops.

The fact that Jess was sitting in a compact car freezing
her buns off, peering out the window across a lake at a
house that appeared to be completely unoccupied, was evidence of just how desperate she was, she mused grimly
as she drained her last sip of coffee. She'd finished off the
hot chocolate long ago. She had plenty of sustenance available in the form of juice boxes, nuts, apples and granola
bars, but nothing that could warm her up.

This was the worst stakeout so far. She'd been here for
four hours, with a cardboard sun protector in the windshield, clothes hung over the windows on the sides that
faced the road, and boxes piled in back so someone would
have to make a concerted effort to see inside. She had a
small peephole through the passenger window, through
which she could watch the Gilpatricks' lake house.

Not that she really expected to see anything. The house
appeared to be locked up tight—no cars in the driveway,
the window shades pulled shut, no smoke coming out of
the chimney. But since Marva had gone to the trouble of
ferreting out the existence of the house and its address
yesterday, Jess had felt compelled to do something with
the lead.

What else did she have to do? She'd completely run out
of work, and though sitting in Lynn's tiny Toyota was less
than comfortable, it still beat reading about herself in the
paper or poring over the law books Lynn continually
handed to her.

She watched until her teeth were chattering and her eyes
burning. If Terry were by chance hiding in that house, he

wouldn't advertise the fact. But sooner or later he would have to come out or someone would have to visit—to replenish his groceries if nothing else. She couldn't imagine Terry surviving on dried fruits and rice. He would need pizza, and fettuccini Alfredo, and spinach artichoke enchiladas, not to mention designer beer.

The solitude would get to him.

The solitude was certainly getting to her. She had way too much time to think, and unfortunately her thoughts weren't good company. They vacillated between the horror of being locked up for the rest of her life...and the fact that she missed Kyle.

With the disaster her life had become, it seemed silly to waste even one thought on a man, especially given the hell the various men in her life had put her through. But she couldn't help it. Time and again she found herself dwelling on memories of their brief but intense times together, the way she'd felt so secure sleeping against him, his breathing like a lullaby. And the way his kisses felt—thrilling, dangerous.

She'd picked a helluva time to fall and a helluva man to fall for. Oh, not that it was love, she hastily reminded herself, even if it felt like it. She was simply at a vulnerable period in her life, and Kyle had come along, offering protection, security, hope. How could a woman in her position resist?

But in real life, he wasn't the right type of man for her. He was too strong and authoritative—dictatorial, even. Sure, when he was on her side he was a dream come true, St. George slaying all her dragons. But what about when he decided to oppose her? With a delicate shiver she remembered all too clearly those first few days of their acquaintance, when he'd hammered at her with his confusing questions, scowled at her until she wanted to dissolve into tears, arrested her, accused her of lying.

He was a formidable opponent, and she simply wasn't

in his league. If she had to have a man at all, better to find a malleable one, an easygoing, flexible, nonargumentative, gentle one...like Terry? Egad, what a horrible thought. She'd believed that Terry had all the qualities she was looking for, and what a monster he'd turned out to be.

Okay, so she didn't know what she wanted or needed in a man. Her judgment was appalling. Better for her to go without.

Certainly better than facing criminal charges every time she turned around.

With that decision made, she vowed to banish all thoughts of Detective Kyle Branson. Any time he popped into her head, she would instead think of...ducks. Little yellow, fuzzy ducklings, something safe and comforting.

An hour later, as she thought of her hundred-and-nineteenth duckling, she decided she despised the creatures. She would think of jack-o'-lanterns instead. It was, after all, only a couple of weeks until Halloween. Oh, Lord, she was going stir crazy. Was this what prisoners in solitary confinement went through? Would they put her in solitary?

A tap on the driver's window nearly sent her through the roof. Don't panic, she cautioned herself. The doors were locked, the keys in the ignition. If the bogeyman was outside, all she had to do was slide into the driver's seat, start the car—oh, God, what if it didn't start? Lynn had been having trouble with the battery lately.

The knock sounded again, more insistent, and she ventured a peek. Kyle peered at her through the window around the sleeve of a blouse she'd hung there. Relief flooded through her, then fury on its heels. She clambered over the console, threw the blouse in the back seat and cranked open the window.

"I can't believe it. You were following me again!"

"No, no," he quickly denied. "I was here first, since early this morning. Unlock the door, huh? It's freezing out here.'' He had his hands in the pockets of his leather jacket, and he stamped his feet against the cold.

With a sigh, she unlocked the door. ''It's not much better in here,'' she muttered. ''Hurry up, get in before someone see you. I'm trying to be unobtrusive here.''

''Hah! This car is about as unobtrusive as a hand grenade in a silverware drawer.''

''Why do you say that? It's brown. It's anonymous.''

''It also has a cardboard sun-shield thingy in the windshield, at a time of year when no one would think of using one.''

''Oh.'' She concentrated on the droplets of moisture rolling around on the black leather of his jacket. Kyle smelled good, like leather and wood smoke. His presence filled the small car, much more potent than her imaginings had been. She couldn't think of ducks *or* jack-o'-lanterns right now...only him. Thank goodness she was tangled up in her blanket so she couldn't reach out to touch him.

''How did you find out about the Gilpatricks' house?'' Kyle asked, sounding exasperated.

''Marva dug it up for me. I know it's a long shot, but...'' Maybe not, if Kyle was here. ''How did you know about it?''

''I found out the same way Marva did, I imagine. I told you I would check it out.''

''I know, but I was afraid that you'd reached the end of your rope where I was concerned. Helping me out almost got you in a lot of trouble.''

''You don't have to remind me,'' he said, grimacing.

''You're not in trouble, are you?''

''I still have a job. That's about the best I can say.''

''But they okayed a stakeout?'' she asked hopefully.

He shook his head. ''I tried for a search warrant. The judge laughed in my face. Couldn't get anyone to okay a stakeout, either. I'm on my own.''

Jess was so touched that she didn't know what to say.

He was really going out of his way for her. She swallowed back tears, unwilling for him to know how much his caring meant to her. It was duty, not anything more personal, that drove him. Still, her voice betrayed her with a quaver when she asked, "How long will you be here? I mean, maybe we shouldn't duplicate efforts. I can watch the house while you're at work—"

"I don't have to go to work. I'm on vacation."

"Really? I... Thank you, Kyle."

"I'm not doing it just for you, you know," he said gruffly. "Now that I've gone and made a big issue of the fact that I believe you're innocent, I've got to prove it or I'll never live it down. Either Clewis or me is going to be the butt of a lot of jokes, and I'd prefer it to be Clewis."

Exactly as she'd just figured out for herself. Then why did she feel so disappointed? Had she expected him to say something along the lines of, I can't bear the thought of any harm coming to you? I can't bear the thought of your being locked away from me forever? In her dreams.

She forced herself to be practical, returning her attention to the view of the house across the lake through her field glasses. "Okay, you're the stakeout expert. Are we wasting our time?"

"I don't know yet."

"How can I be less obvious, blend into the woodwork, so to speak?"

Long moments of tense silence passed before he answered her question. "You can't. This old car looks out of place in an upscale area like this, parked on the street, no matter what you do to it."

"And I suppose a fire-engine-red Mustang is less obvious? C'mon, if the residents notice any strange cars in the neighborhood, they'll notice yours first."

"Not if mine's in a garage."

It took a few moments for that to sink in. "You have a garage out here? You have a *house* out here?" She was dripping with envy. He had a kitchen to heat things up in...no, he had actual *heat*. And a bathroom—something she hadn't thought much about until recently.

He nodded in the direction straight ahead of them. "That third house down the way, with the black roof and tall windows. The patio door affords a perfectly unobstructed view of the Gilpatricks' house."

And she was squinting through tree branches. Well, that couldn't be helped. She would work with what she had. "Given the fact that I don't have a garage, how can I do this job more effectively?"

"You can't," he said flatly. "In fact, your mere presence here puts the operation at risk. If Terry is in there and he sees a suspicious vehicle, he might get nervous. He could smuggle himself out of that house as easily as I smuggled you out of mine the other day. We would never be able to drive around to the other side of the lake before he could get away clean, and we'd have nothing."

"So you're suggesting—"

"That you go home. I've got things covered."

"Oh? And I suppose you won't have to sleep? Who'll be watching then? If Terry's going to move around, he'll probably do it at night."

"I don't need much sleep. Anyway, if Clewis can't get hold of you, he's liable to call out the National Guard."

"I thought of that. I gave Clewis the number for my cellular phone so there wouldn't be any more communications gaffes."

Kyle threw his hands up. "Great. Now he'll assume you're with me."

"Why should he? He thinks he was wrong about his previous assumption." When Kyle merely looked at her as if she were hopelessly naive, she sighed. All right, he wasn't going to let her participate. Whether it was male ego or protectiveness for her or some self-preservation instinct that drove him, she didn't know. All she knew was that his decision to shut her out infuriated her.

And it hurt.

"If you have no advice for me," she said coolly, "then I'll just stay here."

"You'll freeze to death. And don't run the engine just to crank up the heater. You'll asphyxiate yourself."

"I'm not crazy. Besides, I'm dressed warmly—"

"I know. In thermal underwear."

Heavens. He remembered that totally embarrassing moment from their first stakeout. She would have bet he hadn't been paying attention.

"If I can't talk you into going home where it's warm—and safe—then I'll leave you," Kyle said. "I have work to do. But you have to promise me something, Jess."

"What?" she asked suspiciously.

"If you see anything—anything at all—you don't make a move without consulting me first."

Oh! Of all the typically egotistically male chauvinist moronic—

"I mean it, Jess. Promise me, cross your heart, or I'll arrest you for interfering with a police investigation."

"You would not. Besides, this isn't even a real police investigation."

"I'll let them sort that out at the station."

Damn, he wasn't bluffing. "All right, I promise," she ground out.

He didn't bother with a triumphant smile. He was seemingly in too big a hurry to get out of her presence. "You can call me if you need to. I've got a cell phone, too." He scribbled the number on the back of a hamburger wrapper and left it on the dash.

"Wait, Kyle?" she said as he opened the door.

He stopped. "Yeah?"

"What do cops normally do on a stakeout when they have to...you know, use the facilities?"

He laughed out loud. "We use— Never mind. In your case I'd make a run to the nearest gas station. There's one just up the road, by the highway exit. And if I were you, I would just keep on driving." With that he left the car and slammed the door.

Chapter 13

Kyle watched out the kitchen window with relief as the brown Toyota pulled away a few minutes later. His satisfaction was short-lived. In fifteen minutes Jess was back, parked in the same spot. That damn car of hers might as well have had a loudspeaker on it, proclaiming, Here I am, suspicious character. Anyone who saw her would think she was a homeless person, living out of her car. She would be lucky if one of the neighbors didn't call the cops on her.

He would have done it himself, just to get her out of the way, if it hadn't meant she might get arrested for loitering or trespassing, then dragged to some police station. He couldn't do that to her again.

He spent the next two hours staring intently through the binoculars at the Gilpatricks' house. The video camera hummed next to him, recording constantly just in case. Kyle studied every brick, every carefully shuttered window, every overgrown shrub. He could see the electric meter, but not clearly enough to know how fast it was moving. Might be interesting to find out.

When he checked out the kitchen window again, the Toyota was still in place. The windows were thoroughly fogged, which shielded Jess from view. But fogged windows were another dead giveaway that a person was inside the car, breathing.

The temperature was dropping steadily. According to the forecast, they were in for an early freeze tonight, with windchills in the teens. Rain was a possibility, too. He could only hope that the worsening weather would drive Jess to shelter—and that it wouldn't drive her to do something stupid, like storm the Gilpatricks' house. She was just desperate and foolhardy enough to try something like that.

He took a short break about seven for dinner, abandoning his vigil by the patio door just long enough to make himself some instant soup in the microwave. He hated putting down his binoculars even for that short period of time. Criminals made mistakes, and he was confident that Terry would make his. But it might happen in the blink of an eye.

He checked out the kitchen window as darkness began to fall. The wind was whipping the bare branches of the trees into a frenzy as dry leaves danced in minitornadoes and eddies along the street. And the Toyota was still there.

He reached a decision then. Whatever the consequences, he couldn't allow Jess to get frostbite out there. He shoved his arms into the sleeves of his jacket, tucked the garage-door opener—with new batteries—into his pocket and stormed out of the house, a man with a mission.

He didn't bother knocking this time. He simply jerked the driver's door open. She hadn't even locked it.

Jess gave a shriek of surprise before recovering and glaring at him. "What n-n-now?"

Jeez, she was practically blue. The keys were in the

ignition, he noticed. That made things easier. He climbed behind the wheel, adjusted the seat and started the car.

"What d-d-do you th-think—"

"Save it. I'm taking you in where it's warm. You can sit in front of the fire, I'll make us some coffee and then we'll start taking shifts watching the Gilpatricks' house."

She focused on only one thing he'd said. "Fire?"

"The logs are stacked on the grate, ready for a match." It took about twenty seconds of driving to reach his rental house. He pressed the button in his pocket to make the garage door open.

"Wait a minute," Jess objected. "We can't... I mean, I can't hang around in your house. We'll be in the same fix we were last time you offered me your...hospitality."

"It's not quite the same as last time," he said reasonably, using the same arguments he'd used on himself to rationalize his decision. "For one thing, I didn't tell a soul where I would be. I leased the house through an ad in the paper. So unless one of us was followed... You weren't, were you?"

"I d-don't think so."

He knew he hadn't been. He'd meandered around enough side streets to be sure. "Then we're okay. We're safe."

She didn't look as if she believed him. Could he blame her? He'd made similar assurances last time he'd taken her home with him, and look what had happened.

Jess had to fight with her prison of blankets in order to get out of the car. Finally she freed herself and awkwardly climbed out, still visibly shivering. She followed him into the house. "Oh, Lord, it feels good in here. Where's that fireplace you were talking a—" She stopped midword, looking around her in awe. "This place is a palace! You could park an airplane in here."

"It is a bit excessive, but I didn't have much choice. Come on." He guided her by her trembling shoulders from the kitchen into the living room. He helped her peel off her gloves, jacket and scarf, then propelled her into a plump chair by the fireplace. "Sit."

With the touch of a match to the dry kindling—and with a little help from a natural-gas jet—they had instant crackling fire.

Instant atmosphere, too. All in the world Kyle wanted was to curl up in that big chair with her and gaze into the dancing flames, sipping wine and talking softly about nothing more significant than summer vacations and movies they'd seen. He wanted to feel her body warm next to his and loosen from the effects of the wine. And when they were both seriously relaxed he could carry her upstairs to that sinfully huge bed and—

"You said something about coffee?" Jess asked hopefully, intruding on his fantasy.

"Coming right up." Just as well, he thought, as he measured coffee into a paper filter. Even if Jess were willing, he didn't have time to dally in bed with her. Every minute he spent away from that window was a possible lost opportunity to spot Terry Rodin and end this nightmare for Jess.

While the coffee brewed, he made them each a ham-and-cheese sandwich. She smiled gratefully when he handed her the mug of coffee and set a plate with the sandwich and some potato chips in her lap.

"Another few minutes out there," he said as he resumed his seat by the patio door, "and you'd have had icicles growing off your ears."

"I know. I probably shouldn't admit this to you, but I was thinking about packing it in when you showed up."

Kyle thought about that as he gazed out the window into the increasing gloom. If he'd been just a touch more hard-hearted, he would be rid of his problem. Jess would have gone home, and he wouldn't have to deal with her now. Only he had a hard time thinking of her as a problem right this moment. An unwelcome distraction, maybe.

"Are you warming up?" he asked. "No frostbitten fingers or toes?"

"I'm fine."

"Oh, yeah. Thermal underwear. I'd forgotten."

She laughed, a low, throaty sound that Kyle had heard far too rarely since he'd known her. "You'll never let *me* forget it, I suppose." She paused, and when next she spoke she was solemnly serious. "What can you see out there?"

"Well, it's getting dark, and so far I don't see any lights."

"Shoot, the place is probably deserted. Do you think we're on a wild-goose chase?"

He considered lying to her. If she didn't think this vigil would pay off, maybe she would go home, and he wouldn't be constantly aware of her presence. But she'd sounded so defeated that he couldn't stand to disappoint her further.

"Actually, no. I believe there could be someone occupying that house."

"Really?" She shot out of her chair and in an instant was beside him, peering into the night. Even rumpled and exhausted, she was dazzling, at least to his own tired senses. Her body still retained a hint of whatever fragrance she'd used that morning—soap or shampoo, not perfume, he guessed.

"At first glance the house looks deserted," Kyle said, trying to keep his mind on business. "But look at the leaves on the front porch, around the door." He handed her the binoculars.

She took a few moments to locate the house and focus the lenses to her satisfaction. "I don't see any leaves."

"Exactly. Leaves have blown up knee-deep along that face of the house, but there are none right around the front door—which means someone pushed them out of the way to get in or out of the front door.''

"So someone has at least entered the house in the last few days.''

"I believe that's the case.''

"Interesting. Oh,'' she said, sounding surprised.

"What is it?''

"A big security light just came on,'' she said excitedly.

That's what he'd been afraid of. He'd noticed the floodlight by the driveway, atop a tall pole. "Just because it came on doesn't mean anyone turned it on,'' he said as he reclaimed his binoculars. "It's probably on a timer.''

"Oh.''

He looked through the glasses. The floodlight bathed the house, practically as well as daylight had earlier. It would be harder for him to detect interior lights now.

"Kyle?''

"Uh-huh?''

"Why can't we just go up to the house, ring the doorbell and see who's there?''

"Because if it's Terry, he won't answer the door, and he'll know we're wise to him. He'll be extra careful, maybe even find a way to escape from the house without us seeing. I don't want him careful. I'm counting on him being careless, at least once.'' ·

She nodded her understanding. He studied her as she gazed out into the darkness. She was obviously thinking hard about something, judging from the little furrows of worry on her forehead. Finally she spoke. "I suppose I should go. It appears you have everything under control here.''

And he supposed he should let her. To his consternation, the words that came out of his mouth were "No, stay.''

She looked just as surprised as he felt.

"I've realized that one pair of eyes just isn't enough,'' he continued. "You made the point earlier. I do have to sleep, and eat. With the two of us, we can cover the house every second. We could take four-hour shifts. Although the decision is up to you,'' he added hastily. ''If you feel it's too risky for you to stay here with me—''

''I'll stay,'' she said with finality.

He felt elated, even as he acknowledged that his feelings went well beyond what was logical. He had it for Jess, and he had it bad. ''Okay. I'll take the first shift.''

She looked at her watch. ''I'll try to get some sleep, then,'' she said in a very businesslike tone. ''Are the bedrooms upstairs?''

''Two up, two down. Take your pick. I'll wake you when it's your shift.''

''Okay.'' She looked around, then plodded up the stairs. Somehow, he knew which bedroom she would pick.

Jess could only stare in openmouthed shock at the huge round bed with its custom-fitted red satin comforter and matching sheets. This was something she would expect to find at the Poconos, not in the heart of the conservative Midwest.

Such a temptation. How could anyone resist? She peeled off her clothes down to her infamous thermals, folding everything neatly and stacking it on the dresser. That's when she noticed the dresser drawer open a crack. She opened it the rest of the way and found men's socks and underwear.

Kyle's.

Of course, he'd picked the master bedroom as his. That was only logical. And she should hotfoot it down the hall to some other room. But the round bed called to her. Ah, hell, he'd never know she'd been here. She peeled back the comforter and dived between the decadent sheets, laid her cheek against the satin pillow slip and sighed with contentment. She was asleep in seconds.

Some time later she was wakened by a crack of thunder,

loud as rifle fire. Flickering lightning illuminated the strange bedroom, and it took her a few moments to get oriented. Rain poured down on the roof in what sounded like a waterfall.

She slipped from the bed and went to the window. The rainfall was so hard that visibility was nil.

Jess looked at her watch. Kyle had let her sleep an hour past their shift-change time. That was nice of him, she supposed, but hardly fair. She pulled on her jeans and went downstairs.

The living room was dark and eerily quiet, cast in faint orange glow from the dying embers of their fire. "Kyle?" She could make out his form, stretched out in the chair by the door. He didn't answer her.

As she came nearer, the faint sounds of snoring reached her. He was asleep! What kind of lousy stakeout was this, anyway? She bumped his shoulder with the back of her hand. "Hey, Sleeping Beauty."

His eyes flew open and he was instantly awake. He looked at his watch, then out the door where the downpour continued.

She reached for a lamp, but he stopped her. "Don't. At night I want to keep the lights off in here as much as possible. Don't want one of the neighbors to see us with the binoculars and get the wrong idea."

"Good point." She could see all right by the dying fire. "You were sleeping on the job," she said, though there was no bite in her words.

"Just a catnap while it rained. I have the ability to wake myself up every few minutes to check. And as long as it was raining and neither of us could see a thing, I didn't see any point in waking you."

Momentarily mollified, she said, "I'll make fresh coffee."

"None for me, thanks. I'm heading upstairs." He

heaved himself up out of his chair, gave her a distracted wave and made good his word.

It was a full minute later when Jess realized she hadn't made the bed, hadn't taken her shoes and sweater with her when she'd run downstairs. He would know she'd been in his room. She flew up the stairs with the vague notion that she might erase the traces of her trespassing while he was in the bathroom—or, failing that, at least apologize for her presumptuousness.

The door to the master bedroom was wide open. Kyle sat on the bed, removing his tennis shoes. He looked up. "Did I forget something?"

"No, I did. I'm afraid I slept in your bed, and I forgot to remove the evidence."

He grinned wickedly. "Seems to be a habit with you—sleeping in my bed, that is."

"It sure could get to be a habit." The words were out of her mouth before she knew what had possessed her.

He stared at her, looking quite shocked at first, and then his grin returned—even more wicked, if that were possible. "So how was it? The bed, I mean."

"F-fine," she said, her voice almost a whisper.

"Not too hard? Too soft?"

"Too big," she said, amazed at her bravado. But suddenly it seemed totally insane that the two of them should be in this bedroom and not take advantage of it. That's why she'd followed him upstairs. Not to remove her things. Not to apologize. But to take advantage of the situation. "Too big for one person."

Kyle held out his hand. "Come here, Jess."

Powerless to refuse him, she approached with baby steps. He snagged her by the wrist and pulled her into his lap. "Are you suggesting what I think you're suggesting?"

She shrugged. "Well, since it's raining…"

He laughed softly, the sound of it sending pleasurable shivers up her spine, as he wrapped his arms around her waist. His hands were warm where they rested possessively along her midriff. "That's a helluva reason to make love." He grew serious. "I want to make love to you, Jess. I've wanted to from the first day I met you. But I have to be honest. Relationships aren't really my thing."

She found his confession oddly amusing. "I'm assuming you've tried one."

"I've seriously dated a couple of women. But I always find reasons to run them off."

"Like?"

Just when she thought she could gain some serious understanding of this man, he clammed up on her. "It's not important," he murmured against her hair. "But I've seen enough to know that having a woman around could seriously foul up my life."

"And I know, from personal experience, that having a man around can end up wrecking life as I know it. Yet like an idiot I keep gravitating toward them—toward the wrong kind. Incredible how strong our biological urges can be."

"Incredible," he repeated, nuzzling her ear as if to prove her point. "Am I the wrong kind?"

"Would it matter?"

He stopped nibbling long enough to answer seriously. "I'm curious to know what you think is the *right* kind."

She sighed. "Someone kind and gentle and unselfish, not too egotistical. Easygoing. *No* temper," she added meaningfully.

"Sexually compatible?" He resumed his exploration of the sensitive skin beneath her ear.

"Ah, um, that would help. But other things are more important..." Her words trailed off as she drifted into a sensual dream. How could he, how could any man, do this to her with so little effort? Certainly Terry hadn't.

Terry. Funny, when she'd met him she'd thought he was all the things on her list. But it hadn't taken her long to realize that Terry Rodin was a chameleon, capable of showing whatever it was that people wanted to see. He was nothing but a practiced actor, a con man.

Kyle certainly didn't meet many of her ideals. Oh, he'd shown flashes of kindness, when it suited his purposes. And gentleness, like now. But he was all tied up in his professional ego. He'd admitted it—that proving he was right about her innocence was his primary goal right now. And he certainly wasn't easygoing or without a temper.

At least with Kyle, she saw up front exactly the kind of man he was. If she had the option of getting seriously involved with him—which she didn't—she would know what she was getting into.

"A man like you describe wouldn't hold your interest for a week," Kyle said as he pulled the hem of her thermal top free of her jeans and slid his hands inside it. "You'd dominate him, like a whipped dog. You're too strong for someone like that."

"Me, strong? Ah…" She issued a small, pleasure-filled gasp as his firm hands kneaded her flesh, stiff from all those hours in the car.

"Yes, you, strong," he whispered, renewing the assault on her neck. Between butterfly-light kisses he added, "You're the talk of the department, the way you've held up under interrogation."

"I cried like a baby—oh, right there, a little higher—that first day."

"But you improved, didn't you? Adversity makes you stronger."

"Then I should be King Kong by now." Unable to stop her hands from wandering, she did a bit of her own exploring, fondling the rigid cords of his neck and shoulders, the soft springiness of his hair. It was so much softer than it looked. "So, say I'm strong. Does that mean I need a hard-nosed, overbearing man who'll order me around and expect me to subjugate all my needs to his? No, thanks. Been there, done that.''

''Well, you don't need Mr. Rogers.''

''Then who?'' Some fantasy man. Someone who didn't exist.

Her question went unanswered as Kyle lifted the hem of her top and pulled it over her head. This was getting serious. If she didn't stop things now, they wouldn't get stopped.

She found she didn't have the slightest urge to stop. Kyle certainly wasn't a fantasy man.

But fantasies, she'd decided, were for naive girls who believed in equal partnerships and mutual love and respect and happily ever after. Far better to go into any liaison with her eyes wide open than to end up betrayed, emotionally brutalized, terrorized.

That's what men did to her—because she allowed it somehow, she figured. Both times when her relationships had gone downhill and she'd firmed up her backbone and tried to take control of the situation, she'd ended up a victim instead.

Well, no more. She would never again willingly put herself in a situation that gave a man power over her. That wasn't what was happening here, by God. Judging from Kyle's shortness of breath and the way his hands shook as they unhooked her bra, she was the one wielding the power. And that suited her just fine.

''I don't mean to be cavalier about this—'' Kyle said.

''Then I won't take it that way.''

''You do mean something to me. This isn't just a case of opportunity. I think we were destined for this moment, whether now or later.''

Jess knew what it had probably cost Kyle to admit that he cared, even a little. She accepted his assurances, let them settle warmly about her heart. She answered him by placing her lips quite deliberately against his.

And then there were no more words.

Jess wasn't sure what she'd expected, but Kyle's brand of lovemaking came as a complete shock, and a pleasurable one. At first he seemed to be battling for control, his tongue dueling with hers, his arms wrapped tightly around her, subduing her into submission. He twisted his body around, and she found herself atop the naughty red comforter, with him on top.

Just when his overpowering passion began to both thrill and frighten her, he backed off, returning to the teasing kisses and sensual massage he'd started with. He tenderly removed the rest of her clothes, caressing her limbs with velvety touches that soaked into her body like a hot bath, all the way to her core.

She felt overwhelmed—not by him, but by her own responses. She was drowning in desire, almost mindless, and he'd hardly started. Her earthier feelings for him, building over the past few weeks, were pushing to get free like storm tides against a weakening dam. She wanted to let go, but her fear of the unknown kept her alert, fighting for control, even as her body arched against his hand like a wanton cat's.

He removed his own clothes with a lithe grace and total unconcern for himself. In fact, his gaze never left her. His confidence awed her, and she shivered.

Apparently he thought she was cold, because he whipped back the comforter and silently urged her to slip into the red satin cocoon, which she did willingly. She wasn't accustomed to having her nude form studied so thoroughly, and though it was exciting, it was also unnerving.

One step at a time. She'd always been conservative when it came to sex; she couldn't turn brazen overnight.

Or could she? After Kyle slid between the cool sheets beside her, his simple nearness had her questioning everything she thought she knew about herself, her body, her sexuality. He stroked her not as if he were seeking self-gratification, but as a man bent on learning and absorbing everything about her. The effect was both awe-inspiring and evocative. Her body arched against his hand wherever it touched, and she couldn't help the sounds that came from her throat, soft mewling noises that were half plea-sure, half crazed anticipation.

He followed his caresses with his mouth, leaving soft, lingering kisses in places she'd never imagined being kissed before. His beard gently abraded her skin, adding to the bombardment of sensations that threatened to over-load her brain until steam came out of her ears.

At last he returned to her mouth, joining with her there again in a kiss that stole away not only her breath but her soul as well. For those few minutes, at least, he possessed her. She knew it, and she suspected he did, too. This was a man who never did anything halfway.

He covered her body with his, but he seemed in no hurry to complete the act. He gave her the opportunity to accus-tom herself to his weight, his ever-present warmth, the feel of his body hair against her skin. All the while he contin-ued to kiss her, never breaking contact except once or twice so that they could both inhale great gulps of air, only to resume their frenzied coupling.

She wanted this man inside her as she'd never wanted anything in her life. In his arms, everything else faded away. She forgot, for a little while, her upcoming trial, the charges against her, the horrifying possibility of incarcer-ation. For this little while she was free, and she was de-liriously happy.

When he finally entered her in one velvet-smooth stroke, she raised her hips to meet him, joyously laughing at the same time.

He smiled, then, an expression of pure bliss that made her heart flutter as if it was trying to escape from her rib cage. When she'd first met him, she hadn't thought he was particularly handsome. Now she thought he was the most beautiful man in the world.

He moved inside her with infinite slowness, patience. Of course, he wouldn't rush anything. She was fully aware of his presence inside her, his length, the incredible depth he reached, and she felt every inch of the contact to her deepest core. She could feel him in the tips of her fingers and the roots of her hair…and in her heart, which ached with a fullness that was new to her.

Just when she was thinking he was a man who wouldn't lose control, he did. His strokes grew faster, more frenzied, and she moved with him like some crazed flamenco dancer trying to keep up with an ever-increasing tempo.

It was all too much for her. She let go completely, giving herself up to fate and God and whatever else was out there controlling her. The sensations washed over her now, like the wind at the top of a mountain. She heard her voice, and his, but she couldn't make out what either of them was saying.

She knew the exact moment that he found his release from the maelstrom they shared, and somehow or other she became one with his ecstasy until it seemed they'd become part of the same climax.

Which was patently ridiculous, she thought as she gradually became aware of her back against the satin sheets, her hair draped over her face, the harsh breathing of the man who held her, still embedded within her. She was afraid to trust the experience her mind had told her was real. Ordinary human beings didn't have that kind of cosmic trip just by having sex…did they?

She nearly cried when he finally pulled away from her, signaling the official ending of the consummation. There would never be another first time for them. There might not be another time for them at all, period.

She prepared herself for the awkward postcoital murmurings of two people who had just shared the ultimate intimacy but had no future. There would be no false declarations of feeling, just a jarring transition back to the real world.

But Kyle's wry eloquence surprised her.

"You're a lovely woman, Jess. And somewhere out there is the perfect man for you. I can't imagine why he hasn't found you. He must be looking. I'm sure you'll meet him soon."

But I've already met him, an inner voice suddenly informed her. And as a wealth of feelings welled up inside her, she realized she'd done it again. She'd fallen for a man who was all wrong for her. Only this time it was different. Her feelings for Phil and for Terry had been nothing but immature schoolgirl infatuations that had crumbled upon close scrutiny. This was real.

And it was doomed.

Maybe she was lucky Kyle didn't return her feelings, that he had no intention of remaining with her once this stakeout succeeded or was abandoned. She'd admitted to herself all along that Kyle was too much man for her. She would be swallowed whole if they tried to make a go of a relationship.

She mustn't let him know how she felt, she decided. She wouldn't give him even a clue, because if he found out he would feel wretched and awkward, and the rest of their brief time together would be ruined.

"I don't think the right man for me exists," she said with total honesty.

"He has to. They say everyone has a soulmate. But I'll tell you one thing. No mild-mannered Milquetoast would do for you. You'd turn him to ashes the first time he kissed you. You need a strong man, Jess, to match your strength. Anything less, and you'd be bored to tears."

"A strong man, huh? Like you, maybe? Is that what you're suggesting?" She'd spoken in a way that he was sure to understand was teasing. Yet she held her breath as she waited for his answer.

He rose up in bed. "Listen. The rain's stopped. Time to get back to work." He threw the covers off, but she halted him before he could get out of bed.

"My shift, remember? I'll wake you in four hours."

Just like that, they went from passionate lovers to cool business associates. Jess managed to hold on to some semblance of dignity until she'd pulled on her clothes and headed out the door. But as she sat in the recliner positioned by the patio door and gazed through the binoculars at the floodlit house across the lake, she sobbed quietly.

Why had she done it? Why had she let herself taste heaven when she knew it could never be hers?

Chapter 14

Kyle couldn't sleep. He blamed himself for what had just happened between himself and Jess. She was the one who'd come into his bedroom, and only a strong man could have turned his back on her tentative invitation. He was a strong man, wasn't he?

He'd given her fair warning that he wasn't going to fall in love with her, that this wasn't a prelude to some lifetime thing between them. But hell, he could rationalize this thing seven ways to Sunday and he still felt slimy about it.

Deliciously satisfied, but definitely slimy. As if he'd taken advantage of her.

That was ridiculous. She was an adult, an experienced woman. She knew what she was doing. But she'd seemed so naively trusting, his conscience argued. In this day and age, what was wrong with two consenting adults, everything out in the open, sharing a little ecstasy? It had all felt completely right at the time. Perfect, in fact. Then why the guilt now?

For starters, how about the fact that you just made love with a murder suspect? Until he'd crossed that line, he'd been able to vigorously defend, in his own mind at least, his justification for having a special interest in Jess's case. He'd been seeking truth and justice and all that crap.

Now he was starting to wonder. Was he really that committed to justice? Or had his hormones led him astray? Was he grasping at straws Jess handed him, hoping to put them together into her innocence? Or was he no smarter than his former partner, who'd let his love for his wife blind him to the fact that she was a dangerous crack addict?

That was what it all boiled down to. As smart as he and Buck had both thought they were, they'd been taken in by Melissa, by her victim mentality and her pleas for understanding and leniency. Between them they'd thought they knew more than the system, that they could help Melissa straighten up without involving official authorities.

God, how wrong they'd been. Buck, because he'd loved his wife, the woman she used to be, anyway. And Kyle because he'd loved his partner and hadn't wanted to betray his trust.

How different was his current situation? Yeah, he was feeling something for Jess, something strong. Did that make her a good, innocent person? Did that excuse the career-risking moves he'd made in the past few days?

He'd have liked to think he couldn't possibly love a murderer. But that's what Buck had thought.

All he knew was that he'd better tread carefully. He needed to stay alert and think clearly, and that meant keeping his distance from Jess Robinson.

He ordered himself to go to sleep. Rest was essential. Amazingly, it worked. The next time he awakened, it was to find Jess gently shaking his shoulder.

"Mmm, what time is it?" he asked.

"Almost five," she said. "I took a couple of extra

hours. I wasn't sleepy, and I figured you could use the rest.''

He sat up and stretched, suddenly aware of the woman standing so close to him in the darkness. He caught the barest whiff of her scent, musky and womanly and still somehow fresh as a spring day. It made him want to reach for her.

She stood very still, perhaps sensing his urge, waiting for it, maybe even wanting it.

He resisted. He had to keep his reason for being here firmly in mind, and that reason wasn't to tumble Jess every time she came too close to him. Aside from all the other very sensible reasons he'd come up with to keep his distance, he also realized that it was wrong to take advantage of her emotional vulnerability. She was frightened for her fate, and for some reason she found that being close to him offered her a feeling of security, no matter how brief.

He was misleading her by letting her wallow in that security. He wasn't her safety net, or her champion.

That's what he kept telling himself, anyway.

"Any action?" he asked her.

"Nothing. Well, maybe something. I thought I saw a light go on in the house. Then I couldn't see it anymore, and I convinced myself it was a trick of the wind and the mist and the trees moving around, causing weird shadows.''

"Could very well be," Kyle said cautiously, although his hopes spiked at the possibility. He was becoming more and more convinced someone—maybe Terry—was holed up in that house, taking extraordinary precautions not to be detected. It was more than a hunch.

Wasn't it?

"I'm going in the other room to sleep. Four hours and I'll be good to go again.''

He looked at her then. Although she was barely visible

in the ambient light coming through the window, he could see the lines of exhaustion on her face.

"I'm feeling great," he lied. "Sleep as long as you like. I have a feeling it's going to get even more tedious before this is through."

She nodded and all but stumbled out of the room. A few moments later Kyle heard a door close down the hall. Silly, but he'd relished the thought of her sleeping in *this* bed, even without him.

He resumed watch. Morning dawned, the floodlight went off, and things looked pretty much as they had the previous day—cold, gray, windy and no activity at the Gilpatricks' house.

Jess didn't appear again until almost noon, when she crept sheepishly down the stairs, her hair wet, and carrying with her a lovely, soapy, floral scent. She was wearing fresh clothes—black jeans and a bulky, cable-knit sweater. Her feet were bare, and for some reason that bit of vulnerability made him want to bundle her up by the fire again, the way he had last night.

"I grabbed a shower," she confessed. "You should have woken me up earlier."

"Why? I'm doing fine. I got a good chunk of sleep last night." Enough to keep him going, anyway. But Jess's pristine condition reminded him of just how grungy he was. "If you're ready to take up the vigil, I'll grab a shower of my own and then fix us some breakfast." He wondered how he could sound so normal, like nothing earth-shattering had happened between them last night.

Jess seemed to welcome the normalcy, because she smiled, though a bit awkwardly. She came closer. "I'm ready. Anything going on?"

"Just some squirrels chasing each other. Neighbors on either side of the Gilpatricks' got in their cars and went somewhere."

"So the neighbors are around. Maybe we should go talk to them."

"I thought of that." He got up from the recliner and handed her the binoculars. "But I'm really worried about alerting out quarry that we're on to him before we can tighten the noose around his neck. He might slip away again."

Jess nodded and flopped down into the recliner. Soon her eyes were trained out the patio door, and it appeared she wasn't interested in continuing the chitchat.

Kyle showered, shaved, stared at himself in the mirror and gave himself a stern lecture about professional detachment. He went downstairs, whipped up some coffee and instant oatmeal and brought Jess some of each. She thanked him politely, and he said, "You're welcome," with a similar degree of impersonal civility.

And he felt like screaming. Why, he wasn't sure. Wasn't this the way he wanted it? Jess wasn't clinging to him, making demands, displaying any uncomfortable expectations. Their lovemaking apparently had been nothing more than a release for her. She'd never claimed it was anything else.

So why did he suddenly find himself wishing she felt differently? The male ego was a perverse thing, he decided.

They spent the rest of the day in a companionable routine, swapping places every couple of hours. While one was watching out the glass, the other would read or watch TV or catch a catnap. It would have been downright pleasant, Kyle thought, if not for the tension between them. Having sex hadn't dissipated that for very long.

Kyle had brought along plenty of groceries, and for dinner Jess decided to cook—really cook. "Spaghetti? Broccoli? Carrots? Olive oil?" she called to him as she inventoried the cabinets and refrigerator. "You must have been intending some real meals in addition to the TV dinners."

"Not really. I intended to dump bottled sauce over the spaghetti and chop the vegetables up into salad. The olive oil isn't even mine. Some previous tenant must've left it."

"That's okay. I'll make good use of it."

For the next few minutes, sounds of comforting domesticity drifted from the kitchen. Jess hummed as she worked, and Kyle liked the sound of her voice. He was glad she could lose herself in the meal preparations, at least for a little while.

After a few minutes, he got up to get himself a beer from the refrigerator. What the heck. He hadn't even touched the six-pack he'd brought with him. When he entered the kitchen, he saw Jess wielding a big, shiny knife with such expertise and precision that, for a moment, he was hypnotized by the way the lights glinted off the stainless steel as her hand moved rhythmically, reducing a big carrot to dozens of paper-thin slices.

She looked up. "What? What's wrong?"

"Ah...nothing." He tried to recover. "Nothing," he repeated unconvincingly.

Then she looked down at the knife in her hand, and understanding dawned. "Oh, Kyle."

"I just didn't realize you were such a practiced..."

"Knife wielder?"

"I was going to say 'cook.'" He reached for the refrigerator door, intending to get his beer and get out of there. All right, so the picture of Jess holding a butcher knife had caught him off guard. He'd tried to visualize it so many times, tried and failed. Now here she was, in the flesh, proving beyond any doubt she knew how to make a good, sharp knife sing.

She slammed the knife down on the cutting board. "Maybe you'd like to cut up the vegetables?"

"Of course not, Jess."

"Then stop staring at me like I'm Jack the Ripper. You

of all people." Tears clogged her voice. "I thought you believed in me. I thought you trusted me."

"I do. Would I have brought you into my house, or into this house, if I didn't? Wouldn't I have at least hidden the butcher knives?" He walked toward her as he spoke, holding her gaze. When he reached her, he picked up the knife and pressed the handle into her right hand. He had to physically wrap her fingers around it before she would willingly hold it. Then he brought their clasped hands up between them until the blade rested against his neck.

He let go. "That's how much I trust you."

She stared at him, and for one horrendous moment he thought she might be mad enough at him to use the knife. Then sanity returned with a rush. She wouldn't. Of course she wouldn't. She was Jess, the woman who'd made love to him last night with such gentleness, such feeling.

That's when he knew how deep he was into this thing. The knife clattered to the floor and she was in his arms, their mouths locked in a sensual duel. Kyle reached over to turn off the stove, then pulled her into his arms.

"The stakeout—" she started to protest feebly.

He cut her off with another kiss. "It'll keep," he growled. He was out of his mind, and he knew it, but he didn't care. Nothing mattered but staking his claim on this woman, making sure she knew that their being together wasn't some accident, some matter of mutual convenience or availability or a need for comfort. This was meant to be, and not just for an hour or a day or a week.

The realization that he was thinking in terms of the future should have been alarming but wasn't—not when he knew he wanted Jess as part of that future.

He could sense her animal hunger matching his. She sighed when he roughly slid her jeans and panties down her legs in one motion, steadying herself with one hand on the counter so she could step out of them.

Instead of standing back up, Kyle pressed his face

against her abdomen and ran his hands up the back of her thighs, finally grasping her firm buttocks. He hadn't seen her—really seen her—last night, and he was astounded at the perfection of her form. He shuddered at the realization that he'd been primed to abuse that perfection, to sink himself deeply inside her in a desperate quest to satisfy some impossible-to-define desire.

Such beauty didn't deserve that. He kissed her, burying his face in the soft black curls that guarded her femininity, seeking his prize with his tongue.

But instead of meekly accepting his ministrations, she collapsed, and all at once they were both on the floor in a tangle of arms and legs. They kissed passionately once again, almost as if they were trying to devour each other.

"For God's sake, Kyle," she said, panting between each word, "how long does it take you to undress?" She yanked at the buttons of his shirt.

Her urgency ignited him as nothing else could have. He tensed with each touch as she worked with buttons and zippers, pulling this way and that. In her haste she was more hindrance than help, but he didn't stop her, so great was his pleasure in the process.

It wasn't until he was buck naked that he realized how hideously cold the floor was. "If the bed would be more comfortable—"

"Undoubtedly it would," she said. Then she wrapped her arms around him and pulled him down on top of her, obviously with no intentions of changing venue.

So be it. But he did roll over so that his back, not hers, would be against the uncompromising quarry-tile surface.

He had little control over what happened after that. He was rock hard, had been since the moment he'd touched her. She poised herself above him. He felt a momentary concern that it was too soon, that she wouldn't be ready, that he would hurt her, and he couldn't bear the thought.

But when she sheathed him, it became apparent that she was more than ready.

Enveloped in her warmth, with her moving atop him, he could do little more than grasp her around the waist and join in.

Like last night, it ended quickly. The experience was too intense to linger over, he realized in his cloudy mind as he lost what little control he had.

With a series of high-pitched moans, Jess found what she was looking for, too. They moved together through the final, erotic dance of completion, and then she collapsed on top of him, her hair forming a riotous curtain of soft brown curls all over his face and shoulders.

He blew one curl away from his mouth. "Jess."

"Don't talk," she said.

"Why not?"

"I'm not sure I can stand even acknowledging what just happened. I've never…I mean…oh, never mind!" She clung to him, her face buried against his shoulder.

He realized then that she was embarrassed. "It's okay, Jess."

"On the kitchen floor, for God's sake!"

Kyle laughed, low and wicked. "You're not the one with tile imprints on your backside."

She raised her head and looked at him with tear-bright eyes. "Oh, Kyle, I'm—"

He cut off her apology with a quick, hard kiss. "Don't you dare say you're sorry. You were magnificent, the most passionate woman I've ever known. I guarantee I'll never forget this if I live to be a thousand. Anyway, I'm the one who should be apologizing."

She eased herself away from him and sat up. He immediately felt the cold, and he raised himself, too, finding his shirt to sit on. He pulled her into his lap. She resisted only a little.

"All that crap about not wanting a relationship," he

continued. "We've got a relationship, whether I want it or not. Now it's just a question of what to do with it." Immediately upon speaking the words, he felt his guilt ease. In fact, it actually felt right, admitting to Jess that he didn't want to throw what they had out the window once her ordeal was over.

She sniffed. "I'm sure you'd like to have a girlfriend on death row."

"That's not going to happen. We're closing in on Terry. I can feel it. It'll be a miracle if *I* don't kill the son of a bitch when we find him."

"I'd visit you in prison," she quipped. But her casual words didn't mask the very real fear in her voice. "Seriously, Kyle. I can't even think about... I mean, it's not fair to you to even talk about...us...until I'm acquitted or the charges are dropped. I don't have any problem with living for the here and now."

He wrapped his arms around her and squeezed her tightly until he forced her to relax. "No matter what we plan for, Jess—no matter what we *think* we ought to do—this thing between us isn't going to go away. Even if we're dealing with a worst-case scenario, God forbid, I'm with you."

He could hardly believe the words he heard himself saying. But it was true, every bit of it. He wouldn't walk away from Jess.

"Even if..." she started to say, then trailed off.

"What?"

"Oh, nothing." She laughed nervously. "Just scaring myself with worst-case scenarios. Stupid, really. You need to get back to that stakeout."

She was right. He eased her off his lap and climbed to his feet, then helped her up. He gave her one last kiss before grabbing up his clothes. Nothing between them could be settled until they found Terry.

Jess shivered as she dressed, but she was warm inside. Crazy. She had to be crazy to fall in love with someone like Kyle Branson. He was as powerful a man as she'd ever been involved with—not just physically strong, but powerful in terms of his position. He could say anything about her, and who would believe her if she contradicted him? He could claim she'd confessed to Terry's murder. He could manufacture evidence.

Not that she could imagine Kyle doing any of those things. Yet she'd never imagined that sweet, gentle Phil would stalk her and eventually try to rape and kill her. Or that the unambitious Terry would plot such a cunning revenge against her. All because a relationship had turned sour.

Involving herself in another relationship under the current circumstances was just plain stupid. But, as Kyle had pointed out, neither of them seemed to have much choice about it. The bond between them had formed despite their best efforts to avoid it.

"Well, if I can't do anything about it, might as well enjoy it," she murmured as she tried to remember where she'd been in her pasta primavera recipe.

"Did you say something?" Kyle called to her from the recliner, where he'd taken up watch.

"Nothing important," she called back.

She smiled as she chopped the rest of the vegetables. The dish went together quickly, and she served dinner on an end table she'd dragged close to the recliner so she and Kyle could eat together. It was a cozy, companionable meal, and Jess found herself smiling for no reason.

That night they again took four-hour shifts watching out the patio door so they could take turns sleeping, but Jess moved her things back into the master bedroom. Whenever they changed shifts, they lay in bed together for a few minutes, relishing those brief moments of intimacy before parting again. And when it was time for her shift, Jess stared through the binoculars and daydreamed about Kyle, about what kind of relationship they might form after they'd found Terry.

Finding Terry had taken on a new urgency, and Jess renewed her vigilance, never taking her eyes off the house across the lake. If he didn't show himself soon, they would have to flush him out. With tear gas, if necessary. She didn't care how many laws she had to break to get to him.

"How long do we keep this up?" Jess asked impatiently as she and Kyle shared a breakfast of toasted bagels the next morning.

"As long as it takes. Whoever's in there has to leave eventually."

"Realistically?"

Kyle sighed. "Another couple of days. If nothing happens by then, we'll have to resort to something more provocative. But *not* breaking and entering," he hastened to add. "You almost gave me heart failure the last time you did that."

Jess could laugh now about her failed career as a burglar, and she did. "Not to mention put you on crutches. How is your knee, by the way?"

"Nicely recovered. I mean, if crawling around on that freezing kitchen floor didn't bother it, I guess it's okay." He reached over and tucked a strand of her hair behind her ear. For a few moments his touch lingered on her face, and the look he gave her was hot enough to melt her fillings.

Oh, for a couple of weeks of lazy vacation with this man! Under the circumstances she was grateful for the few minutes they could spend together. But this stakeout was hardly conducive to the kind of leisurely exploration she craved.

The sound of a phone ringing startled them both, and they looked toward a lamp table near the fireplace, where both of their cellular phones were plugged in. "Is that yours or mine?" she asked.

"Definitely mine," Kyle answered, pushing himself out of the recliner. "Damn. I wonder what they want? I told 'em to leave me be unless it was important."

Jess had initially been relieved that it wasn't her phone ringing. She didn't want to hear from the outside world, didn't want anything to intrude on the intimate world she and Kyle had created at quiet Lake Weatherby. When she saw the worried look on Kyle's face her apprehension returned.

Maybe it was news about her case—good news, for a change, she thought hopefully. Maybe they'd analyzed the blood on the so-called murder weapon and found it to be chicken's blood, which was what she was hoping.

"Oh, hey, Blayney," Kyle said into the phone. "What's up?" Jess recognized the name as that of Kyle's partner in missing persons. He'd mentioned the name a time or two. He lowered his voice. "Uh-huh...uh-huh. Okay, I'll call him." He felt around in his pockets.

Jess realized he was looking for a pen. She jumped up and brought him one from her purse, along with a scrap of paper to write on. He nodded his thanks. His face, so pleasantly relaxed a few minutes ago, was now wreathed with tension.

"What was that area code again?" Kyle asked. "Six-one-seven. Got it."

Six-one-seven? That was Boston. Who would be calling Kyle from Boston? Jess felt a chill work its way up her spine. All right, she lectured herself, no reason to jump to conclusions. That phone call could be about anything. Kyle worked on lots of cases, not just hers. Maybe it was a lead on a missing person.

Then why was he wearing that dreadful frown as he glanced her way?

"Jess, can you take over at the window for a few minutes? I have a phone call to make."

"Sure, no problem." And why was he unplugging the cellular from its charger and taking it upstairs?

She sat in the recliner and gazed through the binoculars, but the Gilpatricks' house could have been razed by a nuclear bomb and she probably wouldn't have noticed. Her mind was upstairs with Kyle. Who was he talking to? More important, what was he finding out?

She should have told him. She'd wanted to tell him and had, in fact, been on the verge of doing so a number of times, most recently last night after their encounter in the kitchen. But it was so hard to find the words. How did she tell the man who'd put so much on the line banking on her innocence that she really had stabbed a man, almost fatally?

No matter how she explained it, the fact that she was capable of violence looked bad.

Minutes stretched by. After a while, Jess gave up looking out the window. Her vision was blurred with tears, anyway. It was all over. Once the district attorney's office found out about the attempted-murder charge, their case was made. It wouldn't matter that she'd been found innocent because she'd stabbed Phil in self-defense. It *would* matter that she'd not come clean about the Massachusetts trial from the very beginning.

Marva might be able to have the evidence suppressed, but she doubted it. The fact that the stabbing had taken place had never been questioned. Her trial was a matter of public record. But it wasn't the ultimate damage to her case that had her stomach tied up in knots. It was Kyle, and what he would think of her. She should have trusted him with the information.

She heard the stairs creak and knew Kyle had returned. She almost couldn't bear to turn around and look at him, because she knew what she would see—the pain of betrayal. She did turn, because she had to face this. And what she saw stole the breath right out of her body. He wasn't just disappointed in her for concealing the truth from him. He was angry—nail-spitting, flame-spewing furious. And for the first time since Jess had met Kyle, she was honestly frightened of him.

"Why the hell didn't you tell me you'd stood trial for attempted murder?" he ground out, his rage on a tight leash.

Jess got up from the recliner and stood to face him, trying not to flinch. "Because I was afraid to. Because I knew how it would look. Because I was hoping no one would find out about it." Suddenly she felt a thread of her own anger. Why had this source in Boston called Kyle and not Clewis?

"You acted so damn innocent, so damn bewildered that anyone would think *you* could commit a violent crime. When all the while you were hiding—"

"I wasn't hiding anything," she snapped back. "I never lied about it. I just didn't go out of my way to enlighten the police. I was only following Marva's advice. She told me not to discuss it unless I was forced to."

"Don't try to shift the blame to your lawyer. I'm not talking about some minor incident that might reflect badly on you. I'm talking about you stabbing a man. With a butcher knife from your kitchen. Sliding it right between his ribs and nicking his heart. He could have just as easily died as lived."

"It was self-defense!" she cried. "How was I supposed to know that years later I'd be charged with another crime, and the fact that I once blindly stabbed at someone to protect myself would make me look guilty now?"

"You should have told me," he said, lowering his voice. "I would have understood if you'd just explained it to me—"

"Oh, sure. And you wouldn't have run right back to

Clewis and Easley with the news that 'Guess what? Our prime suspect stabbed another guy!'''

He appeared stunned that she would make such an accusation. "After what we shared, after all we've been through together, you really think that's what I would have done?"

"You're a cop first," she said. "No matter what your personal feelings for me, you wouldn't have withheld evidence that has a bearing on the case. I know that much about you."

He opened his mouth as if to object, then halted, merely staring at her, his breathing coming in great gasps.

"Can't deny it, can you? You and your holier-than-thou, you-should-have-trusted-me routine. Am I still supposed to believe that you were strictly trying to help me? I guess that person who called from Boston was just a friend, and by chance you happened to start talking about old cases?"

She could see she'd scored a point by the way he flinched. And she should have stopped there. But she didn't.

"It's all clear now. You were working me over even while you were digging around in my background. Good cop, bad cop—that's what Marva called it. Pretending to side with me against Clewis, all the while hoping I'd drop my guard and give you some juicy tidbit you could use to hang me. The free sex was an added bonus."

Kyle's mouth became a tense white line on his anger-reddened face. He shoved down the antenna on his cellular phone with so much force that it broke off in his hand. He threw the whole mess down into a chair. It bounced onto the carpet.

Without another word, he turned on his heel and marched toward the kitchen and ultimately the garage.

"Where are you going?" she demanded.

"Out. Before *I'm* the one who has to be brought up on murder charges."

Chapter 15

Jess was numb for the first few minutes after Kyle left. She sank to the floor where she stood, hugging her knees to her chest. Gradually, however, the numbness receded and an almost incomprehensible pain took its place.

Kyle had betrayed her. Kyle, the man she'd fallen in love with. She sure knew how to pick 'em.

All right, maybe she'd made the wrong decision to withhold information about Phil Cattrone. But that was a calculated risk she'd taken, and it had backfired. She would suffer the consequences.

Oddly, the fact that the D.A.'s office now had a juicy bit of ammunition didn't bother her nearly as much as Kyle's part in providing it. He'd been investigating her all along, even when he pretended to want to help her. He'd obviously been lying when he'd said he was off the case. What else had he lied about?

Was it all a lie? Did he feel anything for her at all, or had the whole thing been an act designed to lull her into trusting him? Had he ever believed her innocent?

Thinking about it gave her a headache.

Would he come back? she wondered. Or was he even now heading to the station to offer his pièce de résistance to Clewis? How would he handle the congratulations? Would he accept them grudgingly, or bask in the praise?

She'd made everything ten times worse by lighting into him the way she had. If he'd had even an ounce of compassion for her, she'd destroyed it with her accusations. Not that she really believed he would ever have protected her to the extent of withholding important evidence. But if there'd been even a slim chance, she'd blown it.

Hadn't she learned her lesson by now about men? They held all the cards. They were bigger, stronger, and every time she went head-to-head with one of them, she ended up getting trounced—stalked, framed, betrayed.

She was done with the whole damn gender.

With renewed determination, she pushed herself up and resumed her seat in the recliner. Everything was up to her now. No white knight was going to save her from her fate. If anyone was going to track Terry down, she would be that person. At least Kyle had left his good binoculars.

She hadn't been watching five minutes when she saw something. It was a small thing, so insignificant that she could almost believe she'd imagined it. Almost. But a window blind had wiggled, as if someone had separated the slats to peek outside.

Terry was in that house. She could almost smell his presence. And she was tired of waiting for him to make a mistake.

She came to a decision with surprising ease. Maybe Kyle's abandonment had made her reckless—who knew? She decided to stop waiting around for other people to decide her fate. She was taking matters into her own hands. She was going to confront Terry and, through reason or intimidation or brute force, she was going to make him come forward and end this nightmare once and for all.

Jess got up from the recliner and, with quiet deliberation, put on her shoes and a down jacket. She found her purse, her keys and headed out to her car. Her stomach was knotted with apprehension, but she ruthlessly ignored her body's own defense mechanism. So maybe she was headed for disaster. How much worse could it get? In her misery she didn't care.

The garage door opened with an encouraging roar when she pushed the button by the door. Unfortunately, when she climbed into her car and turned the key, her car didn't follow the garage door's example. In fact, nothing happened.

"Oh, great!" She'd been struggling with a weak battery in her sister's car for a while now. What a rotten time for it to finally give out. Maybe it was a sign from heaven, she thought pessimistically. Maybe God didn't want her to embark on this vengeful venture.

Nah, that was stupid. She would find a way to that house across the lake if she had to walk. Or swim. Or...of course! There was a dinghy with a trolling motor tied up to the dock. Use of the boat went with the house rental, Kyle had mentioned, and Jess remembered seeing the key somewhere.

Back inside the house, she found the key, neatly labeled, in the silverware drawer. "Hah," she said as she grabbed it up. That would teach fate to try to thwart her. She pushed the recliner away from the patio door and exited the house, walking down a short flight of stairs to the dock.

It was bitterly cold near the water, and Jess belatedly wished for a hat, scarf, gloves. She could get them, she reasoned, but she decided not to. She didn't want anything to slow down her mission. She also didn't want to give herself any opportunity to chicken out. The trip across the lake would take only a few minutes. She wouldn't freeze to death in that time.

Determinedly she shook the accumulated rain off the

blue plastic tarp cover and pulled it off the dinghy, folding it haphazardly and stuffing it into a storage container on the dock. She climbed gingerly into the shaky boat.

Boats weren't really her thing, and when it came to actually inserting the key in the motor, she almost lost her nerve. But all she had to do was think of Terry and the hell he'd put her through, and she kept on her course toward a confrontation. The realization that it was going to end, one way or another, in a few minutes exhilarated her and quickened her movements.

Then Kyle would have to swallow his lack of faith in her. His information from Boston, so carefully ferreted out, would be meaningless—just like their lovemaking had been.

All right, so she was lying, she thought as she untied the bow and stern of the boat and pulled the bumpers in. Regardless of what it had meant to Kyle, making love with him had meant everything to Jess. Right now she might hate the man, even more intensely than the day he'd interrogated her. But she still loved him.

She was a pathetic case. There was something wrong with her.

The trolling motor buzzed reassuringly to life. It was quiet, like a cat purring, not like the outboard motors Jess remembered. After a couple of false starts, during which she almost ran the boat up onto the bank, she figured out how to reverse the dinghy. Some more maneuvering and she was in business, heading steadfastly toward the Gilpatricks' house.

She had no idea what she would say once she faced Terry, but she was counting on the momentum of anger to carry her through. The anger made her strong. She couldn't fail.

Jess pulled up to the Gilpatricks' dock. With her eyes trained on the house, she cut the motor and quickly secured the boat. Nothing moved. Good.

Now, how to approach the house? A brazen foray right up to the front door was tempting, but chances were Terry wouldn't just open the door and let her in. She would be giving him time to plan an escape strategy. She wished now that she'd thought to bring some tools with her.

A basement window? Her specialty. Then she could sneak upstairs and confront Terry, giving him the shock of his life. And if one of the neighbors saw her breaking in and called the police? Perfect. It was a good plan.

She found a fist-size rock in a neglected garden behind the plain gray brick house. Then she selected a basement window at random. As she crouched down, ready to do the window violence, she tried not to think about what would happen if she was wrong—if the resident of the house wasn't Terry but some reclusive Gilpatrick grand-mother instead. She'd likely give the poor thing a heart attack and wind up in jail for breaking and entering to boot.

But she wasn't about to abandon her plan now. She closed her eyes, swung her hand back, gathered her strength…

Then someone grabbed her by the wrist.

She screamed and dropped the rock, which landed on her own foot with a painful thud. Her eyes flew open. She expected to see Kyle standing over her—Kyle, who'd had a change of heart and returned, discovered Jess missing, figured out her plan and followed her to prevent her from doing something irredeemably stupid.

But it wasn't Kyle standing there with her wrist in a vise grip. It was Terry. His hair was cropped short and dyed brown, and he'd grown the beginnings of a mustache, but she had no trouble identifying him. A surge of pure relief warred with more sinister emotions as she looked up at his smirking face.

"Well, well, what have we here?" he said, yanking her to her feet. He released her arm, and that was a mistake, because without warning Jess hauled off and socked him in the jaw hard enough to snap his head back.

"You son of a bitch," she heard herself saying, "where's your smirk now?"

He rubbed at his face. "That's gonna cost you, Jess." His voice was low and menacing, as she'd never heard it before. "Come on, we're going inside." He grabbed her by the hair and yanked, forcing her to accompany him as she yowled in protest. Kyle's warning flashed through her mind: *"He might be dangerous. Don't underestimate him. Don't approach him on your own. Call the cops. You'll do that."* Belatedly she realized she should have screamed bloody murder outside while she had the chance. Now that he had her inside the house... She shivered. Surely not.

Terry didn't release her until they were in the kitchen. There he pushed her into a chair with a snort of disgust. "I didn't give you enough credit, Jess," he said. "How did you figure out I was here?"

"I'm not the only one who figured it out," she said. "The police suspect you're here, too. I've been working with an off-duty cop. We've been staking out this place for two days. We have a house rented across the lake, and we've been watching this house day and night."

"Sure, Jess," he said, pouring himself a cup of coffee with total unconcern. "If that's true, where's your cop friend now?"

"He had to go out. While he was gone, I saw you at the window, and I decided to make a move. He'll be right behind me. When he gets back and sees I'm gone—"

"Save it, Jess. You never were much of a liar. Want some coffee?"

"No, I don't want coffee!" she exploded. "I want your head on a platter!"

Terry clicked his tongue. "So much violence under the calm, serene exterior. You'd better not lose your temper like that in the courtroom during your trial. It won't look good at all.''

"There isn't going to be a trial, Terry. Don't you realize that? The game's over. I won. All I have to do is reach for that phone on the wall and dial 911.''

He actually smiled at her suggestion. "Be my guest,'' he said, gesturing toward the phone.

"All right, I will.'' She jumped to her feet and made a grab for the phone. Why was he letting her? she wondered even as she dialed. What does he have up his sleeve?

"This is the 911 operator. What is your emergency?'' a preternaturally calm voice asked.

"This is Jess Robinson. I'm the one accused of murdering my ex-boyfriend. But I've found him alive and I need you to—''

"Your name again?''

"Jessica Robinson. I need the police to come—''

"And what is your emergency?''

She looked up at Terry. He was smiling, not in the least worried. And then she figured out what Terry's game was. So simple.

"Just send the police to this address—18 Meadowlark Road,'' she cried as frustration built up and exploded. "There's about to be violence done.'' She slammed down the receiver, then addressed Terry. "You're planning to leave before they get here.''

He nodded. "It takes about five minutes for the cops to get here. I'll be long gone, and you'll look like a total idiot, desperate, psychotic, resorting to breaking into strangers' houses to fuel your pathetic delusion that I'm alive.''

"Why?'' was all she could think to ask. "Why are you doing this to me?''

That smile again. "Because I can. Because I didn't like the way you threw me out of our house—''

"*My* house.''

"—without an ounce of regret for what you were throwing away—"

"What? We had nothing! No, let me correct that. I had nothing. You had a free ride. Any sane person would have thrown you out on your ear long before I did."

"—so calmly, with no emotion. I bet you're feeling emotion now, huh, Jess?"

She realized then that he hadn't heard a word she'd said. He was still wrapped up in his fantasy revenge. Reason wasn't going to prevail. Still, she kept trying.

"Your fingerprints are all over this house. They'll know you were here, that I wasn't lying."

He laughed. "Oh, Jess, haven't you learned anything hanging out with the police? They could pick up my prints here from now till doomsday, but if they don't have prints on file for comparison, they're useless."

"And yours aren't on file," she concluded miserably.

"Not under the name Terry Rodin, anyway. All right, that's enough chitchat. Don't think you can stall me until the police get here. I'm not that dumb." He headed toward the garage door, carrying nothing. No doubt he'd left nothing behind that would identify him.

"Wait, Terry, you can't do this—"

"Of course I can. And you can't stop me. That's the beauty, isn't it?" With a casual salute he turned and resumed walking.

That's when desperation took Jess over. She saw the knife block on the kitchen counter, and a split second later a long, gleaming butcher knife was in her hand. She ran at Terry full throttle, slamming into him with the force of a freight train. The collision knocked him against the wall, and the air whooshed out of him in a surprised grunt.

Jess had the knife at his throat. "Drop to the floor, you SOB, or I'll plunge this knife into your throat faster than you can blink. If I'm going to be executed for killing you, I might as well enjoy the actual act."

His hand twitched, and she could see the thoughts whirring through his mind. He was calculating his chances, wondering if she really had the guts.

"I almost killed Phil Cattrone, remember?" she said breathlessly. "I have no trouble stabbing someone when I'm desperate. Now drop!"

"My God, Jess, you've lost it." He blinked, and his eyes showed fear. Good. She didn't think she could actually draw blood in this situation. Her life wasn't in danger. This wasn't exactly self-defense like stabbing Phil. But Terry didn't know that. His gaze remained locked with hers as his knees bent and he slowly sank to the floor.

"Sit on your hands."

He did.

"Don't move a muscle. Don't even blink." Where were the damn cops? What if the 911 operator had thought she was a crank and had ignored her call? She knew they were supposed to take every call seriously, even if it sounded bogus, but there was always the chance of a slipup.

"You're crazy, you know that?" Terry said. "They ought to lock you up and throw away the key."

"*I'm* crazy?" she asked incredulously. "You perpetrate a hoax on me and the entire Kansas City Police Department that must have taken months to plan, and you think I'm crazy? Don't talk," she added when he opened his mouth to protest. "Don't say another word. What the police will do to you isn't nearly bad enough, and I'm still sorely tempted..." She pressed the knife against his throat for emphasis and prayed for the sound of sirens.

Kyle had no idea where he was driving to or how long it would take. But he felt in a hell of a hurry to get there. The speedometer pushed seventy, then seventy-five, then eighty. His police scanner chattered in the background.

Jess, his sweet Jess, had stabbed a guy. An ex-boyfriend. She'd been arrested and tried for the crime, and had gotten

off only by pleading self-defense. He'd heard that one before. The plea of a guilty person who had nothing else to
fall back on.

People didn't change. The chances were good that if
she'd done it before, she could do it again. And maybe
take it one step further.

He was fuming. She should have come clean with him.
If only she'd been honest up front, he would have...what?
Would he have gone straight to Clewis, as she believed?
Or would he have kept the information to himself, crossing
over that ever-shifting ethical line?

As the car ate up a few more miles, reason prevailed.
Jess had made a good point: why *should* she have trusted
him? Sure, they'd made love. That didn't change the fact
that he'd deceived her, pretending to be a free agent when
he was really working for Clewis. If she'd held back, it
was probably because her instincts were on target.

It still hurt.

When he noticed the speedometer pushing eighty-five,
he lifted his foot off the gas. No sense in getting himself
or someone else killed just because he was having a temper
tantrum. He took the next exit, turned under the highway
and got back on going the opposite direction, still unsure
of his destination.

Even now, he felt an urge to forget he'd ever learned
about the trial in Barnstable County. But that was out of
the question. The new evidence would damage Jess's defense and damage it badly. After all, if it had *him*, her
staunchest supporter, wavering, imagine what an impartial
jury would think.

And did he really think, now, that Jess was guilty?

He considered the matter for some time, and finally concluded that, no, he still didn't believe she'd murdered
Terry Rodin. He was angry enough with her that he almost
wanted to believe it, but he couldn't. Was it naive to think
he couldn't fall in love with a murderer? If he was wrong

about her, then his police instincts were nonexistent, and he should retire from police work forever.

It took him a moment to absorb what he'd just realized. Somehow, despite his best intentions, he'd fallen in love with Jess Robinson. Love was blind, and maybe he was as blind as Buck had been, continuing to believe in Melissa's innocence despite overwhelming evidence. Now Kyle understood why Buck hadn't listened to him when, toward the end, he'd pleaded with his partner to turn his wife over to the authorities. When you loved someone, you had to believe they were ultimately good. Otherwise, what did that say about you?

So here he was, stuck with his belief in Jess. Stuck in love with Jess, whether he wanted to be or not. Committed to protecting her, whether she deserved it or not. He would have to tell Clewis about the trial in Massachusetts, he decided. He couldn't live with himself if he held that back. But he would double his efforts to find other evidence that would be just as compelling—evidence that would prove Jess innocent. If he was a fool for believing he *would* find it, that was tough.

He would have to go back to the rental house and talk things over with Jess. He would give her a chance to explain, to clarify. And though he was still angry with her, he would work with her on coming up with some new ideas for catching Terry...or Terry's real murderer. Maybe they could lay a different kind of trap, plant something with the media that would flush him out. Something.

The police scanner squawked, and he reached for it, intending to turn the obnoxious thing down, when the dispatcher said something that brought him to full attention.

"Any available unit to a disturbance at 18 Meadowlark Road."

He knew that address by heart—the Gilpatricks' house. His blood turned to ice water. What in God's name had Jess done? What had he driven her to?

He heard a highway patrol officer respond to the request. Kyle noted the officer's location. Not nearly close enough. It would take several precious minutes for him to arrive at Lake Weatherby. Kyle could be there in two minutes flat if he pushed it.

He did. He had no gun because he'd left it at the rental house. But he did have a nightstick under the seat. That would have to do. Jess was in trouble.

As he drove like a maniac toward the lake, he listened to the rapid-fire conversations overlapping each other on the scanner. It appeared the 911 dispatcher couldn't elaborate on the nature of the call she'd received. She said only that there'd been a request for police assistance.

Had the request come from Jess? he wondered. Or had Jess broken in on an innocent party, and they were the ones who'd called for help, mistaking her for a burglar?

He didn't bother with caution as he approached the Gilpatricks' house. It was all or nothing now. He roared up into the driveway, apparently the first police to arrive. Without much thought to his own safety, he flew out of his car, clutching the nightstick, and sprinted to the front door. Everything looked quiet from the outside.

He banged on the door with his fist, then stepped to the side. "Police. Open the door!" Nothing. He repeated his announcement. Nothing again. Then he thought he heard something, a female voice, thin and thready.

"Kyle?"

That was all it took. He broke down the door with two karate kicks and a well-placed shoulder. A window might have been easier, he reflected as his shoulder exploded in pain, but he hadn't had time to debate it beforehand.

"Jess?" he called out as he broke through the splintered wood.

"In here," she responded from what he guessed was the kitchen. "Please, help..."

He was too frightened for her to pay much attention to

police procedure. Instead of entering with caution or waiting for backup, he stormed into the kitchen like an avenging knight, the nightstick raised above his head. He would tackle a grizzly bear with a submachine gun if he had to.

When he reached the kitchen, all he could do for a moment was stare in shock. Jess didn't appear to be the one who needed help. She was sitting on top of a guy Kyle had never seen before, a knife at his throat. "Jess?"

"I caught him!" she said triumphantly.

"Caught...who?" he replied as he slowly lowered the nightstick, keeping his words calm and even.

"Who do you think?" she said impatiently, almost hysterically. "Terry!"

Kyle stepped slowly closer, peering at the man on the floor. "You're Terry Rodin?"

"My name's Howard Ghetty," the man said, obviously scared half out of his wits. "Are you police? Please, get this crazy woman away from me."

"Oh, for God's sake!" Jess cried. "It's Terry. He's dyed his hair and grown a mustache, but I'm telling you it's him." She looked up at Kyle, pleading for him to believe her.

He didn't know why he should. If the stranger she was holding captive really was Terry, he was doing a good job of impersonating someone else. But, oddly, Kyle did believe Jess. She might conceal something from her past, but she wouldn't out-and-out lie to him. He had to believe that.

"Put down the knife, Jess," he said, still calm, "and ease off him. You," he said, pointing to the man, "don't move until I tell you."

"Hey, I didn't do anything wrong—" the man started to object, but Kyle silenced him with a quelling look.

"Don't you worry, we'll straighten everything out," Kyle said.

Jess seemed only too happy to drop the knife on the floor and back away. She inched over to a kitchen chair and raised herself onto it. She was shaking violently, looking more frightened than her victim. Her face was oatmeal pale. In the background Kyle could hear a police siren.

"I have a driver's license," the man said, "that proves I'm Howard Ghetty—"

"And probably several other fake identities, as well," Jess broke in, her voice gaining strength. "No wonder the police had such a hard time looking into your background. Terry Rodin didn't exist until you invented him four years ago."

Kyle turned his attention toward Jess, intending to tell her to please leave the interrogation to the police. But in the split second he took his eyes off the other man, the man made a break for it. He was out the back door in a half second flat.

"Oh, hell, I'm too old for this," Kyle muttered as he took off after Rodin—and it had to be Rodin, he realized, or why would he have split?

Terry had several years less mileage on his body than Kyle, and judging from the way he was running, he didn't have a bum knee to contend with. But Kyle managed to stay only a few paces behind. Terry ran down the driveway of a neighbor's house and over a fence.

Undaunted, Kyle followed, wincing as his knee protested the landing on the other side, but it didn't give out. He chased Rodin through the yard, around a doghouse—Kyle could only hope the dog was absent—and over the fence on the opposite side. That's where Terry ran into trouble. The hem of his jeans caught on the top of the chain-link fence, flipping him upside down. The harder he struggled, the more securely he got stuck.

Kyle scaled the fence with an easy vault, landing gently on the other side. His prey hung upside down from the fence like a rabbit caught in a snare.

Kyle grabbed him by the throat. "Did you suddenly feel

the need for some fresh air, Rodin? Or some exercise, perhaps? Surely you weren't running from the police."

"Get me down," he grated out. His face was turning red.

"Say the magic word." Kyle said.

"Please?"

"I was thinking more like, 'I really am Terry Rodin and I framed Jess Robinson for my own murder.'"

"Yes, yes! Just get me down before my head explodes."

All right, so as a confession it lacked something, aside from the fact that it was obtained under duress and would be totally useless in court. Kyle wasn't worried about that any longer. If Jess said this guy was her ex-boyfriend, the man she identified as Terry Rodin, then that's who it was and the truth would come out. She was off the hook. She hadn't killed anybody.

Not that Kyle had ever truly believed she had, not after he'd gotten to know her. But he'd had fleeting moments of doubt. As it should be. Blind faith might be fine in theory, but in practice it could kill you. It had killed Buck. Whether Jess would agree with Kyle was another story, however.

Two highway patrolmen careered around the corner in Keystone Kop fashion. "What in the holy hell is going on here?" one of them asked, his hand caressing his gun, though he kept it holstered.

Easy, Clint Eastwood, Kyle thought, though thankfully he hadn't said it out loud. "I'm Kyle Branson, Kansas City Police Department, off duty. This red-faced gentleman is Terry Rodin, who's been missing for several weeks—"

"Rodin? I thought he was dead," one of the patrolmen said.

"He sure don't look like the picture in the paper," the other observed skeptically.

"Can we debate my identity later?" Rodin pleaded. "Just get me off of this fence!"

"Whoever he is," Kyle said, "he was running from the scene of a crime when I, er, apprehended him. Hold him for questioning. Do *not* let him go. When you get him loose, follow me."

Kyle left it to the other two officers to free the sputtering Rodin from the fence. Eventually they all ended up in the kitchen of the Gilpatricks' house. Jess, looking drained but not quite so pale, was only too happy to tell her story to the amazed highway patrolmen. Rodin, handcuffed to a kitchen cabinet, offered nothing except a driver's license, expired more than a year earlier, that did in fact identify him as Howard Ghetty. But in the picture he was blond with no facial hair, and quite obviously the same man who'd been passing himself off as Terry Rodin for the past several years.

Kyle took great pleasure in notifying the Kansas City Police Department that he had Terry Rodin in custody. He spoke with Clewis personally, who grudgingly agreed to send a squad car out to pick up the "alleged" victim-turned-culprit. No one was sure what exactly he would be charged with, but Kyle was determined the man wouldn't walk free.

Clewis, with his usual lack of professional courtesy, demanded the presence of the two highway patrolmen, too. They went willingly. It was a weird enough case that they were interested, and they also were lured by the prospect of seeing their names in the paper.

And finally, Clewis wanted Kyle and Jess at the station without delay. He wanted them there so badly, in fact, that he insisted they ride in the patrol car that came to pick up Terry.

Picturing the bloodletting that would take place if either he or Jess were forced into the same car with Rodin, Kyle just as adamantly insisted he would drive Jess to the station himself.

If she would even get in the car with him. Judging from the looks she cast his way every so often, she might have preferred riding with Terry.

Chapter 16

"What in the world were you thinking?" were the first words out of Kyle's mouth once he'd gotten Jess alone in his car. He'd intended to start on a much more conciliatory note, but once his adrenaline had receded and he knew Jess was safe, anger had taken its place.

"I was thinking I wanted to save my hide," Jess replied indignantly. "What innocent person in my position would have volunteered information about a previous stabbing?"

"That's not what I was asking," Kyle said quietly when he realized they weren't on the same track. "I understand about that. I want to know why you did something so stupid as to confront Terry Rodin on your own."

"It did the job, didn't it?" she snapped. Then her voice changed. "You understand?"

"I'll admit I was mad as hell at first that you'd kept it back. I guess I thought that if you cared anything about me, if you trusted me, you should have told me everything. But...I wasn't a hundred percent honest with you, either. Guess I was using a double standard."

"It wasn't a lack of trust that kept me from telling you, believe me. Oh, won't this car ever get warm?" Even with a down jacket on, she was shivering.

Kyle cranked up the heater.

"I trusted you, Kyle Branson, whether you deserved it or not. I believed you were a certain kind of man."

"Really? What kind?"

"Dedicated and ethical. If I'd told you about my troubles back in Massachusetts, your sense of duty would have dictated that you turn that information over to Clewis. Even if you didn't want to hurt me."

"And has your opinion of me changed?"

She hesitated. "No. Obviously your duty as an officer of the law is more important than anything else."

His duty? Where had she gotten the idea that he was some paragon of ethics? Somewhere along the line, his feelings for Jess had stomped all over duty. He honestly wasn't sure what he would have done if she'd told him about Phil Cattrone. He *thought* he would have brought the information to Clewis, but he still wasn't sure.

"So you kept your secrets for *my* sake?" he asked. "To save me from having to make a painful decision?"

"Oh, all right. As long as I'm being totally honest here, I was scared to death to breathe a word of that story to anyone. The information was just too damaging, even if I'd willingly volunteered it.

"But," she continued, "I wanted to tell you. I almost did, several times. Like when you first said you knew I wasn't capable of violence. I wanted to point out that anyone, under the right conditions, can be violent. A mother protecting her children, a woman protecting her...well, whatever." She dropped her head and stared into her lap.

"My God, Jess, is that what happened? The man was trying to rape you?" The thought nauseated Kyle. His source in Boston hadn't mentioned rape.

"He'd been stalking me for weeks," she said, lifting

her head to look directly at Kyle. "He'd never threatened violence, just kept promising this sick sort of eternal love and vague things like 'I'll make sure no other man ever loves you the way I do.' The police wouldn't do anything. They didn't take it seriously."

"And so he came into your house?"

"He forced his way in while I was carrying some groceries inside. Pushed me up against the kitchen counter. There was no doubt that he intended to rape me. He made that abundantly clear. And I might have stood that. I might have survived it. But I wasn't altogether clear that he was going to let me live afterward. So I grabbed the first weapon I could lay my hands on, a knife in the dish drainer."

Her voice quavered, but she went on. "I didn't threaten him or try to scare him, because I knew Phil, and I knew that wouldn't work. So I stabbed. Viciously, and with intent to hurt him."

"You don't have to tell me this, you know," Kyle said.

"Of course I do. I owe you this explanation, I think. I only wish I could have given it to you before you stormed out of the house."

"Point taken." He gripped the steering wheel until his knuckles turned white. "I'm sorry. My temper gets the better of me sometimes. I think you pointed that out recently. Fortunately, I cool down pretty fast."

"Does that mean you're not mad anymore?"

"Hell, I don't know. In your position I might have done exactly the same thing. It was just such a shock finding out that you…"

"That I'd stabbed someone. Even in self-defense. I know. People have a hard time believing a gently bred, middle-class, Midwestern lady can do something so bloody and unsavory."

"It's not that, Jess," he said, suddenly intense. "I have

no problem believing a 'nice' woman can do violence. I've seen it.'' Without warning he took the next exit.

''Where are you going?''

''We're stopping for coffee. I have to tell you something.''

''But Clewis—''

''Clewis can wait. He'll have enough to do for a while with Terry and the highway patrol guys. I could use some caffeine.''

Kyle said nothing more until they'd pulled into a non-descript chain café and ordered their coffee. But Jess sensed there was something heavy on his mind. He tapped his spoon against the thick ceramic mug, biding his time, perhaps choosing his words just as she'd chosen hers.

''A few years ago I had a partner named Buck Palladia,'' he began. And as Jess listened to the tragic, unsavory tale of Melissa Palladia's downward spiral into crack addiction, she began to understand a lot of things about Kyle Branson—about why he'd been so suspicious of her at the beginning. And why, when he'd wanted to believe in her innocence, he'd fought it.

He hadn't wanted to be naive, like Buck, who'd ended up with a bullet in his brain when his wife had finally gone over the edge.

No wonder Kyle had reacted so strongly when he'd discovered Jess's duplicity. He'd suddenly seen Buck's situation all over again—a guy taken in by a pretty face, lulled into a false sense of security by sex and protestations of innocence.

When Kyle's story ran down and he fell silent, she shook her head. ''It's a wonder you didn't give up on me,'' she said, a trace of wonder coloring the statement. ''Or did you just come back to Lake Weatherby because you heard the 911 call over the scanner?''

''No, I was coming back, anyway. After thinking things

through, I'd realized that no matter what, I still believed you didn't kill Terry.''

"And what did you think when you walked into the Gilpatricks' house and saw me sitting on a strange man with a knife at his throat?" She managed a smile. What a picture that must have been.

"I thought you were the most beautiful avenging angel I'd ever seen."

"Liar. You went white."

"Okay, the scene did give me a turn." He reached across the table and took her hand. "But only for a moment. Because I'd realized something else when I was driving around. I realized I love you."

Jess's heart beat double time, then stopped altogether for a moment. Had she heard him right? "You mean, like…"

"I mean I love you. How else can I say it? And no matter how bad things looked, I had to give you the benefit of the doubt. I'd already screwed up once by not doing that."

Amazing. She'd blown up at him, let him have it with both barrels…and nothing awful had happened. He hadn't turned against her. He *loved* her. Her heart grew wings and threatened to burst out into the open. Then something else occurred to her. A small matter, really, but she had to mention it.

"When I told you the guy on the floor was Terry, you didn't believe me at first." She softened the admonishment by rubbing her fingers across the back of his hand.

"He didn't look like Terry. It would have taken blind faith to believe you without question. I don't know if I'll ever have that kind of faith again, Jess. Not even with you."

At least he was honest. "I'm not sure blind faith is such a good thing, anyway," she said, resigned. "It's certainly gotten me into trouble a few times. I guess a bit of healthy skepticism is okay, as long as it's combined with a good strong hunch that the person you love is decent and honest... That's enough, isn't it?''

One corner of his mouth turned up. "It works for me." He stared at her over the rim of his mug as he took a long sip. "So I just told you I love you. What are you going to do about it?''

She hesitated. "Love you back?"

"Aw, Jess. You don't have to say it if it's not true. Neither of us planned for this..." He shrugged helplessly.

"Idiot. Maybe I haven't always been *completely* honest with you, but you don't think I'd lie about something like this, do you?''

He answered her by leaning over the table and capturing her lips with his. Steam from their coffee mingled with their own self-generated steam, and only a disapproving throat-clearing from a passing waitress made them stop.

"I could get used to that," Kyle said, his voice husky.

"Me too.''

Abruptly his demeanor changed. He gulped down the rest of his coffee in a few swallows, then wiped his mouth with his napkin. "C'mon, drink up. I'm anxious to get back to the station and force Clewis to eat a big helping of crow.''

Jess stretched languorously in Kyle's bed. This was the second time she'd awakened here. Unlike the first time, she and Kyle hadn't spent the night in innocent sleep. She was deliciously sore in places she hadn't imagined.

She realized Kyle wasn't in bed with her. He was probably one of those annoying early risers, she decided. She'd have to break him of that habit, at least on his days off.

A sound thump on her bottom brought her more fully awake. Kyle was standing by the bed looking huggably rumpled, holding two steaming cups of coffee and a folded

Kansas City Star. All right, maybe it wasn't so bad having him wake up before her.

"Did you just thump me with a newspaper?" she asked suspiciously.

"Mmm-hmm. I thought you wouldn't mind, since the front-page story is about you."

"Really?" She sat up and rubbed her eyes, then sipped greedily from the cup of coffee Kyle handed her.

"Scoot over. We'll read it together. I think it might answer some of the questions you've had. An 'inside source' gave the paper some details we didn't know about."

"You've already read the story," she concluded as she made room for him under the covers with her.

"While the coffee was brewing. Couldn't resist. You'll like it."

Even with Kyle's recommendation, she was still leery of reading about herself on the front page. But she soon found he was right. The press, which had vilified her in every story over the past couple of weeks, now thought she walked on water.

"Murder 'Victim' Found Alive and Kicking," the banner headline read. And beneath, "All Charges Dropped Against Jess Robinson." She liked it so far.

The story went on to detail Terry's demented plan to punish Jess for rejecting him. Apparently not the least bit ashamed, he'd bragged of his cleverness to the police.

"Who gave all this information to the press?" Jess wondered aloud. "It couldn't have been Clewis. This whole thing makes him look like a fourteen-karat turkey."

"No, not Clewis," Kyle agreed. "Maybe Easley. He's apologized to me ten or twelve times already, and I think he wants everything out in the open so it can be digested and forgotten as quickly as possible."

Jess continued to read, fascinated. Terry had started his plot against Jess by disposing of the shower curtain and storing the rug in Kevin's basement. Then he'd faked the shaving cut and planted the blood—a drop on his shirt and a casual suggestion that Mrs. Tanglemeyer might have some good stain remover. More blood had been splattered on the rug. And lots of it—two pints of human blood appropriated from the hospital where Kevin worked—dumped all over the bathtub, sink and washing machine. Terry had carefully coached Kevin, who'd thought the "practical joke" nothing more than a harmless prank at first, on what to tell the police.

He'd rented a U-Haul truck, then failed to pick it up.

He'd stolen Jess's knife a few days before his disappearance, but hadn't actually planted it under the porch steps until he'd needed more evidence against Jess. The crank phone calls had been designed to disrupt Jess's sleep and make her doubt herself.

He'd even thought to dispose of the shirt with the bloodstain so no evidence would corroborate her story. Finally, he'd hidden his personal possessions—keys, wallet—under Jess's mattress. Since he'd intended to assume a new identity, he didn't need those things.

Terry was charged with fraud—it was the best the D.A.'s office could come up with. But the resultant investigation turned up some interesting facts about Terry Rodin, a.k.a. Howard Ghetty, a.k.a. a half dozen other identities. He was wanted for forgery in three different states.

"I knew he was not quite right," Jess said, shaking her head. "But I had no idea..."

"Don't feel too bad, Jess," Kyle said, sliding his arm around her shoulders. "He's taken in a lot of people. The good news is he'll be mired in the legal system for some time to come."

The story went on to describe Kyle and Jess's unsanctioned stakeout and Jess's daring move to take Terry on her own. The wording managed to make Jess sound courageous instead of desperate and foolhardy.

When she finished reading, Jess laid the paper down. "Well, that was pretty thorough," she said. "But the ever-vigilant members of the press did manage to overlook one very juicy detail."

"They did, didn't they?" Kyle said with a satisfied smile. "Maybe we should enlighten them."

"No way," she said flatly. Much as she enjoyed seeing the reporters take back every nasty word they'd printed about her, she didn't want any more personal details of her life splashed across the pages for anyone to read.

"Guess they'll have to find out about our marriage when we send 'em the wedding announcement," Kyle said, nuzzling her neck.

"Mmm, that would be refreshing—keeping our private affairs private. But I don't understand how they missed the fact that we applied for the wedding license not more than an hour after the charges against me were formally dropped."

"I don't know, either…but I don't really care." He took her coffee from her hand and set it on the nightstand, then pushed the newspaper out of the way and concentrated on thoroughly kissing her ear.

Neither coffee nor newsprint held much interest for Jess at that point.

* * * * *

In April 1997
Bestselling Author

DALLAS SCHULZE

takes her Family Circle series to new heights with

TESSA'S CHILD

In April 1997 Dallas Schulze brings readers a
brand-new, longer, out-of-series title featuring the
characters from her popular Family Circle miniseries.

When rancher Keefe Walker found Tessa Wyndham he
knew that she needed a man's protection—she was
pregnant, alone and on the run from a heartless past.
Keefe was also hiding from a dark past...but in one
overwhelming moment he and Tessa forged a family
bond that could never be broken.

Available in April wherever books are sold.

This summer, the legend
continues in Jacobsville

A LONG, TALL
TEXAN SUMMER

Three **BRAND-NEW** short stories

This summer, Silhouette brings readers a special
collection for Diana Palmer's LONG, TALL TEXANS
fans. Diana has rounded up three **BRAND-NEW**
stories of love Texas-style, all set in Jacobsville,
Texas. Featuring the men you've grown to love from
this wonderful town, this collection is a must-have
for all fans!

*They grow 'em tall in the saddle in Texas—and
they've got love and marriage on their minds!*

Don't miss this collection of original Long, Tall Texans
stories...available in June at your favorite retail outlet.

INTIMATE MOMENTS®
™ Silhouette® Extra

For an *EXTRA*-special treat, pick up

THE PERFECT COUPLE
by
Maura Seger

In April of 1997, Intimate Moments proudly
features Maura Seger's *The Perfect Couple,* #775.

Everyone always said that Shane Dutton and
Brenna O'Hare were the perfect couple. But they
weren't convinced...not until a plane crash
separated them, leaving Brenna at home to
agonize and Shane to fight for his life in the frigid
Alaskan tundra. Suddenly they began to realize
just how perfect for each other they were. And
they prayed...for a second chance.

In future months, look for titles with the
EXTRA flash for more excitement, more
romance—simply *more....*

INTIMATE MOMENTS®
™ Silhouette®

IME2

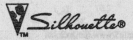

From the bestselling author of *Scandalous*

Cam Monroe vowed revenge when
Angela Stanhope's family accused him
of a crime he didn't commit.

Fifteen years later he returns from exile, wealthy
and powerful, to demand Angela's hand in marriage.
It is then that the strange "accidents" begin. Are the
Stanhopes trying to remove him from their lives
one last time, or is there a more insidious,
mysterious explanation?

Available this March at your favorite retail outlet.

IN CELEBRATION OF MOTHER'S DAY, JOIN
SILHOUETTE THIS MAY AS WE BRING YOU

a funny thing

HAPPENED ON THE WAY TO THE

DELIVERY ROOM

THESE THREE STORIES, CELEBRATING THE
LIGHTER SIDE OF MOTHERHOOD, ARE
WRITTEN BY YOUR FAVORITE AUTHORS:

KASEY MICHAELS
KATHLEEN EAGLE
EMILIE RICHARDS

When three couples make the trip to the delivery
room, they get more than their own bundles of
joy...they get the promise of love!

Available this May,
wherever Silhouette books are sold.

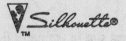

MD